THE SEARCH

for

CHRISTOPHER GORDON

a novel by
Gordon R. Lawrence

191 Bank Street
Burlington, Vermont 05401

The Search for Christopher Gordon is a work of fiction. The names, characters, places, dialogue, and incidents are either products of my imagination or used fictitiously. Other than the historical events surrounding the First Vermont Cavalry, any resemblance to actual events or locales or persons, living or dead, is coincidental.

"The Host of the Air" was written by William Butler Yeats. It appeared in *The Wind Among The Reeds* published in 1905 by J. Lane, New York. It is in the public domain.

"The Minstrel Boy" was written by Thomas Moore. It is in the public domain.

If you wish to make comments to the author, go to the comments section at:
www.GordonRLawrence.com

Copyright © 2019 by Gordon Lawrence

All rights reserved. No part of this publication may be reproduced, distributed, or transmitted in any form or by any means, including photocopying, recording, or other electronic or mechanical methods, without the prior written permission of the publisher, except in the case of brief quotations embodied in critical reviews and certain other noncommercial uses permitted by copyright law.

ISBN: 978-1-949066-29-6

LCCN: 2020900682

Onion River Press
191 Bank Street
Burlington, VT 05401

Printed in the United States of America

ACKNOWLEDGEMENTS

I wish to thank each of the following individuals and institutions from the depths of my heart.

Jeff Bukowski, Lin Stone and Emily Copeland guided me during the early stages of writing the novel.

Annie Dalton directed me to resources at Burlington's Lakeview Cemetery and Fletcher Free Library.

The City of Burlington and the Roman Catholic Diocese of Burlington maintain a number of cemeteries. I've walked every one of them and love the stories they tell.

The microfiche records of The Burlington Free Press, found in the Howe Library at the University of Vermont were invaluable as were the University's Special Collections records and staff.

Dr. Dennis Plante joked with me while answering medical questions.

My wife's book group (Andi, Barb, Collette, Diane, Paulie, and Red) offered honest insight, criticism, as well as few laughs.

Fiction Editor Janice Obuchowski struggled to make me a better writer. I hope someday she succeeds.

Sarah Lyman of Lyman Media waded through all of the details to produce the printed copy.

Ed Desautels bought a boat in 1966. The rest is history.

Mary Navin, a lifelong friend, read multiple revisions of the story. After each, we'd discussed her thoughts over Chardonnay. Her insight coaxed me into paying more attention to the characters Walt and Catch. Her sense of humor reminded me why I asked her help in the first place. I hope I meet her expectations

Tom Lawrence is an artist at heart so I asked him to design a cover for the book. Split Rock looks just like Jack would have painted it.

Jeff Lawrence reads everything he can get his hands on. He devoured each revision to the story, offering suggestions, criticism, and a great deal of support. He loves the feel of a book.

Paulie Lawrence read every version of every chapter. She listened to my thoughts again and again though she knew every detail. She encouraged, encouraged, encouraged. She always sees the best side. That is her way.

To Paulie

Brennan-Gordon-LeClair Tree

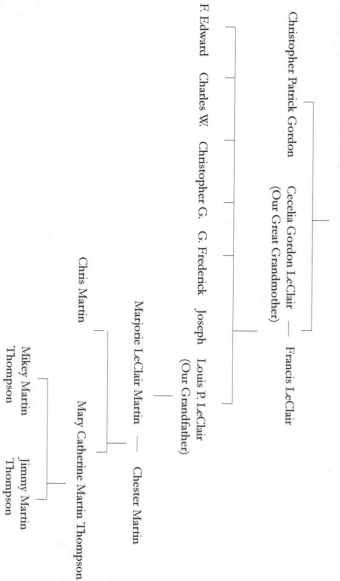

Christopher Patrick Gordon

Cecelia Gordon LeClair
(Our Great Grandmother)
—
Francis LeClair

F. Edward   Charles W.   Christopher G.   G. Frederick   Joseph   Louis P. LeClair
(Our Grandfather)

Chris Martin

Marjorie LeClair Martin
—
Mary Catherine Martin Thompson
Chester Martin

Mikey Martin Thompson

Jimmy Martin Thompson

1

At the top of Queen City Academy's central stairway, Chris Martin stepped through the swinging doors and halted. The third floor's academic corridor stretched out before him like a gauntlet. As the teacher watched the classroom doors close one by one, he struggled to recall where he'd left off during the previous day's American Heritage class. He couldn't.

The lone student in the hallway said, "Hi, Mr. Martin!" as he hurried by, but Chris ignored him. The Academy's distinguished alumni, looking down from their dark 19th-century portraits above the wainscoting, witnessed this most unprofessional behavior. Chris sensed their disapproving glares but didn't care.

He paused outside C44 and listened for any chatter coming from his senior history students inside. He'd become more attentive since finding his car wrapped in toilet paper the previous Saturday morning. It must have been the seniors, he thought. Not hearing anything suspicious, he entered and lumbered down the aisle, his eyes darting from desk to desk. When he noticed the word *talisman* scribbled across the top of T.D. Glover's notebook, he was intrigued. The skinny, red-haired athlete didn't know the difference between a talisman and a snowman.

Michael Andover slipped into the room just behind Chris. He fist bumped T.D. as he went to his assigned seat in the window row. The dark-eyed, dark-haired student stood six feet two but appeared taller because of the preppy, patrician way he tilted his head. After unbuttoning his Academy blazer and pushing his long hair back, he glanced at Madison Amore. The pixyish senior smiled then draped a tissue over the side of her desk, wiggling it. It was their signal.

When the Academy's metallic-sounding horn announced seventh period at 1:24, the room became like a crypt. Chris lifted his lesson planner and seating chart from his tote bag. He placed the seating chart on the corner of his desk before opening the lesson planner. The only thing written under October 16th was "meeting."

"Attendance please."

Madison Amore stepped forward, pushing her short blonde hair behind her ears. She opened the seating chart and compared it with the students present before punching the all-present code into the digital keypad on the wall.

"Thank you, Miss Amore," Chris said as she returned to her desk.

C44 wore a fresh coat of educational beige, newly installed fluorescent lights, and triple-glazed windows that provided optimal lighting conditions. But man does not learn by light alone. Not a single timeline graced the walls. There were neither Colonial maps nor portraits of dead presidents to inspire. No posters announced homecoming or after school activities. The bulletin boards were barren except for two Teacher of the Year certificates dating back to the eighties.

Even Honora Webster, the History Department's self-proclaimed chef extraordinaire, displayed a sports calendar and homecoming poster on her bulletin board. Those hung alongside copies of her favorite recipes under her "FUN/FOOD/FACTS CORNER" sign.

The sound of Chris turning his notebook pages reverberated through the emptiness.

"Please turn to page 52 in *American Heritage*. Begin reading, Miss Hasan," Chris said, pointing to a tiny, olive-skinned girl in the second row who was wearing a blue hijab.

"The French and Indian War, sir?"

"That's where we left off yesterday."

Michael Andover turned toward T.D. and rolled his eyes. T.D. shook his head.

"Yes, sir. The French and Indian War. 'In the mid-1750s, the British and French Empires clashed on the North American continent in a series of battles...'"

Chris unlocked his desk, lifted out his green-and-gold mug, and took a long sip of cold coffee. Over the edge of the mug, he noticed T.D., holding his thumb up to Michael. Michael nodded. Madison wiggled her tissue.

"'The conflict began again in 1754...'" the girl read.

Chris stood and then went to the windows. Glancing over his textbook, he noticed Michael Andover had written the day's date, after which was the outline of yet another crouched snowboarder. Then he looked out to Main Street hill, beyond Municipal Auditorium. Suspended over the roofs of the business district, the Lake Champlain Valley stretched north and south like an impressionist's canvas. Cobalt blue and ultramarine waters glittered with flecks of reflected sunlight. A sloop with titanium white sails tacked westward from the breakwater. Far beyond, the autumn-gilded Adirondacks wore spots of purple cast down from floating castles of cumulus clouds.

The Queen brothers, the Academy's founders, chose to erect their edifice on upper Main Street, facing westward toward Lake Champlain and the Adirondacks, both to inspire students and to look down on everything and everyone else in the valley. Old Hall was constructed in the 1860's, using Redstone from the brothers' quarry in the city's south end. The ground floor, A level, housed a cavernous two-story lobby surrounded by administrative offices, a teacher's lounge, and the library. B and C levels above contained the classrooms. New Hall, added in the 1960s, ran perpendicular to Old Hall. The gymnasium, auditorium, and cafeteria were on A level. The Science and Music Departments were on B level. The buildings were connected by a long brick-lined corridor called the central artery.

Academy students referred to the two sections as Old Money and New Money.

Chris followed the ridgelines from the far shoreline toward the high peaks, where he thought he noticed patches of early snow. The reader's voice had faded, but it didn't matter. Chris knew every word. He'd chaired the textbook committee a half dozen years before, and the section on the French and Indian War was only three pages long.

"Thank you, Miss Hasan. Please continue, Mr. Chopras."

Michael Andover closed his eyes and shook his head as he continued to sketch.

"'Native Americans and the French enjoyed a unique partnership. It began…'"

Chris took his notebook from his tote bag before going to the whiteboard. He wrote three review questions before returning to his window spot. Michael had added to his drawing. The snowboard sat atop a thunderbolt, flames spewing from behind.

"'Jesuit priests paddled into the wilderness to live among Native …'"

Across the lake, a wisp of diesel smoke stretched out above the far shore, north of Rensselaer Island. Chris glanced at the clock. Amtrak's Albany Flyer was on schedule, and there were only minutes left before the day's early dismissal.

"'…alliances developed out of the French-Native American trade relations.'"

"Mr. Andover. Please continue."

Michael's pencil dropped to the desk as his head jerked from his sketch to the textbook. He jabbed his finger toward the top of the page, running over each line. After skimming the page twice, he turned toward Madison who mouthed, "Third paragraph!" but Michael's fingers continued searching.

Chris's book was already closed when Michael's hand shot up.

"Mr. Martin! Mr. Martin!"

"Page 56. Paragraph three."

"It's not that, sir. I have a question."

"Yes, Mr. Andover," Chris said, removing his reading glasses.

"Mr. Martin. You know my dad's in the history department up at the college…" Michael leaned back in his chair and pointed toward Chris's coffee mug.

He's also the school board chairman, Chris thought.

"...and he's always talking about what really happened here. You know Fort Ticonderoga and *The Last of the Mohicans* stuff. That was a great movie, by the way. I loved Daniel Day Lewis. And Magua! Wasn't he great?"

"Your question, Mr. Andover?"

"Yes, sir. Why isn't any of that in here?" Michael said, holding up the text.

"Do you mean Fort Ticonderoga or *The Last of the Mohicans*, Mr. Andover?"

"I mean the Champlain Valley. Our text books never mention any local stuff. They just talk about barrels of pork and which army had the longest supply lines. And that's pretty boring, if you get my drift."

T.D. Glover lowered his head and ran his skinny fingers through his hair. The beginnings of a smile emerged and his shoulders began to shake as if he were trying to suppress a volcanic laugh.

"So?"

"So what really happened here, Mr. Martin?"

Oh, shit, Chris thought and inhaled.

"The simplest way to explain it, Mr. Andover, is to say that both empires understood the strategic value of the Champlain Valley-Lake George-Hudson River corridor. The Native Americans alternately used the waterways for trading and warfare."

The clock watchers began closing their books.

"Later they shared their knowledge with their allies. French trappers, French and English scouts, and French and English armies all used the corridor, beginning with Champlain's visit in..."

The Academy's metallic sounding horn interrupted him, screaming out early escape to teacher and students alike. Michael's face hardened.

"There will be a quiz tomorrow. Hint, the Enlightenment!" Chris called over the din, pointing to the review questions on the board.

As the seniors filed out, he returned to his desk, placing the seating chart and lesson plan back in his tote bag. As he reached for his coffee mug, a shadow blocked the sunlight crossing his desk.

"Mr. Martin!"

Michael Andover was staring down at him. T.D. and Madison waited near the door.

"Yes, Mr. Andover."

"I didn't mean the general stuff. My father talked a lot about Crown Point. Do you know how large that fort was?"

"Yes, Mr. Andover. I do."

"He said thousands of troops were stationed there. Thousands! It was the largest British outpost in North America. Larger than New York! That's not in the book." Chris forced a smile and shook his head. "Have you ever been there, Mr. Martin? To Crown Point?"

"I have."

"Why doesn't the book mention it? Why don't you? I mean, that's important stuff."

Chris felt as if he were being dragged toward some cliff. He removed his reading glasses.

"I'm sorry, Mr. Andover. We'll have to discuss this some other time. I have a ..."

"Yeah, yeah I know. Superintendent's meeting!"

"Michael, are you coming?" Madison said from the doorway.

Michael buttoned his blazer and went to the door. As Chris reached for his books, he thought he heard "Loser!" whispered and, looking up, noticed T.D. Glover's skinny thumb and forefinger in the shape of an L at his side. But before Chris could react, the nasal voice of Anita Small, Principal Wentworth's secretary, interrupted with final announcements over the paging speakers.

"ATTENTION, TEACHERS! PLEASE REPORT TO THE ADITORIUM. THE SUPERINTENDENT'S MEETING WILL BEGIN AT 1:50.

ATTENTION STUDENTS! THE LATIN CLUB IS

HOLDING ITS ANNUAL POMEGRANATE SALE IN THE LOBBY. FOR ONLY $3.85 PER POUND YOU…"

Chris locked his grade book and coffee mug in his desk drawer. The desks were lined up and the blinds level but a crumpled piece of paper on the floor near the doorway created minor disorder in the room. He picked it up, stuffing it into his jacket pocket before stepping into the congested hallway. He felt pulled and tugged in the human flow as if trapped in one of the eddies at the Salmon Hole beneath Weaverton Falls where his Uncle Jonathon used to fish when he was sober enough. Chris drew his tote bag up to his chest like some flotation device. He felt the pressure again. It was mild at first but grew as he walked, making him wonder whether any of the smothering students knew the correct ratio of compressions to breaths in case he needed CPR.

Libby O'Connor, waiting outside C36, appeared more a business professional than a history teacher in her trim navy blue suit. After the Academy had hired her in August, Chris had mentored her. Standing on tip toes, her faun-colored eyes searched through the young faces. Each time she turned, her straight auburn hair rippled around her neck. When she finally noticed Chris's ashen face, her smile dissolved.

"Did something happen?"

"I don't know what to do about that kid."

"Andover?"

"Yeah. He tried using the French and Indian War to piss me off. It's all about winning with him. He's just like his old man. There's no purity. It's not about discovery. He doesn't care about the facts. He just wants to…"

"Excuse us, Mr. Martin."

Chris forced a smile before sidestepping a group of noisy sophomores. "To show me up. That's all. Shouldn't this stuff be meaningful on its own?"

"Come on, Chris. Kids aren't excited about history the way we were. They have the History Channel and smartphones. Media and technology are tough competitors."

"And they have video football games, too, but nobody can throw a damn pass."

"Touché."

"Hey, wait up, guys!" K.J. Wheeler, a lanky, curly haired teacher, came up behind them. Though a teacher at the Academy for nearly 30 years, he maintained a youthful look with bright eyes and a cocky smile. Only his graying hair betrayed his middle age. "Hi gorgeous," K.J. said to Libby, who smiled. "Excuse me, Chris, but you look like crap. What's up?"

"I think my seventh-period seniors are scheming. Maybe planning to steal my coffee mug."

"She's a beauty. I'd steal it," K.J. said. "Green Mountain University's colors and initials on the front. Fire Up 66 on the back."

"What's that all about?" Libby said.

"A frat brother picked it up at a college reunion I missed."

K.J.'s blue eyes lit up, indicating some switch had been flipped. He pushed his glasses back up his narrow nose. "During my senior year in high school, we had this trig teacher who kept bumping into things. We thought he drank gin or vodka—the one that doesn't smell—so we planned to steal his coffee mug." K.J. pushed up his glasses again. "Urban legend! The guy was just a klutz. He saved us a detention by knocking his cup off his desk one afternoon. After it smashed, we were all kind of disappointed. Took the wind out of our sails, I guess. I'd lock yours away if you want to keep it."

"Already done."

"I never tried anything like that when I was in high school," Libby said.

Chris led them into the central stairway where they blended in among the navy-and-gray clad students. Chris turned toward the beige brick walls rather than face the students. When the three reached the first floor, K.J. said, "I think we're in for some surprises this afternoon."

"At the superintendent's meeting?" Libby said.

"I prefer to think of it as a press conference. Listening to Dr. George is like listening to a politician. He evades everything. As for Brent..."

"Are you saying our esteemed leaders don't tell the whole story?" Libby said.

"Those guys could use a course in…"

"Any idea what this thing is really about, K.J.?" Chris said.

"Anita showed me the agenda. Brent is going to disclose the new recertification guidelines. It sounds like we've got more shit to do."

"K.J.!"

"Well, it's true. All businesses are the same. The managers devise new ways to impress the higher ups, and we groundlings get to bust our butts. Kind of poetic, I must say, but we'll know for sure in a few minutes."

At the lobby, K.J. and Libby turned left toward the central artery and the auditorium beyond. Chris turned right toward the teacher's lounge. "I've got to stop for a minute," he said. "Save me some coffee."

A group of students momentarily blocked the path toward the central artery but stepped aside when K.J. said, "Excuse us, please! We have a very pressing conference to attend!"

2

Honora Webster's granite voice rumbled through the teacher's lounge door, reminding Chris of a freight train's thunderous approach to the Blue Bridge trestle over the Weaverton River.

"You think you've been forgetting things! Yesterday, it was my keys. Today, I…"

Chris stepped behind Honora before closing himself inside the lavatory. The rushing water drowned out all background noise. He dipped his hands into the flow and lifted the coolness to his pale cheeks and high forehead. Patches of color returned. He dried his face, forced a smile, and stepped out into the lounge, where Honora nearly trampled him like one of Pamplona's finest on her way toward the door.

"Sorry about that, Honora."

Honora, a big Wisconsin farm girl who had grown up, Chris suspected, on massive portions of bratwurst, beer, and cheese, placed her hand on her rounded hip. "You should be!" She walked into the lobby. Her light-colored bouffant hair never budged an inch.

Chris picked up *The Daily Freeman* from the coffee table and scanned the obituaries. Not recognizing any names, he left for the auditorium. While crossing the lobby, he noticed Anita Small through the principal's office window, raising her hand, signaling him in.

"What's up?"

"I'm glad I caught you. Have you heard about Walt?"

"What about him?"

Before she could answer, the principal's line rang. Anita held up her index finger. "Principal Wentworth's office, this is Anita Small."

The tiny woman's eyes closed. Whatever she heard caused more wrinkles to form around her eyes and mouth, yet her smile endured. Her mousy hair, pinned high, was disheveled. She wore another drab, pleated wool skirt and baggy cardigan. K.J. liked saying Anita dressed like the valedictorian at Auntie Em's Academy of Haute Couture.

"It's Brittany!" Anita whispered with one hand over the mouthpiece.

"I'll stop by later."

Chis left and found K.J. and Libby lingering beside the refreshment table outside the auditorium. He poured a half cup of two o'clock coffee, drawing it back when Libby offered the creamer. "I've put on some weight."

"Speaking of put on!" K.J. said, nodding toward the auditorium door.

They turned to Principal Brent Wentworth walking toward them. "Hello, my friends. Great to see you all." He reached to shake Chris's hand, using both of his own. K.J. called Brent's two-hand technique rock snotting, a reference to a slimy sediment, rock snot, recently discovered in the Mad River and reported on in *The Daily Freeman*.

"Is everyone having just a great day?" Brent said, reaching for Libby's hand.

"Fine, Brent. And you?"

"Wonderful! I just visited the integrated sciences lab on New Hall B. Our Mr. Little is such a wizard. His juniors—or maybe it was the seniors—are doing some nifty experiments. He's got them using lasers and studying mouse-population growth."

Brent turned to K.J., but instead of reaching out, he just nodded. K.J. nodded back then pushed his glasses back up his nose using his middle finger.

"This stuff is all smoke and mirrors to me. We never did experiments like that when I was in school. The only things we ever…" Brent stopped, noticing Brittany Newport, the school dietitian, strutting across the lobby. Her honey-blonde hair bounced in perfect time with her breasts. She looked over her shoulder and smiled at Brent the same way she smiled at the hormone-driven senior boys in the lunch-ticket line.

"Box of rocks," K.J. whispered to Chris.

Once Brittany disappeared into the central artery, Brent turned back to Chris. "By the way, I need to meet with you during eighth period tomorrow."

"Sure. What's going on?"

"You haven't heard? Walt was rushed to the hospital. You're the History Department chairman until he returns. You've got to get up to speed."

"What is it?" Chris said, feeling himself off balance.

"Is he OK?" Libby said at the same time.

"It may be a stroke. I told Anita to call the family tonight for an update. Until he's back, we'll just have to adapt. You'll have to tighten up your computer skills if you want to keep up. But we'll worry about that later. Won't we?" Brent winked at Chris before being distracted by some disorderly sugar packets on the serving table. He returned them to their bowl, then tidied the napkins and rearranged the coffee stirrers in their plastic holder. He glanced at his watch. "Excuse me. I nearly forgot. I've got to start this meeting. We've got education on the plate. Besides, look, Dr. George is pacing."

The tall, bearded superintendent was pacing back and forth across the stage, holding index cards in one hand while stroking his trimmed salt-and-pepper beard with the other.

"How do I look?" Brent said to Libby, adjusting his cuffs. "We could really use some better clothing stores around here. You know, the big guys. They're just aren't enough choices."

Libby returned a compulsory smile and nodded. Brent always looked the perfect spokesman: a sculpted build, square nose, dimpled chin, and neat sandy brown hair. He started for the stage, rock snotting every hand he could grasp along the way.

"Typical city boy!" K.J. said. "Moves to Vermont to escape urban ills then complains there aren't enough box stores. And look. He's even wearing his tasseled loafers. Always wears them when Dr. George is around."

To Chris Libby said, "Congratulations! I guess. But

that's awful about Walt. You OK?"

"Yeah." Chris took a deep breath. "I just hope he's OK. That's all. I can put up with anything until decisions are made."

"You've been friends a long time, haven't you?"

"We go way back to Green Mountain University. I wouldn't be here if it weren't for him. He saved my…"

K.J. said, "You don't know him yet, Libby, but he can be a prankster."

"Walt, a prankster!"

"Tell her about Walt's lawn, Chris."

Chris smiled. "Last Saturday, he invited me over to watch the Notre Dame game. When I arrived, a couple of freshmen boys were outside raking the lawn."

"He's always finding ways for kids to make a buck," K.J. said.

"I said hi and went inside. About half way through the third quarter, the doorbell rang. Walt answered and I could hear him laughing with the kids. A minute later, he came in and asked to borrow five bucks. Said he didn't have enough cash to pay them. Later, in the middle of the fourth quarter, he called upstairs to his wife, "Come on, Bebe, we're going out to dinner." She came down and he said to lock up after the game. It seemed strange because USC had started a comeback, but I was into the game. Well, Notre Dame intercepted a few minutes later and stopped the drive. After they'd won, I locked up and headed out. The kids had done a nice job on the lawn, but, when I reached the car, all the leaves were thrown in my back seat. Without bags! When I saw Walt Monday morning, he started laughing and said "You paid them!" I think he was still laughing during third period."

Libby raised her hand to her mouth to hold back a laugh.

"Listen to this. Walt tells people he's got this invisible dog, Spot," K.J. said. "He's always dropping food on the floor and saying, "Spot, come and get your supper!" Drives his wife nuts."

A smile appeared on Chris's face but faded in an instant. "This doesn't seem real."

"Is there anything I can do?" Libby said.

"Me too," K.J. said. "I can help with the computer stuff."

When Brent finally reached the stage, he grasped Dr. George's hand before stepping to the microphone. Dr. George sat down, easing the index cards into his jacket pocket.

"Please take your seats, everyone. We have a lot to cover…"

A screech belched from the loudspeaker. "Testing. Testing."

Chris gulped down his coffee, refilled the cup, and hurried to join Libby and K.J. behind the rest of the History Department a few rows down the main aisle. He sat just as Brent finished fiddling with the microphone.

"Thank you all for coming today. We've got a lively program ahead and then Dr. George, our favorite superintendent, is going to inspire us. Applause! Applause!" He raised one hand in the air. Scattered clapping came from around the room.

"Ass kissers!" K.J. whispered.

Honora turned and cleared her throat.

"First, we have a few announcements." Brent reminded the teachers about the pomegranate sale, noted new items Brittany Newport had added to the lunch menu, and cited changes to the bus schedule. Next, he called the head librarian to the microphone to explain the Academy's new borrowing policy.

As she talked, Chris was remembering a young Walt tossing a football across the Theta Alpha Chi fraternity lawn. That picture dissolved into a vision of the all-night study pit beneath the college library where he and Walt had gone to prep for the History 241 final. They were on their hands and knees, searching through Walt's papers, which had all fallen from his desk and scattered across the floor. Chris's eyes welled up as he thought of holding

Walt's daughter, Janet, during her christening at the First Congregational Church.

"If there is no response to the second notice, I have the authority to…"

Walt may be dying and this idiot is worried about collecting nickels. Chris finished his coffee, placed the cup on the floor, and slid further down into his chair. The discomfort in his chest began creeping back, so he closed his eyes and took a few deep, slow breaths. Within minutes the tension began draining from his body like wine drops falling from some ancient spigot on to a cellar floor.

"The next item is progress reports and parent conferences. We'll use the same format as last year. All reports must be in the database before Nov. the 19th."

"Have you begun writing yours?" Libby said, breaking into Chris' quiet space.

"We've still got a couple of weeks."

"… parents between 6:30 and 9:30 on November 22nd. No classes on Friday. If you need to finish up Saturday, doors will be open but it's your nickel."

When a few groans rose from the audience, Brent barked back, "It's in the contract. You signed it! Now for some big news." Brent shuffled through his papers.

"You know he drives a CTS?" K.J. whispered to Chris. "Big shots in Italian shirts always drive Caddies."

"I own an Italian shirt," Chris said.

"We all do. One! Brent has a whole fleet. And I bet he doesn't get his at the seconds store off I-89. He probably drives all the way to the Albany mall. I went there once. The guy measuring my arm kept pinching my bicep, but I didn't like the way…"

"Shhh! This is important," Honora said, looking back at K.J.

Libby smiled and held her finger before her lips as Brent began speaking.

"Myra Spelling over at the State Certification Standards Board informed Dr. George there are major problems implementing the new recertification standards. As you know, the board's legacy system shut down when the Waterbury complex flooded last spring. The new system and its software are still being debugged. Neither system works. Computers! What are you going to do? The board came up with a paper alternative. Those guys are clever, aren't they? Drum roll please."

Chris thought Brent looked vaudevillian, shrugging his shoulders and raising his palms. K.J. must have been thinking the same thing, because he turned to Libby and whispered, "He reminds me of Henny Youngman."

"Who?"

K.J. rolled his eyes. "You're such a kid, Libby! Pretend I said Rodney Dangerfield."

"It's a quick fix, one time only, to let the state use all its resources on tuning up the new system. Here's how it'll work. If you must recertify this academic year but haven't met the requirements yet, you can acquire credits using an individual portfolio action plan. You design your project, do your course work, and submit a statement saying you've met the criteria. The state will grant you six of the mandatory nine credits. As I said: a once in a lifetime opportunity so be imaginative. Try something you've never done before. There is one caveat. Department heads will act as gatekeepers. You must get their approval by November 15th.   Work with them if you want to use the portfolio-plan alternative. You can still use the normal procedure, but doing so will take state resources away from the new systems. So think about helping out."

"How many credits do you need, Chris?" K.J. said.

"Six."

Muffled conversations could be heard around the auditorium.

"I think I just heard a few sighs of relief. Great! It's cheaper for the Academy too, if we don't have to reimburse GMU for your courses for one semester. Everybody wins!"

"That guy's all about money." K.J. whispered. "Doesn't he have anything important in his life?"

"I'll give copies of the guidelines to your department

chairmen," Brent said, waving a handful of papers in the air.

"This could be fun. Imagine concentrating on something you enjoy," Libby said.

"Why should I care?" Chris said. "I'm not sure I'm even coming back."

"Don't say that!" Libby said. "That's a big decision. Give yourself a chance. You might enjoy the challenge."

"The president is about to speak, Libby. Shhh!" K. J. said.

Libby closed her eyes and shook her head.

"We may have a few more surprises for you this year but right now, it's time to hear from our special guest. As you know, Dr. George Baker came to the Queen City from the wilds of northern New Hampshire to lead our district in a new direction. Under his leadership, we've out performed our neighboring districts in all statistical categories."

"What a joke." K.J. whispered.

Libby turned to him. "What do you mean?"

"… a serious guy, with serious ideas…"

"He's talking about Weaverton. They've always struggled. No tax base. Crumbling schools. Diverse population. Every obstacle you can imagine."

"This man has inspired me personally…"

Dr. George's head bounced along to the cadence of Brent's compliments.

"…so now please welcome our good friend, our superintendent, our guru, Dr. George Baker."

The superintendent stepped forward to polite applause as Brent grasped his hand before slithering off to a chair further back on the stage. Dr. George stood at the lectern like Moses, prepared to enlighten the misguided. "Thank you, Brent. And thank you, fellow educators."

K.J. elbowed Libby. "You don't see nice corduroy suits like that much anymore. It's woodchuck chic."

"K.J.!"

"We've come a long way, but we have a long way to

go! A 150 years ago, the founders of this Academy built our sacred temple of learning from the red rock quarries at the city's south end. Their objectives: provide quality education to locals and boarders alike, create independent leaders for tomorrow's challenges, and elevate the masses above the slough of mediocrity. Noble purposes all. But recently, we've suffered. Our magnificent temple of learning became soiled."

"Here we go," K.J. whispered.

"It doesn't take a rocket scientist to know there are times when elbow grease is more important than computer chips, so we rolled up our sleeves and dug in. We reconnoitered and brought in new leadership." Dr. George turned and bowed toward Brent. The principal's eyelids fluttered. "It was dirty work, but, once the triage was complete, we took up the guidon and designed the databases. We built the databases. We implemented the databases. Now our benchmarks are up and the opportunities endless. And our students just love being here.

But we must not rest on our laurels! Time is too short. We need to future manage our crises and prepare for the unknown. As Godlewski said, 'The mind is the door to infinity. Unlock it and breathe in the cosmos.'"

"Who is Godlewski?" Libby said, leaning toward K.J.

"Another irrelevant educator, I guess."

"And we must seek. As persistent seekers, educators, cosmopolitans, we must strive for the cusp of the cutting edge…"

Brent, staring at the good doctor who appeared closer and closer to some orgasmic nirvana, took his handkerchief from his pocket, bent forward, and wiped off his tasseled loafers.

"…the eyes of eagles…"

K.J. made a spastic slap at the last fly of summer.

Chris looked away, but instead of relief he found aggravation. The seniors' pranks, Walt's sudden illness, new certification alternatives, Honora's attitude, and a hundred other nuisances prodded and poked him.

"...down the digital autobahn..."

Whenever Chris's world became too cluttered or tightened around him, he would restore tranquility by thinking about the lake.

"...the words of Zollikofer..."

He closed his eyes and imagined a vista of blue water dotted with emerald islands. Driven by a light southerly breeze, tiny ripples danced across the surface. His breathing slowed, his muscles relaxed, and he felt warm—comforted like a child embraced after some injury. Even when storms rolled eastward off the Adirondacks, the lake consoled him.

3

After concluding his remarks, Doctor George stepped back from the podium, inducing Brent to rush forward with his hands extended and the teachers to stand and begin filing toward the auditorium doors. As Libby stood, she said to Chris, "I think the portfolio idea has potential. You?"

"I'm not sure. Sounds like a lot of effort."

"It's ingenious!" K.J. said. "Imagine getting credit for being creative. I've taken enough mandatory courses on HVAC standards and classroom attire for a lifetime. I'm in."

"I am too! I..." A short burp vibrated from Libby's purse. "Excuse me." She found her smartphone, glanced at the call detail, grimaced, and then began scrolling through texts.

"Everything OK?" K.J. reached for his own device and scanned for messages.

"It's my mother! Another recipe, I guess. I'll call her later."

Chris glanced at the two. "I don't get it. I drove cross country when I was in college and didn't talk with anyone back home for two months. Nowadays, people notify the world whenever they burp or fart."

K.J. smiled, but Libby just shook her head.

"I've got to go," she said. "Cross-county practice at 4 pm. You done for the day, K.J.?"

"Comic Book City. Rumor has it they've come up with a few original *Teenage Mutant Ninja Turtles*. Still wrapped in original plastic! I just need April and December '93 to finish my collection. And my better half gave me permission."

"While you two play, I've got to prepare a quiz," Chris said and walked toward the central artery.

When Chris got back to C44, he flipped through the

text, searching for the section on the Enlightenment. He kept trying to write questions, but, after multiple attempts, crumpled the paper, closed his book, went to the file cabinet, and retrieved the previous year's quiz. He covered the date with a whiteout strip, wrote in the current one, and walked down to the teacher's lounge, where he made 20 copies.

Barney, the janitor, had just finished wet mopping the central artery when Chris walked through it toward the parking lot. Beyond his car, the girls' cross-country team was warming up along the edge of the soccer field. Libby paced around the team, hands on her hips, wearing an Academy t-shirt and gold running shorts, her auburn hair back in a short ponytail.

Chris loosened his tie and unbuttoned his blazer, thinking how much he loved Indian summer. Finding the crumpled paper in his jacket pocket, he opened it after tossing the blazer on the back seat. "You don't belong here!" it said.

He became distracted when a light breeze lifted Libby's coaching voice above the murmur of traffic cruising up and down Main Street hill. "Stretching's mundane compared to running, but you won't perform well unless you've stretched properly. It's like doing homework. If you've done it, you're prepared. If you haven't, you're taking a chance. Only two weeks before the state meet. Until then, we'll work on stretching, running techniques, and concentration. We'll follow our routines, stay focused. Think about each step you take. Don't be distracted by how you want to look in the victory photo or what you'll say picking up the trophy. Keep your eyes on what is right in front of you. The moment! Always live in the moment! The race is in the running, not the finish line. Now, captains, set the pace. Let's go"

Libby noticed Chris standing beside his car and waved as she began running with the team. The girls jogged down the back drive toward Maple Street. Though Libby ran near the center of the pack, she stood out from the others. She had strong, smooth legs that glided in a powerful fluid rhythm. She possessed a grace and beauty that reminded Chris of antelope he'd seen on his trip across the Great Plains. Once he'd become so distracted watching them he'd veered across the center line, nearly running head on into a semi carrying pigs toward Sioux Falls.

The depth of Libby's tan made Chris wonder whether she'd spent her summer lying on the sand at North End Beach. He imagined her athletic body in a bathing suit, dripping with tanning oil and beach sweat.

"Running saved me, Chris," she'd told him early on. "Even when it's dark and cold, I feel a sense of accomplishment after I've run."

After the team had left the lot, Chris started his car. As he shifted into drive, he remembered his friend Jack, thinking he'd better tell him about Walt, so instead of turning left at the end of the drive, he took a right and headed down Maple.

Lake Champlain's deep blue beckoned. The autumn sky and the Adirondacks joined in. Chris wondered if the waters out at North End Beach where Aunt Harriet used to take him were still summer warm or if the autumn evenings had taken their toll. At the first stop sign, he reached into the glove compartment and found the old cassette, eased it into the deck, and fast forwarded to number seven. The drums, setting the '60s beat, was followed by the piano and strings. The Isley Brothers started to belt out "This Old Heart of Mine." It was from a time Chris just couldn't let go. He stepped on the gas.

His foot began tapping as it had summers before, and he started singing along. He felt the red Glastron rise up on its own wake after he'd pulled back on the throttle. Thunder Rock lay off the port bow. Blue sky. A fresh southerly breeze kissed the mirror surface, leaving a trail of ripples for miles. There was a light scent of gasoline. The fallen skier treaded water 20 yards off the stern. Straight ahead, the tops of the Adirondacks, August green, formed a jagged line for 30 miles south along the western shore. His college girlfriend, Susan, sat beside him.

He remembered turning to her and looking into her dark eyes. They promised forever. Everything was perfect when she smiled back.

He reached the light at the bottom of the hill, then drove across the tracks and pulled into an empty space in the Salt Dock parking lot. The dock had evolved from a utilitarian macadam work space, where cargoes of lumber were once loaded on sailing canal boats bound for Montreal, to a public viewing area, complete with a walking path and lined with picnic thick grass.

Once the song ended, he turned off the engine. The afternoon sun silhouetted Jack, a solitary figure atop chiseled grey granite blocks at the end of the dock. He was wearing a beret and holding a fishing pole, gazing off toward the breakwater and Thunder Rock. Chris locked his car walked toward him.

A few sailboats defied the calendar at moorings near the Redstone breakwater, 350 yards off shore. They rocked back and forth on the gentle swells. A shackle clanged against a distant mast, casting haunting echoes atop the breeze. Sun beams licked the tops of the ripples.

Jack hadn't moved since Chris parked the car and began walking across the grass strip toward the water. Perhaps something nibbled at his bait. Perhaps he was hypnotized by the lake, the mountains, or the sun. He reached for a 16 oz. beer can at his side, taking a long tug before placing it back alongside a couple of empties.

Jack's features were rugged though worn. His ponytail had turned salt and pepper long ago. He pulled a pack of Camels from the breast pocket of his leather jacket and looked up at Chris while lighting his cigarette. He inhaled a long drag before clenching the cigarette between his front teeth. The smoke formed a haze around him before drifting skyward.

"Any luck?" Chris asked.

He looked up at Chris, while tending his line. His eyes were tired, their complexion milky, and his teeth were tobacco yellow. He pursed his lips and shook his head.

"What the hell do you think, doofus? Did you see the fucking Reggie's Seafood truck waiting to pick up the day's catch? I don't come here to fish. I'm here for that." He nodded across the lake. "This is the best view in the world. That's why I'm here, to look at those beautiful Tetons. Any luck! Shit."

"You deserve an Oscar for over acting."

"Over acting! Hey! Give a drink to a man with an accordion and you're bound to hear a polka."

Jack's shtick forced Chris to savor the moment. He smiled and gazed westward where Thunder Rock floated in the distance like Bali Hai, out of reach. Beyond it were Rensselaer Island and the High Peaks. The purity of that autumnal moment softened an otherwise turbulent afternoon, but it couldn't last. "Walt's in the hospital."

"Poor bastard. What is it?"

"A stroke. A heart attack. They don't know yet."

Chris glanced at the horizon, drawn to the breakwater's south end where a speedboat was entering the harbor from the broad lake. The sight triggered memories from an autumn night, decades before. There were dark waters and flashing lights, the crunching sound made by fiberglass colliding with the redstone breakwater and the feel of Walt's strong hand yanking him upward out of cooling unconsciousness. The thought shook him, and, when he turned, Jack's gaze was fixed on the same spot.

"Don't go back there," Jack said. "She is gorgeous today. Remember that."

"I won't forget," Chris said.

Jack pulled back his pole and began reeling in the monofilament. The cigarette between his teeth flapped up and down in synch with his reeling hand. The hook was clean.

"You know, I've given up naming my worms. It hurts when you lose friends."

He held the shank of the hook while rummaging around the bottom of the rusted Hill's Brothers can. Cigarette smoke floated up into his eyes. When he uncovered a fat, juicy night crawler, its future was immediately in jeopardy because Jack's tremor might shake it to death before it ever faced a perch.

"Damn annelids. They think they can squirm all night and skip paying the piper in the morning." An evil little smile crossed Jack's lips. "Not this guy. Pay up you bastard!" He gouged the crawler before tossing the line into the lake.

"Will you be at the Club meeting Friday?"

"Wouldn't miss it. It's the only time I get to hang out with successful people. Besides, I win all the hands. None of you ever could play cards. And you still can't fuckin' bluff."

"Nice jacket," Chris said.

"Ayyah."

"Where'd you get it?"

"Some girl." Jack leaned forward as if to peer below the surface. His cigarette slipped from between his teeth and fell into the water. He pursed his lips and reached for his pack of Camels. He lit another, taking a long drag while gazing off at the horizon. Setting his rod down, he raised his arms out in front of him and closed one eye. Stretching his thumbs together and raising his forefingers, he panned the horizon.

When Chris left the parking lot, he followed Bluffs Street north along the lakeshore. The city had rooted there in the early 19th century. After the Queen Brothers built the wharves and breakwater, lumberyards dominated the shoreline. Nearby were small homes, tenements, and mansions. Uncle Jonathon loved to tell those old stories of how Queen City grew upward from the lake. Now there were open vistas, city parks, hotels, and marinas.

Chris drove past Main, turned east at College Street, and climbed up through the area known as the Slough. Hotels, boutiques, and restaurants stood where the brothels and bars of the 1860s once operated. Traffic slowed below a crawl when Chris reached the pedestrian mall intersection at Center Street. On beautiful days, the crowds at the heart of the business district crossed the street more like divas than sprinters.

A block further, College began another climb through the hill section up toward GMU. As Chris approached the light, sirens shrieked from the firehouse on the opposite corner. He braked and froze in place. His heart pounded. After the fires engines screamed passed, he remained frozen until an obnoxious tooting horn behind him broke his trance.

A few blocks further up College, he turned into Wells Court, a dead-end street of gilded-age houses where he lived. He parked and walked toward his door. Down the street, a little man walking a tiny rat-faced dog watched him as he picked up his mail.

Inside, the air in the hallway smelled richly of yesterday. Chris loved the feel of the dark oak banister and the craftsmanship chiseled into the wainscoting and thick oak doors. The brass knobs shined.

The neighborhood's giant Victorians once harbored Queen City's ambitious lumber barons, bankers, and boat captains, whose lives filled Uncle Jonathon's stories. But if Uncle Jonathon were still alive, he wouldn't recognize the neighborhood. During the '70s, developers had chopped most of the hulks into tiny apartments and attached four-story condominiums on their backs to rent to the college crowd. They'd refurbished carriage barns and hung out signs for antique shops and real estate offices. Emerald lawns, where croquet and lemonade were once Sunday traditions, vanished beneath black asphalt parking lots. Chris's landlady followed a different path, however. She closed off a few doorways on the second floor and added some cabinets and a kitchen sink. The rest of the house and yard waited for children or grandchildren to return.

The poster of a young Bob Dylan greeted Chris as he entered his apartment. "Hey, Bob," Chris said, placing his tote bag down. He tossed his coat across the couch on the way to the galley kitchen. A single TV dinner was left in the fridge, which he placed in the oven, setting the timer before sitting down at the round kitchen table near his bulletin board. Odd notes, appointment cards, and a few black-and-white photos were tacked up there. He shuffled through mail until he noticed his retirement-fund envelope mixed in among the bills. It was the same green color as a traffic light. His thoughts returned to Walt, so he put down the envelope and called Walt's house phone. After a few rings, the call went to voicemail. Walt's voice took him by surprise. "Hi. You've reached the McCormack's. Please…"

"Hold on a second!" Another voice said over the recording. There was a click on the line and the recorded message stopped. "Hello. Sorry about that. This is Bill Hudson."

"Hey, Bill. This is Chris Martin. How's your father-in-law is doing?"

"He's in the ICU, Chris. They think it's a stroke. He's all wired up. Everything's out of whack."

"What happened?"

"I don't know much. Janet's mom called late last night. She found Walt on the bathroom floor and called the ambulance. Janet talked with her today, but they were still doing tests. I just left her at the hospital and brought the baby here. No place for a kid who needs to go to bed."

"Can I go see him?"

"You don't want to see him now. His face is all bruised from the fall and he isn't moving. Just stares. Besides, the room is full of guys in white…" A child started to cry in the background. "Chris, I've got to run. This little girl's really fussy."

"Let me give you some numbers where you can reach me."

Bill took down the numbers as the baby continued crying. "I'll call you once we know something. Gotta go."

"Thanks. Give my love to Janet and her mom."

Chris grabbed the remote and clicked on the big screen. He muted it, but as the reporter's lips moved, Chris heard Dr. George and Brent's voices. Their words reminded him of the pep talks officers gave to praying soldiers as they rode toward beaches in landing craft. Time stood still until the oven's buzzer sounded.

After chewing spongy tortellini, Chris called his sister, Mary Catherine. There was no answer, so he reached for the green envelope and searched for his notebook and calculator, finding them atop a Clancy Brothers LP near the turntable. The boys smiled back at him from outside Carnegie Hall in the '60s.

Chris punched the new figures into his calculator. They were less inspiring than Dr. George's talk, leaving him to imagine several more years at the Academy. That odd feeling returned to his chest. It was one of many ghosts that tried to haunt him when he was alone, but he'd already had enough worries and needed sleep. His doctor's appointment was a still a few weeks away, so he'd worry then. He took three antacids, climbed into bed, and closed his eyes.

4

After midnight, Chris sat up in bed to find a path of light streaming between his disrupted blinds. And then he heard, high up in the air, honkers honking away. Lost geese? Lost souls? He peeked between the blinds for the errant flock to discover a landscape bathed in the creamy light of an autumn moon. The scene awakened him as the summer moons of his youth once had. He was up in an instant, dressed, and tiptoeing across the apartment.

"I'm going out for a little walk," he whispered to Bob Dylan.

Chris turned up College Street to find the entire neighborhood asleep except for a green VW bug parked with its motor running on the front lawn of one of the fraternity houses. No one in sight. How strange. It wasn't even the weekend.

At the top of College, GMU's campus green stretched out into the darkness. He crossed Pinnacle Street in front of Waterford Hall to walk along the green. It was lined with walkways and dotted by statues and trees. He avoided the walkways, leaving tracks where his Dockers sank into the thick, moist grass. The breeze wiggled the maple leaves and the tops of the white pines. He smelled something sweet and licked his lips.

In the middle of the green was a fountain, its water just trickling out under nighttime pressure. He'd nearly driven into that pool once when celebrating a fraternity brother's return from Vietnam.

After walking up a long incline, he reached the far side of the green. A single car approached. The green VW's driver waved as he putted by. Once across the street, Chris walked to the north end of Sci. Hall and started up the fire escape. The metal stairway creaked with each step. He finally sat down on the ledge outside the third floor quant lab, remembering how shaky he'd felt at that height when, in college, he'd watched sunsets from the same perch.

Downtown's lights blinked through the treetops, revealing the college's flagpole on the green. Beyond it, Chris could just make out the outline of the former Queen City general hospital across from the northwest corner of the green. After the current hospital was constructed a few blocks away, the old hulk was sentenced to become doctors' offices. Chris thought back to the summers when he worked at the hospital while in college. That's when he'd first met Jack.

***

Chris had been hired as an orderly at Queen City General Hospital the summer after his sophomore year in college. He'd completed the mandatory training and spent a few weeks following one of the day staff around before being assigned to the evening shift. Most of the evening duties were completed by 10 o'clock, so orderlies often ended their shifts playing cards in the equipment room. It was dismal space, located below ground level, well beyond the reach of air conditioning, leaving it hot and stuffy most of the time. A large, gray metal desk sat in the concrete-block room's center, surrounded by a half dozen folding metal chairs. The rest of the space was crammed floor to ceiling with wheel chairs, sitz baths, gurneys, and other passé medical debris. One humid July evening, during a game of five-card stud, Chris pleaded with Jack, the newest orderly, to try out a local diversion. As Jack studied his cards, all Chris could see were Jack's stubby fingers, piercing eyes, and close-cropped, brown hair.

"You think I'm from some cabbage patch? I've heard all the checkered paint and tent stretcher stories," Jack said. "Somebody's always trying to cajole the new guys to try the same stupid shit they're embarrassed about. Then, when something goes wrong, they say, 'Just bad karma.' Well, I don't have to make stupid mistakes before I can condemn 'em. As a matter of fact, I can condemn something even if I don't know anything about it. I've got that kind of power."

"Won't you at least watch?" Chris said, tossing down another losing hand.

"Of course! It can't hurt. Besides, what you said about the free beer has a way of making stupid things sound a little sweeter. You know, beer's my name?"

"What?"

"Piwowicz means hops or rice in honyock, so that means beer, right?"

"I guess." Chris shrugged his shoulders.

The two punched out after the end of the shift and headed across the parking lot. Chris grabbed a six pack from the cooler in the back of his Aunt Harriet's old red Dodge Wayfarer. After a couple of swigs, the boys walked across the street and up the diagonal walkway, crossing the GMU green toward Sci. Hall. The flagpole waited near the top.

As they neared the pole, Chris said, "Wait here." He glanced around.

He chugged the last of his beer and tossed the empty on the grass beneath the Ira Allen memorial pine tree before shimmying a few feet up the flagpole. He untied the rope from its cleat and slid back down. The rope swung free.

"The guards use a little stepladder. I wonder what they think in the mornings when they see the rope flopping in the breeze."

"Maybe they don't. There not real cops."

Chris wound the rope around his hand before backing up as far from the pole as the rope would let him go. He took a deep breath then ran down the walkway away from the flagpole. When the tether stretched tight, the pole bent forward slightly under the tension before snapping back and lifting Chris into the night. He whirled through the darkness in a giant arc around the flagpole. His feet clipped small branches and needles off the towering Ira Allen pine while he was 15 feet off the ground. As the momentum died, he came down and landed in a run slightly uphill of the pole.

"Wow! That looked just as bad as I thought it would. You cajoled me just right." Jack took a long swig from his beer.

"Be sure to wrap the rope around your hand about three times. You don't want to fall because it's a long way down."

"I don't want to fall because it might hurt."

Jack wiped the sweat from his forehead then bit his cigarette between his teeth. He wrapped the rope round his hands, backed as far as the tether would let him go, then ran down the walkway. In an instant, he was catapulted into orbit. The cigarette flew off into the night.

"Lord love a duck!" he said as he came down and hit the ground running. He caught his balance and a toothy grin lit up his face. "I'd do that again even if there was no free beer."

And they did, over and over, giggling like children each time, until Chris noticed a college security cruiser driving through the parking lot beside Waterford Hall. The boys dropped the rope, picked up their empties, and walked back toward Chris's car.

"Let's get some fries," Chris said.

"There's nothing open at this hour."

"Yeah, there is. Benny's!"

Benny's was a yellow 1940's school bus filled with refrigerators, a grill, and deep-fat fryer. From May to October, it parked at the entrance to Bluffs Park every evening except Mondays. Benny's sold hot dogs, hamburgers, and greasy fries until the wee hours. On summer evenings, families picnicked on the park lawn, ate fries, and listened to concerts. After parents took their children home to bed, there was a lull until business picked back up after midnight. As the bars emptied, the park refilled. Cars pulled in and poured their occupants into a long line. The later the night, the larger the crowd. Townies said when the bars closed down, the bums went to Benny's.

Queen City was a small friendly place where everyone

knew everyone else or some relative. People came from all over the county to eat hot dogs and fries together. Sometimes people sat at the picnic tables, on the stone wall, or up in the bandstand until the sun came up.

Chris ordered a quart of fries and a couple of Cokes from Benny before walking back toward the old red Dodge.

"Let's eat up in the bandstand." Chris pointed toward the shadow lurking in the center of the park. "You can see everything."

They emptied their cups at the curb, refilled them with beer from the cooler in the Dodge, and walked to the bandstand. The story-and-a-half high structure resembled the turret of a careworn castle and was made of pebble-studded stucco. The surface was just bumpy enough to provide footholds for nighttime mountaineers. Chris climbed up first while Jack held the food below. He handed it up then followed. The entire park was visible in the half light of distant street lamps and moon glow. Benny's bus stood near the north entrance, General Well's statue guarded the southeast corner, and a low stone wall rode the crest of the bluff on the west, 250 feet above the lakeshore. Dannemora Prison's beacon flashed ghostly warnings across the black waters.

"Beauteous!" Jack said.

"You wouldn't say that during an August thunderstorm."

"I can say what I want. Doesn't mean it's true." Jack stood, holding his arms like the town maestro, pretending to direct a march and turn the pages of the silent music. Chris picked the last of the fries from his container.

"My Aunt Harriet used to bring us here for fries as kids."

"Who's Aunt Harriet and us?"

"My sister Catch and I…"

"Catch? You're not helping. Make it simple for me."

"My sister, Mary Catherine. I call her Catch. We lived with our Aunt Harriet and Uncle Jonathon over where the Hill Section—you know, the hospital university area—and the old North End meet. Quiet little street, near downtown. Everybody there owns a dog and kids walk to school."

"Sounds like *Leave It To Beaver*."

"Not quite. Uncle Jonathon has some issues…" Chris said, pointing his thumb to his mouth and raising his fist like a bottle. "So Aunt Harriet would get protective, especially when Uncle Jonathon would come home early and head to the garage. That meant there could be trouble. She'd call us and say, 'Let's go for a swim.' We'd jump in her old Dodge and drive over to North End Beach, leaving Uncle Jonathon to do whatever. We'd play around in the shallows and try to catch each other. Get it? 'Catch?'"

"I'm not as dumb as I look."

"We'd make sandcastles, play on the swings, maybe just stare off at the mountains while Aunt Harriet read. When it got late, I'd beg to stay. She'd promise to bring us back but must have felt guilty, so she'd bring us up here for fries and dogs." Chris reached out. "Can I have some of your fries? What brought you here? Queen City's not exactly the center of the universe."

"It was an accident, I guess. My old man pushed me out, so I joined the service. Corpsman, USN. The Navy loaned me to the Brits in Scotland, and one of the guys came from Queen City. We got pretty tight, called each other Chumley. Hung out in the pubs after hours and sang with the locals. I loved it. I would've stayed forever, but I couldn't stand the haggis. Old Chumley got out before me and dropped a few postcards. When my tour was up, I was headed home, but as the bus pulled into Port Huron, all the old shit came back. It never goes away. Then I found one of Chumley's postcards in my jacket pocket. I just sat back down and came to Vermont."

"Brothers and sisters?"

"Two of each. And my mom's great. How they can stay with my old man is beyond me. Thank goodness he was gone so much."

Chris searched through the vinegar drenched fries for the little crunchy pieces that fall through to the bottom of the container. "Where?"

Jack finished his beer. "Green Berets. He'd disappear for months at a time, training recruits to eat snakes and shit like that. It warped him. When he came home, he couldn't figure out how to deal with me, so he'd order me around like some new Joe. Hell, he could've taken me fishing or played catch, but I guess he was too busy being angry or drunk." Jack's face tightened. "He'd have a few shots of Yukon Jack, then stick his finger in my chest, push me backwards. One time, I was out late with some of my team-mates. He was waiting on the lawn, yelled 'You're AWOL, soldier,' and made me pull down my pants in front of my buddies. Took off his belt and spanked me like I was a fucking convict. Hell, I was only a couple of minutes late! You'd think I'd started the missile crisis."

"Jack, that's awful!"

"I looked him in the eye and clenched my teeth. He wanted me to cry but I'd learned not to show my hand. Once football was over, there was no one to hit back, and I got pretty angry. I knew I had to leave. The day after grad-uation, I was off to boot camp."

"Uncle Jonathon never abused anyone. He'd just have a few out in the garage. Sometimes, a friend would come over and they'd sit out there and tell stories until it was pretty late. But just the thought of it put Aunt Harriet in a state of..." A humming sound was coming from North End Avenue. The noise grew louder and louder until it became a roaring mechanical precision as a dozen chopped Har-leys and a couple of old Indians glided single file past Ben-ny's into the park. The biker's revved their engines, pulled to a halt, and lined up side by side along the curb. After some unseen signal, every one of them shut down at the same instant. The bikers climbed from the saddles before strolling toward the yellow French fry bus, laughing and talking.

"Who the hell are they?"

"The Wild Dogs. They're the local motorcycle pack. They come here most nights along with everyone else.

Come on!"

"Families, statues, symphonies, motorcycle madness. This is really an eclectic place."

The boys climbed down from the bandstand. Some of the Wild Dogs were already in line outside the serving window when Chris and Jack reached the bus. Most of the pack were dressed in their colors: dungarees, engineer boots, and black leather jackets. Their emblem, a chopper pointed at a star with a snarling wolfhound in the saddle, decorated the back of their jackets.

As Chris and Jack neared the bus, a single Honda 90 pulled into the park. A stocky kid with windblown blond hair got off. He wore cutoff jeans and a white t-shirt.

"Hey, Logan! What's up?"

"Hey, Chris. Just came out to play with the big kids and get some fries."

"Jack, this is Logan Cassidy," Chris said. "I used to work with him."

The two shook hands just as Benny's head stuck out the window of the bus. "Sorry, boys. Just dogs and drinks left. Just dogs and drinks!"

Logan looked up at Benny, pretending a sad face. "Man. I just drove all the way down here for a cheeseburger and fries, Benny. Can't you help me out?

"Sorry, boys. Just dogs and drinks."

People in line grumbled, but the scene had a cathartic effect on Jack. He inhaled, pursed his lips like a trumpeter, and blew through them while raising his arm in a slow, graceful arc. The ballerina-like movement contrasted sharply with the primitive noise coming from the air forced through his lips. The noise transformed the park into a jungle where wild, hungry dogs turned to the trumpet of his pachyderm.

"Sweat, beer, and French fries. And an elephant! I love this place."

***

Chris felt a chill and noticed the moon was partially hidden behind a cloud. He took hold of the rail, stood, and started back down the fire escape. His tracks were still visible on the college green, so he followed them toward Waterford Hall and his bed beyond.

5

The Academy's routines were comfortable. Chris found that once the confusion of September had passed, seasons differed little from year to year, allowing him to be in the patterns of an organized and structured world. He knew the facts: the facts never changed. He understood the expectations: texts were followed and progress recorded. The only variables were the individual students, and though his interaction with them was limited by class size, period length, and schedules, the possibility always existed that disturbances could threaten his routines. With Walt's sudden illness, another variable had been added to the mix.

Chris dropped his tote bag off in C44, picked up his coffee mug, and went to the teacher's lounge for his second cup of the day. Honora's back was to the door when he entered. She was listening to Millicent, one of the English teachers, as Chris reached for the coffee pot.

"But they are cheap. I bought one of those 10 packs over at Cost Plus. I keep a pair in my car, one at my desk, one in my purse. If I misplace one, I just grab another."

"I never lose mine. This little chain's my savior," Honora said, lifting off her glasses and displaying the imitation rhinestone chain that secured them to her neck. "My niece, Little Honey, gave it to me. I'd do anything for her. I told Brent it would be so much fun to have her classroom next to mine but when the Education Department's computer flooded last summer, they couldn't verify her credentials, so Brent had to hire Libby. That just wasn't fair."

The teacher's room door swung open again as K.J. and Libby entered. Honora changed trajectories. "So, Millicent. Are you still thinking of retiring next year?"

"I was until my annual statement arrived yesterday. I don't understand. I've worked for 40 years but still don't have enough to live on."

Chris picked up *The Daily Freeman* from the coffee table

and thumbed through the local section until he found the obituaries.

"Recognize any lottery winners?" K.J. said over Chris's shoulder.

"Lottery? I was checking the obits."

"Yeah, I know. That's the first thing most people check, but saying it sounds morbid so I call it the lottery. After all, they're both the same."

"I don't get it."

"Hey, you never know when your number'll come up."

"Oh, Chris. Hello!" Honora said.

Hearing his name, Chris recalled K.J. saying how Honora's voice sounded like sleigh bells on a snowy Christmas when she wanted something. He turned to find himself staring at her rhinestone necklace and the large cold sore on her lower lip. "Brent said you're the department chair while Walt's out."

"I guess I am."

"I have this wonderful idea for my recertification project. Can we talk?" Honora said, leading Chris to the far side of the room. "I think it would be just fabulous to host a series of historical dinners. We could charge $4 each and…"

"Honora, the projects aren't meant to be fund raisers. And besides…"

"Oh, I know, I know. But hear me out, Chris. Please! Walt always did!"

Chris took a deep breath and steeled himself. "OK. What's your idea?"

"Well, I only need three credits anyway, so this isn't really important. Besides, I've taken all the courses up at GMU."

"What's your idea, Honora?"

"I was thinking of picking out two or three crucial historical events—say the signing of the Magna Carta or the Norman Invasion—then do some research into what they were eating." Honora appeared to enter a trance-like state: her eyes glassed over. "I have some superb European recipes. Of course, I'd do all the cooking and the kids will sell the tickets, wait on tables, and print up menus. There's a gorgeous French scrip we could use for the font. A nice touch, don't you think? We could invite GMU's madrigal singers to…"

"I don't think that fits the criteria."

"Really, Chris! This has a lot of potential. Think of all the important decisions that have been made over boeuf bourguignon. Imagine Charlemagne and Pepin at a long table with silver chalices of Pinot Noir, swords hanging nearby. Imagine warm French bread! It's inspiring just to think about what they ate. And to taste it! To really taste it!"

"French bread! I'll take a couple of loaves, Honora. How much?" K.J. said from the couch.

"I hadn't thought of that. We could bake extra loaves! Let's see, 300 is a good number. We could keep the cost down if …"

"I'm sorry, but I don't think it's going to fly," Chris said.

"What about a Middle Eastern theme, Honora? Say 1001 Arabian bites? I'd like to sit next to Scheherazade," K.J. said.

Chris wanted to punch the skinny son of a bitch but held his temper.

"We could all dress up. Little Honey will help out of course. She is quite a seamstress."

Lord have mercy! Honora and Little Honey in costume in a kitchen was almost more than Chris could bear. He could hear the pots and pans pounding against the counters and imagined servers dressed in tights, wearing little jester hats with bells!

"Honora, the guidelines are clear. This is a once in a lifetime thing. Something you've never done! And there has to be academic value. We all know you've done historical dinners, and they were wonderful, but…"

"How about a night with the Medicis? I love gnocchi," the wiry teacher said, kissing his fingertips. "Fantastico!"

"But I don't think a dinner will work this time. Perhaps doing a research unit on nutrition during a particular time period would be more appropriate, but not another…"

Honora spun about before Chris could finish, began muttering, and left the room. Chris inhaled before taking a long sip of coffee.

"Ah, but for some boeuf bourguignon!" K.J. said.

"And a nice Beaujolais. What's that all about?" Libby said, walking over.

"I don't need this."

"Well, boss. I have a great idea for my project." K. J. said.

"Seriously?"

"Of course." K.J. said, clasping his skinny hands together. "It's got everything the good doctor—excuse me—President George would want. Databases, research, student involvement, artifacts, and—ah—did I mention databases?"

"Sounds exciting. Tell us more," Libby said.

"I call it shared historical information technology research. The acronym will be SHIT'R."

Chris closed his eyes and shook his head.

"Seriously, here's what I'm thinking. First, I'll ask Raji in IT to scare up some space on the PROC TLG server. Then my kids will design a questionnaire. It'll be an inventory sheet for a database. I plan to list the historical resources available in each of Vermont's 251 towns."

"Not all of them have resources or even libraries," Libby said.

"Doesn't matter. The less the better. I'm looking for re-certification not the Nobel Prize."

K.J. used the Bixby Library in Vergennes as an example. It had hundreds of artifacts on the second floor—arrowheads, pottery, and tools—but outside Vergennes, very few knew about it. He said Raji could build a site with links to the state libraries homepage, and his students would collect similar data from around the state and populate the database on the server.

"Bingo, every school in the state knows what's available, where it's located, and how to get it."

"K.J. That's brilliant," Libby said.

"It is. Just what the doctor ordered. Besides, it gives new meaning to the old expression, 'I'm going to the SHIT'R.'"

"Mr. Monroe!" Libby said, pretending to slap K.J.'s wrist.

"What about you, Libby? Any ideas?"

"I'm not that far along, but I'm thinking of designing a unit for AP students in which we compare different versions of the same historical events."

"Like the two movie versions of *The Last of the Mohicans*?" K.J. said.

"Sort of. I was thinking of investigating how scholarship and time changes our perception of people and events. Native Americans, for example, appear quite different if you compare the captivity narratives of the 18th and 19th centuries with the research of current historians like Colin Calloway. Or we could compare perspectives on the French and Indian War by looking at the writings of Francis Parkman versus Fred Anderson. Chris, any ideas?"

"I haven't thought about it much."

"I've got some demography books. You could design a data-collection project," K.J. said.

"Maybe."

"You might even try something fun," Libby said. "The county genealogical society's website says there's an open house next weekend. I bet they've got ideas you could use."

"I almost took their intro course a while ago. I have an ancestor, Christopher Gordon, who I was named after. I was told he fought in the Civil War so I was going to…"

"Gordon?" K.J. said, wearing a big smile.

"Yeah. The Gordons came from Scotland. What's so funny?"

"Nothing really, boss, but I've always thought of you as a George."

"I know a teacher over at Weaverton High who could help," Libby said. "She uses genealogy in her classes. Her kids love it—especially when they discover oddball stuff about their own families. What do you think?"

"Maybe. I'll think about it." He took another sip of coffee as the door opened.

Doctor George and Brent entered the room and began greeting the other teachers.

"Careful about thinking too much. And look, Brent's tassels are erect. Do you think that's Freudian?"

"Everyone's looking great today!" Brent said crossing the room.

Chris nearly spilled his coffee when Brent reached out to grasp his hand.

Dr. George just nodded, his face was no more expressive than the sand on North End Beach.

"Chris, Dr. George and I would like to talk with you."

"Sure."

Chris followed them into the conference room and closed the door as Brent began.

"Myra Spelling over at the State Certification Standards Board is holding an all-districts conference call after lunch today. We wondered if you had any feedback yet on the recertification alternative."

"Not much. We just found out yesterday."

"Can you share what you're hearing? We don't want to be caught blind if Myra pulls the trigger," Dr. George said.

"Everyone seems positive."

"Ideas?"

Chris's eyes darted between the two. "They cover a broad spectrum. One's an imaginative media study. Another is a great technology application. One, well, ah…"

"Honora wants to do another dinner, I suppose?" Brent said. Chris nodded and gulped more coffee.

"Keep pressing them. We can't slow the train. There's a lot of bandwidth to fill if we're going to stay on the curve," said Dr. George.

"What about you, Chris? Do you have something, yet? You are the new chair." Brent's eyes narrowed, making Chris feel like a witness on the stand.

"I've had a couple of ideas. But it's still early."

"Let us in."

"They're really just in the formative stage."

"Yes? And?"

"We'll, it's so early. I may have to change everything."

"Your leadership is important. *You* are the chairman," Dr. George said.

Chris's breathing become labored as tension tightened around his chest. He sensed Dr. George and Brent circling him until his options had run out.

"It's all preliminary, but I'm thinking about a genealogy project. It may involve the county genealogical society. There's a teacher at Weaverton High who uses genealogy in her classes. I have to discuss my ideas with her before I commit. You know databases…" Dr. George smiled. "…records research, data gathering, etc., but I'll need to work with my contact. I'll let you know."

"Who is it?" Brent said. "Your contact? Who is your contact?"

The belt around Chris chest began to tighten again but slacked off the instant the Academy's metallic horn sounded attendance period.

"I've got to run, guys. Attendance then World Outlook up on C level. I'll keep in touch."

"I like the database stuff."

"Don't forget our eighth-period meeting."

Chris caught up with K.J. and Libby outside the central stairway. "I'm in it now."

"What do you mean?" Libby said.

"I'll need to talk to your friend over at Weaverton."

"Don't worry. We'll figure this out."

The constriction in Chris's chest had nearly disappeared by the time they'd reached the top of the central stairway, but as they stepped through the swinging doors into the corridor, Chris noticed Michael Andover and T.D. Glover walking toward him and the tension returned.

6

Chris floated through the rest of the day as if programmed by some inner operating system over which he had no control. He arrived at the appropriate classrooms at the appointed times, assigned readings, and even verbalized correct responses to the most difficult student inquiries. He felt only able to comprehend what was directly in front of him. Somehow the hours whisked by, which surprised him since a meeting with Brent was normally not high on his list. Today, it was even lower. After his seniors filed out at the end of seventh period, his stomach began to flutter.

He cleared his desk, picked up his coffee mug, and hurried toward the central stairway. The crowding had already dissipated so he could move quickly. He reached A level in half the normal time, so he detoured into the teachers' lounge, where Honora and some of the English teachers were discussing the benefits of soluble fiber in a white-bread world. Chris refilled his green-and-gold mug with the remnants of the day's coffee and waved to K.J., who was correcting papers on the coffee table by the couch. He checked his mailbox—empty—then noticed Libby enter the room. She walked over to him. "Are you ready for Brent?"

"I think so. He doesn't bite."

"I wouldn't go that far." K.J. said from the couch. "There are rumors."

Libby's eyes widened. Honora turned from her conversation. "Rumors?"

"The usual drivel. His wife always wears longs sleeves, or she missed the faculty party because she walked into a door," K.J. said, pushing his glasses back up his nose.

"He's anal, not brutal," Chris said and started for the door.

Anita Small looked up from her keyboard when Chris

entered the principal's outer office.

"Hi, Chris. Right on time."

"Anything new on Walt today?"

"I've left a message but no call back."

Anita smiled with the compassionate grace of the Madonna. It reminded Chris why K.J. called her "Our Lady of the Academy."

"With all the concern over Walt, I haven't asked about your brother lately. How is he?"

"He's been down. Doesn't think I should have to take care of him, but what am I to do? He's got nothing. No insurance. And it just keeps eating away at him."

"St. Peter's got a halo for you."

"Just as long as I don't have to die to get it."

When the clock turned to 2:20, the metallic horn sounded and Brent's door opened. His hands preceded him.

"Chris, Chris! So glad you could make it." He glanced at Anita. "I'll be in conference until quarter of." Brent looked at the papers on Anita's desk and flicked his hand toward them. "Tidy this up. I'm expecting some alumni Monday. You can never tell what they'll think. Come on in, Chris."

Brent's office also had been redecorated over the summer. Though it was painted the same educational beige as Chris's room, there were differences. Chris room didn't have an Afghan rug, wing back chairs, and a desk the size of a billiard table. "Nice rug, Brent."

"Yes, yes. The muted blues and reds really accentuate the hardwood floor. And a new desk too. Did you notice? Mahogany polishes so well!"

A sparkling blade putter leaned against one of the new Cardiff House arm chairs. Brent repositioned it against his bookcase, placing it beside a pair of white golf shoes resting on a fluffy red towel. Chris glanced around the room. An electronic picture frame on the bookcase flashed photos of Brent playing golf or shaking hands with other tan men wearing visors and short-sleeve shirts. One photo showed Brent accepting a trophy from a man wearing a Catamount Valley Club jacket. It faded away. The next displayed Brent chipping out of the "big beach" sand trap on the 15th fairway. The sand floated toward the camera in a nearly perfect semicircular arch. That image repeated every fourth spot in the rotating sequence.

The bookcase also held a few ornamental coffee table volumes. Beside one stood a large frame displaying a photo of Brent and Dr. George with arms over each other's shoulders as they stood before a Catamount Valley Invitational banner. The shelves were filled with golf trophies, golf knickknacks, and golf balls. One tiny frame on the top shelf pictured Brent speaking before a student assembly. Chris squinted, trying to recognize any of the students.

"You've got some great photos."

"This is my favorite." The sand wedge shot appeared right on cue. "I shot just two over that day. Great game! And look at my feet. Perfect position! Golf teaches us a lot, Chris. When you're all alone on the fairway with your clubs and the ball, you have to take chances. You have to go for the gold."

"I suppose."

"You've never been an athlete, Chris, so it's hard for you to understand but..." Brent looked down at his chronograph. "We'll get to that another time. I'll cut to the chase. We need to talk about your new responsibilities in history."

Chris thought of Walt. "Have you heard from Walt's family?"

"I haven't had the time."

"I talked with his son-in-law last night. Didn't know much. His wife's been sick, too, you know."

"I told Anita to get in touch..."

"For God's sake, Brent, he's worked here 40 years, and you haven't tried to call." Chris's heartbeat accelerated and the discomfort returned to his chest, but he bit back the emotions stirring inside.

"There's really nothing we can do, so let's get our jobs done."

Just what he expected. Chris folded his arms.

"There's a lot of pressure right now. Dr. George has high expectations. He doesn't want anything to suffer because Walt's out—especially in light of the break we're getting from the certification people. Myra is a big help. Have you decided what you're going to do?"

Chris blinked quickly. "Not yet."

"Well, since you haven't, here's an idea. You know Myra's put herself out on a limb so many times that, ah, Dr. George thought it might be a nice gesture to do something to help her look good. And you're the chair."

Chris thought of the air raid sirens that proceeded Luftwaffe attacks over London. "So?"

"GMU doesn't hold a corner on the historic-preservation market. It was Myra's specialty, you know. I bet she'd really appreciate it if you had your kids to do something like—oh, I don't know—identify historic houses in the Old North End. They could build a diorama of the old neighborhoods. Could be a great photo-op. Imagine a group of Academy kids standing in front of the doors at the old bus garages or Fassett's Bakery or the Ten Commandments. *The Freeman* would eat it up. I'll bet it would improve relations with GMU. Regan Andover runs historic preservation, and he's not happy with you right now."

"What?"

"He called with some questions about your credentials. His son's been complaining about your classes. He told Regan they're rather flat."

Chris watched the rotating picture of the sand-trap shot come up again. The pressure behind his breast bone seemed to be increasing. Brent stood, picked up his putter, and walked over to the synthetic green rug in the corner, where he lined up an imaginary putt.

"Now, has anyone in your department handed in a proposal for certification yet?"

"I told you what I knew this morning. They're not due till November 15th!"

"I know, I know but we've got to keep the pressure

up. You're too laissez faire. You'll never gain legitimacy as chairman that way. We can't miss this one. If anything fails, the board won't look favorably upon you remaining chairman."

"I thought this was a temporary thing."

"Yes and no. If Walt can't come back, the contract says I have to offer the chair to the senior teacher in the department. If you want it, that is."

Chris clenched his jaw.

"But don't make any mistakes. The union really pushed for that clause. They wanted us to buy local instead of going outside. They'll be after you to prove it was a good decision, and the board will be looking for leadership. In either case, you've got to perform."

"What if I don't want it?"

"Get out now. It will be better for everyone. I'll just appoint Honora, and she can take the heat. She's next in line. Actually, you'd be doing me a favor by stepping aside. Everybody knows she's going to fall. She's still living in the '60s. Historic dinners for credit! Even I know that's crap!"

"You want to fire her?"

"No! Just nudge her out. Once she's gone, the contract says I can go outside the system and pick who I want. That'll mean two vacancies. By the way, what do you think of Honora's niece, Little Honey? The state just squared away her credentials, and she wants a job. We could slip her right in. Very stylish too. We need new blood!"

As Brent lined up another putt, Chris's fingers dug into the arms of Brent's wingback.

"I can see you're busy, Brent. How much time do I have? I mean, what's the contract say about when I have to decide?"

"If Walt stays out, you've got till the last day of school to sign a contract."

"Just like the other teachers?"

"We want them back by May first, but officially all contracts are due the last day of the school year. This year, that's, let me see." Brent walked to his desk and flipped through his calendar. "The day after Memorial Day."

"I'll let you know."

"I know you don't want this, Chris. You can just bow out and save us all, I mean, yourself, the aggravation."

Chris was at the door before Brent's hands could extend, leaving Brent leaning over his desk, off balance. He recovered then pressed the intercom button as Chris passed Anita's desk.

"Anita, I'm going to try to get nine holes in. Weather's still good. If anyone calls, tell them I'm in conference."

Chris drove home after work. When he parked outside his apartment, his neighbor and his neighbor's little rat-faced dog were just rounding the corner. He picked up his mail and climbed the stairs and smiled at Dylan before sitting down at his tiny kitchen table with the bills and advertisements that seemed to fill his life. He tossed the junk mail into recycling, leaving the bills in a neat stack off to one side. Above them, old black-and-white photos hung on his bulletin board in a montage of his past.

A young Chris and a teenage Catch stood on a porch along with Aunt Harriet and Uncle Jonathon, a stern faced woman in a calf-length house dress and a bald man wearing a double breasted suit. Another pictured a group of young men in chinos and button-down shirts laughing while sitting on stone steps. An old car with big headlights; two little boys seated in a Radio Flyer. The last was much older: a baseball diamond with tall elm trees in the background. Several lanky teenage boys were lined up along the third baseline wearing old baseball uniforms that said Lakeside. Someone had circled in pencil the face of a boy in the back row.

7

Chris had not recognized the bald man in the brown suit, but Catch had nodded, which gave Chris permission to follow the man into the house. They walked through unfamiliar rooms, cluttered with black-and-white photos of people Chris didn't recognize and trophies for teams that no longer competed. One, picturing boys in uniforms, holding bats and gloves, stood alone on a side table.

"Who are those guys, Uncle Jonathon?"

"That's me."

"You don't look very happy."

"I've only cried a couple times. Once, when old Doc Tomasi said I'd never play again. The other when those guys shipped out for the South Pacific." He lowered his head and walked out to the back porch.

Aunt Harriet pointed toward another boy. "Your father before the war. Wasn't he handsome?"

Catch smiled but Chris just studied the unfamiliar face.

"Come with me. I'll fix you something to eat." Aunt Harriet led the children into the kitchen, where she made peanut-butter-and-jelly sandwiches and poured glasses of milk.

Once she'd served the food, Aunt Harriet lifted her apron over the top of her perm and excused herself to step outside to speak with Uncle Jonathon, who was standing outside the garage.

"I don't like this place, Catch."

"It'll be OK."

"They're not very friendly."

"They don't know how. They don't have any children of their own."

***

The early summer was filled with the sounds of baseball being played across the street at Pomeroy Park. Chris joined pickup games until July turned torrid and the regulars disappeared. Then he pushed himself on the front porch glider and sorted his Topps cards while Catch practiced the piano. A calm afternoon could change if Uncle Jonathon came home early from the bakery. Aunt Harriet would watch him for the clues disguised by tight lips and piercing eyes. She'd listen for abruptness and displeasure. If they showed themselves, she'd gather the children.

"Let's go for a swim," she'd say and they'd pile in her red Dodge Wayfarer for the drive to North End Beach.

Chris loved the big maroon sedan with its big round headlights, chrome bumpers, and long sloped-backed roof. It smelled showroom, and the cloth bench seats felt like sofas. A radio dominated the center of the dash with letters on each of the five station buttons, spelling out Dodge.

Once they arrived, the children carried their inner tubes from the lot through the beach house to the lakeside steps. Then they hurried down, sprinting blanket to blanket across blistering sand for the water. Aunt Harriet followed with her low beach chair and placed it in ankle-deep water. She read while the children splashed, or made sand castles, or gazed off at the Adirondacks. When the sun reached the tops of the mountains, Aunt Harriet began folding her chair.

"Can we come back? I love this place."

"As often as you like, Chris" she'd say. "Now, let's go to Benny's."

After dark, Chris would sneak into Catch's bedroom, carrying his father's baseball mitt, and lay on the floor beside his sister's bed.

"Do you miss them? I know I do," Catch would say.

He'd pound the dried out leather mitt and stare at the ceiling.

"It's OK to be sad. We all are."

He'd continue to pound the mitt.

"Someday, I'm going to hit the ball clear over the fence and break slates off Madigan's roof, just like the big guys."

Catch's bedroom was at the rear of the house, above the driveway. When her window was open, they could hear Uncle Jonathon talking with his pal Mick Finnigan in the garage below. Mick, a brawny man with a boxer's nose and puffy eyes, managed Mount Saint Brendan's Cemetery for the Queen City Diocese. Aunt Harriet never let alcohol in the house, so Uncle Jonathon moved the Dodge out and sat with Mick in the dark, chewing the fat while sipping from quarts of Ballantine Ale.

"When I was a kid, I delivered *The Freeman* up in the Hill Section," Uncle Jonathon said one night. "Hell, the bankers used to set their watches by me. Old Colonel H. Nelson Jackson was the best of that bunch. He'd be waiting for me on his porch with his coffee. He'd talk about his father-in-law, General Wells, the one who won the Medal of Honor at Gettysburg. The Colonel even opened me a savings account at Queen City Savings. Back about nineteen aught three, the Colonel drove his Winton cross country. He brought his dog. Can you believe…"

"Speaking of cars, I ever tell you bout the parade they held for silent Cal?" Mick interrupted.

"What parade?"

"The president and the missus come up to Queen City to visit Grace's family and, a course, all the politicians wanted a parade." Mick took a long sip. "They needed a fancy car, so they called Ernie Jefferson, the bootlegger. He was nuttin' but a bum but looked sharp. Funny, ain't it, how the bellhop manager at the Hotel Vermont always wore a double-breasted suit? Big Al! He had 'bout the best car in town, a big Packard Phaeton, deep brown, fast. Polished it so she shined just like a banker's coffin."

"God damn it, Mick. That's funny."

"Chris!" Aunt Harriet stood in the doorway and pointed toward his bedroom.

"Why can't I listen?"

"It's late."

"But it's summer."

"Well, it's…that's not for children."

"Why not? They're just telling stories."

"Chris, they're drinking, and they don't behave the way they should. Now, that's between you and I and the lamppost." She held her finger to her lips. "Now off to bed with you. And, Mary Catherine, you too."

Chris felt torn, looking into his aunt's melancholy eyes. He loved her but also liked listening to Uncle Jonathon's stories. He stood, placed his hand against the wall, and guided himself down the dark corridor to his bedroom. Peering into the darkness above his bed, he folded his hands together. "God, please don't make me choose. I can't. I promise to be good if you make Uncle Jonathon stop drinking."

***

Mick and Uncle Jonathon continued their story telling ritual each summer. One evening, during the spring after Chris started high school, he overheard Mick complaining.

"Can't get good help at the cem no more. I got one stupid kid working for me. Sent him up in the horse barn for checkered paint, and he's gone near an hour, for cripe's sake. Idiot! He near walked into an open grave one time. I thought he broke his…"

"You need help? My nephew's a smart kid, and he could use a few bucks."

"Send him over. Now, the kid's name is Carter. The boys pick on him mercilessly, askin' him where he keeps his Little Liver Pills. Kid just don't get it."

The Catholic diocese had a big budget for Mount Saint Brendan's in those days. Four or five men worked out of the horse barn from April to October. They raked leaves, cut the grass, watered the geraniums, and even helped the vets put out tiny flags for Memorial Day.

When Chris reported for work the next morning, another local kid, Logan Cassidy, was there too. The foreman showed the boys how to gas up the mowers, change the oil, and sharpen the blades before sending them off to mow. Chris cut in the cemetery's top section that day. Pushing his machine around the large granite stones, he noticed familiar local names. Fitzsimons, McMahon, Casey, Finnigan, Gillis, Cassidy, Lonergan, and Cashman were all families Uncle Jonathon and Mick told stories about. They had been contractors, lawyers, priests, or even bootleggers. They'd built Queen City and Weaverton, and they'd become rich and famous—or infamous, depending on Uncle Jonathon's story.

After lunch, Chris noticed Logan's mower running unattended beneath a maple tree near the gazebo, but Logan was nowhere in sight. Chris eventually spotted him: he was high up in the maple's branches, watching the gates to the cemetery. When Mick's big black Lincoln rounded the corner at the top of Archer Street, Logan jumped down and started mowing where he'd left off. After Mick parked, he called everyone together and ordered the boys to fill the potholes in the dirt drive.

"The undertakers get pissed when the hearses scrape bottom!" he said.

"Mick's more worried about scratching his own Continental than the hearses," Logan whispered to Chris as he pushed his long blond hair from his eyes.

Once Mick drove off, Logan restarted his mower and climbed back up the maple.

***

Chris felt lost when Catch started attending Trinity College and moved to its campus, but he called her daily. After meeting Mike Thompson at a sock hop in the gym, she told Chris, "He walked up and said I looked just like Natalie Wood and asked me to dance. I felt like I was in a cocoon when he wrapped his big arms around me."

She told Chris everything. They laughed and cried and sometimes they sang songs they'd heard on the radio. After Catch married Mike, they had less time to talk. Chris's oldest nephew, Mikey, was born two years later, and Jimmy arrived the year after that. Because Catch's life was no longer her own, the brother and sister postponed their conversations until her boys were asleep. Chris watched the clock then stretched the phone cord to the dining room closet. He'd sit beneath the long coats and tell Catch stories of his friends, and the sports he played, and the tests he'd taken until she couldn't keep her eyes open any longer. Later, Chris babysat for his nephews so his sister could work the evening shift at the Hotel Vermont to help pay for the new house.

***

"I'm going to GMU," Chris told Aunt Harriet during his senior year at the Academy. "It's cheaper than going away, and I can walk to class."

His first semester was a blur of classes, studying, and sleep. He slept away much of Christmas break before hitting the books again in January. During his sophomore year, he took calculus, English, history, French, ROTC, and chemistry. He added a PE course, choosing basketball because the running would help recover from his freshman fifteen.

The PE classes were a mixture of conditioning and competition. After stretching and passing drills, they scrimmaged. Chris's team played together all semester. He and Pat Carmichael, a six footer with long brown hair, usually played guards, bringing up the ball. Jim Underwood played center. He was taller and more muscular than Pat, and he had a thin chiseled face and elbows that banged up most opponents. There were others. Their approach wasn't sophisticated, just pushing the ball up to the first open man and shooting. As Chris left the showers after one of the scrimmages, Pat Carmichael called to him. "We have a hoop over at the frat house. Come on over on Saturday and meet some of the guys. We'll play a little three on three."

"What house?"

"Theta Alpha Chi. You know, TAC."

TAC was a block north of GMU's green. On Saturday morning, Chris walked over to the massive, three-story brick building sitting atop a Redstone foundation. Chris knocked several times before Pat answered the door. "Nobody ever knocks. From now on, just walk in."

Pat led Chris into a wood-paneled hallway. A fireplace was before them, a staircase off to the right. In a smaller room, several fraternity brothers lay across some old stuffed chairs and a threadbare couch. There was a banged-up upright piano against the far wall with a Zenith portable TV on top. Someone had attached a twisted coat hanger in place of the rabbit ears. *Sky King* was playing but the reception was so snowy that one of the brothers kept getting up to wiggle the coat hanger.

"Hey, guys. This is Chris," Pat said from the doorway. A couple of the brothers waved. "I said, this is Chris. What do we say when we meet someone new?"

Other brothers turned and smiled, but Pat would have none of that. He called each by name and made them get up and shake Chris's hand. Jim Underwood from PE was there, along with a few guys Chris recognized from the corridors of Lafayette Hall, including Walt McCormack. Then Logan Cassidy walked into the room.

"I didn't know you were a brother," Chris said.

"He's a legacy." Underwood said. "His great grandfather built this place."

After the intros, the brothers returned to *Sky King* but Pat led Chris through the house.

"Now you have to meet El, our house mother."

Chris followed Pat through the living room, where the walls were covered with framed black-and-white photos of former fraternity brothers dressed in tuxedoes, reminding Chris of the photos in Uncle Jonathon's living room. Next, the dining room was long and narrow, paneled in dark wainscoting, which was topped with an eye-level shelf, where the brother's beer mugs stood on display. A single red coffee mug sat beside them. Chris pointed at it.

"El's. She tosses her pension money in, just in case

someone runs short of cash."

At a dinged wooden table, a plume of cigarette smoke rose from behind an open copy of *The Daily Freeman*.

"El!"

A couple of coughs sounded from behind the paper. "Excuse me. I'm still primping. I'll be down shortly," a whiskey voice said.

"El, this is Chris. Chis, this is Eleanor Masterson."

The paper inched downward, exposing a long, thin face. El's blue eyes were slightly bloodshot, her skin alabaster white. Bobby pins corralled most of her auburn/gray hair but some had broken free, giving her the windblown look of a girl raised on the Great Plains. El ran her hand through the mess, pushing fractious strands from her eyes. "Hi, Chrissy Chris."

"Hi back."

"El's our house marm, and she knows how to keep boys in line. Twenty five years in the WACs."

El forced a smile, stood up, and took a long Garbo-like drag from an unfiltered butt before walking into the kitchen. "You guys better straighten out this dump today," she called back. "Or you'll be sorry."

"El, I love it when you're angry. Please yell again. It really turns me on."

"Honeybun, bug-a-boozer, cut the crap. Some of the alums are coming to Sunday's chapter meeting. If this place doesn't look good, they'll be pissed."

Chris looked over at Pat. "A few of the prewar brothers still show up for the meetings. They trade war stories with El. Most come so they don't have to drink alone, and there's always someone here to order around."

"Cut the crap!"

"And they're our advisors. We're supposed to glean whatever wisdom they impart."

"You'll laugh out of the other side of your mouth, honeybun."

"She means well," Pat whispered before raising his voice again. "And we all love her."

"Cut the crap, and clean up this dump."

Pat signaled Chris to follow and started toward the living room, but Chris stopped and peeked in the red cup. It was filled with fives and tens. Back in the TV room, Pat turned off the Zenith.

"OK, guys. There's a chapter meeting Sunday. Here's what we're going to do."

He ordered the brothers to gather the trash, clean the bathrooms, and move the furniture back into some sort of order. Chris, Logan, and Walt were to wash windows. By midafternoon, the house was presentable, and Chris knew all the brothers. When he spoke with Catch that evening, he told her all about TAC.

"Sis, I love it. It feels more like home than Uncle Jonathon's ever did. The next time I go over, I'm going to bring Jack."

"He's not a student."

"I don't think it matters to those guys."

***

Jack was the ideal pledge but for the fact that he wasn't a student. He played sports, drank beer, memorized poetry, and stayed up late. The house had no formal rituals or secret passwords so if someone liked the place enough, he was considered a brother. Jack's acceptance, however, was called into question at a late-April house meeting.

"He can't join!" Underwood said. "He's not a matriculated student."

"Hold on," Pat said. "The Greek statutes and the house bylaws leave a lot of leeway. We'll just make him a social associate under some bullshit rule or other."

"What the hell does that mean?" Jack said.

"You pay your dues in cash, but you can't vote or be in house pictures."

"What if I can't pay? I work at a hospital!"

"We'll figure something. Next item on the agenda is…"

"Not according to Hoyle," Underwood said. "And get

your feet off the couch, Jack!"

"Screw you, Underwood," Pat said. "I'm pre-law; you're business. He's in. Next item!"

Jack smiled. "I feel like an altar boy. Sit up front at Mass and don't have to give to the collection."

Logan Cassidy handed Jack a beer as Chris put his arm over Jack's shoulder.

"Congratulations, brother!"

***

Chris signed up to take Romantic Literature the following semester. He was late for the first lecture in Lafayette Hall, arriving just as Dr. Brown called his name. He took the empty seat in the third row and found himself next to Susan Boisvert. He blushed when she smiled. Her face was cherub-like with bright hazel eyes that seemed to look right through him. She wore her long light-brown hair back with a barrette. He took out his notebook and decided to find out more about her.

Outside Lafayette Hall they talked after their third class. He asked what courses she was taking and where she lived before she hurried off.

The following week, Chris overslept and missed a lecture. Susan shared her class notes so he thanked her by inviting her to the dairy bar that afternoon. She liked maple walnut ice cream, she said. They ate their cones, walking across the campus green toward the traffic light at Main Street.

"They say Dr. Brown was a war hero, that he was wounded in the South Pacific."

"I've heard that, but it can't be true. He's so passionate about poetry. Men like that don't kill others. They can't," she said.

"I don't know. People adapt to their circumstances. If you're being fired at..."

"Nobody changes that much. You're either weak or strong."

"What are you?"

"Wonderful! Don't you think so?"

Chris couldn't hold back his smile. "Yeah. I do!"

The longer they walked, the more comfortable he felt. They slowed near the corner, then stopped, talking through a half dozen changes of the stop light.

"Hope to see you soon." She said, stepping away.

Chris's heart pounded as he ran all the way to Weaverton Ave.

***

TAC's homecoming party was the first weekend in October, the evening after GMU beat the Black Bears 21–14. When Chris arrived at the house, kegs lined the hallway and dancers packed the living room, where the Hardly Worth Mentionings, a local band, blasted out nearly recognizable covers from a small platform in the corner. Logan handed Chris a red plastic cup filled with draft. He took a sip before dancing through the living room to see who was there. He greeted a couple of friends after the song then headed for the kitchen.

Jack was dealing cards in the dining room. Holding them close under his chin, he glanced from player to player. Chris walked by, tapped Jack's shoulder, and winked. "Sandwich?"

Jack shook his head before spreading his cards on the table and saying, "Pony up, Dido!" to his latest victim.

El had left an overcooked turkey on the kitchen shelf with paper plates and plastic forks nearby. Chris dug out a few pieces of moist meat from below the drumstick before opening the cupboard, looking for a loaf of white bread. Closing it, he found himself facing Susan. "What are you doing here?"

"Same as you. Listening to the music and dancing. I hope. He brought me." Susan nodded toward Jim Underwood, who stood beside the stainless-steel milk dispenser. Underwood's index finger was pointed into the face of some poor freshman.

"Excuse us, Chris." Walt and his tiny blonde date squeezed past Chris and Susan on their way towards the living room.

"Hey, Walt."

"Hey, Chris. Meet Mini."

"Nice to meet you, Mini. This is Susan. How are you feeling? That Bears tackle pushed you around a lot today."

The big lineman's face wore the reds and blues of battle where elbows and fists had found their way through the opening between his face mask and helmet, leaving Walt's nose, bent long ago in some fight, looking puffy. Still, he smiled. "He was a maanster. A gaad damn maanster, but I kicked his ass in the second half and can still dance. Can't I, Mini?"

"He sure can! But he only likes the slow ones. I like everything."

The shapely blonde in the tight red skirt pulled him toward the music as the Mentionings's lead guitar played the intro notes to a surfing song.

"Walt, don't forget, Aunt Harriet's expecting you for dinner tomorrow."

"See you around noon," Walt said over his shoulder.

The volume kept increasing, becoming so loud Chris couldn't understand what Susan was saying, so he led her through the kitchen, tapping Jim on the shoulder as they passed. "She's in my English class. I need to ask her about the midterm." Chris pointed toward the porch door.

Jim nodded before turning back to the unlucky freshman.

The noise softened once they were out on the porch though they felt the drums pounding.

"I'm glad you're here. I never expected it."

"I met Jim last year. He asks me out sometimes."

"Are you..."

"No. We date others. I just let him tell me his problems. This is a great house. Do you belong?"

"I guess I do. I joined last spring. There are some really

great guys here."

"Jim says some of them can get out of hand."

"I don't know about that. Can I get you a beer?"

"No thanks. I can't." She held out her hand out like a traffic cop.

"Can't?"

"Family problems. My dad. Let's not get into it now. You were telling me about the fraternity."

"My Uncle Jonathon can get out of hand. Is it bad?"

"Please. It's embarrassing. I'd rather not."

"OK. The house: it's more like a boy's clubhouse than a fraternity. The guys are great. And there's always something going on. Are you in a house?"

"Takes too much time. I usually go home weekends. Big family."

"Well, maybe you could stay some weekend and let me take you out."

The door opened, and Jim stepped out on the porch. He belched. "Come on, Sue. We're going to dance."

Jim took Susan's hand and led her inside but she turned back and whispered just as the door closed. "I'd like that."

Chris looked up at the stars. He took a swig of beer, but it had turned flat so he left the cup on the rail and squeezed back through the kitchen crowd. Jack was sitting behind a pile of quarters in the dining room. The living room and front-hall dance floor were packed with moving couples. Chris squinted into the darkness, searching for Susan but among the blurred moving bodies only one couple stood out: Walt and Mini. They were gyrating to a thumping beat from the base guitar. And all the brothers were focused on Mini's red skirt and what she let the music do with it.

***

The brothers held their annual hay ride late in October. Chris gathered up his courage and asked Susan to go with him. She accepted. A lover's moon rose as the brothers and their dates piled on to the hay wagon at Queen City Orchards. Chris and Susan sat near the middle.

"We can wrap up in this," Susan said covering their legs with a red-and-black checkered blanket.

They threw hay at each other, sang "Kumbaya" off-key, and sipped hot spiced cider from a large thermos Susan had brought along. The stars sparkled through a frosty veil.

"Chris, want to add some hard stuff? It'll keep you warm," Logan said, holding a flask.

"No thanks. We're warm enough," Susan said, pulling the blanket up and snuggling next to Chris.

Later, Chris took Susan's hand in his as they walked through the parking lot toward Aunt Harriet's red Dodge. They drove back to the fraternity, where couples danced to the Lettermen in the darkened living room. Chris then drove Susan back to her dorm for curfew. On the steps outside, he asked her if he could kiss her goodnight. She just closed her eyes and leaned forward.

***

Chris cherished his TAC brotherhood. Everything about it contrasted with his past. The brothers didn't sweep his questions into closets like Aunt Harriet had when she'd said, "That's between you and I and the lamp-post." Instead everything was faced, debated, challenged, and even mocked.

He loved the spontaneity, camaraderie, and excitement. People walked into the fraternity living room at all hours with a case of beer or a cousin. They'd talk with anyone still awake about anything. Soon, lights were flipped on and music blared as if it were midday. Bob Dylan, Ray Charles, and the Beach Boys blasted from the stereo. When the Clancy Brothers were on, everyone sang.

"Up the rebel!" someone would shout and young men with no political knowledge or aspirations found purpose in the dreams of previous generations who'd believed in freedom from tyranny and music. Brothers recited poetry by Behan or Yeats. They sang up the ghosts of Roddy Mc-Corley and Kevin Barry before joining in "A Jug of Punch" or "Johnson's Motor Car." The songs, brotherhood, and emotions were inspired by youthful invincibility, charged with testosterone, and fueled by cheap beer. Filled with a new vitality, Chris joined brothers with glasses raised and arms entwined as the music became somber and "The Minstrel Boy" went off to fight. Afterward, the wayward drifted home as brothers and visitors found beds.

Chris grew close to some of the visitors. Individuals showed up out of nowhere, talked, and were invited to stay. Some lived on the third floor for entire summers. They ate meals with Chris and the brothers. They talked with El. They played cards and joined in whatever activity was taking place until vanishing into addresses and phone numbers scribbled on scraps of paper, taped to the fridge. Then those scraps vanished also. But Chris felt all the richer for it.

8

Halfway through his fourth-period European History class Friday morning, Chris realized he was out of lunch tickets. He'd have to be creative if he wanted ample time for lunch so as the clock counted down, he resorted to an old technique. He closed his book, packed his tote bag, and began walking down the aisle about ten seconds before the mechanical horn was due to sound. He reached the door just as it went off and continued into the hallway ahead of the student onslaught. There was still no congestion in the central stairway, which allowed him clear sailing through the lobby to the central artery. At that point, several students hurried past him in a near trot. The bottleneck formed at the ticket window.

Brittany Newport was efficient behind the cafeteria ticket window. That wasn't the problem. During each of four 28-minute lunch periods, she often waited on as many as 170 customers, handing back the correct change and smiling. That was the problem. The boys, especially the senior boys, wanted her to smile provocatively back at each one of them so, they bought their tickets daily rather than weekly. The wait could consume half the lunch period.

There were just four students ahead of Chris when he lined up behind T.D. Glover. The senior didn't stop moving some portion of his body the entire time they waited. Finally, it was T.D.'s turn.

"Hi, sugar."

"Just one."

When Brittany handed T.D. his ticket and smiled, the back of T.D.'s neck turned deep maroon indicating that some basic, animalistic reactions flushed through his system. Chris could only imagine T.D.'s face.

"Thanks."

"Have a good day, sugar."

Chris asked for ten tickets.

"Sure, sugar."

He stepped over to the serving line, where he heard T.D. begging for an additional scoop of shepherd's pie. Chris asked for a half serving but couldn't resist a large piece of pineapple-upside-down cake that winked at him from the desert shelf. T.D. was flirting with the student cashier so Chris left his ticket and walked around him.

There was only one unoccupied teacher's table left. Chris stepped around the table where Miss Hasan and her brother, Basil, were speaking in whispers as they ate. Her eyes were closed, her hand squeezing his wrist. Madison Amore and Michael Andover were also seated nearby, talking. Madison handed Michael some papers as Chris sat down at the teacher's table.

"Thanks, Madison. I'll look through them before the test."

"Hey, bro! Hi, Miss M," T.D. said as he arrived at their table.

"Hi, T.D. As I was saying, Michael, take the SATs again. December 8th is your last chance to raise your scores before applications are due."

"Hey, Michael." T.D. said. "What do you think of Ashley Kruger?"

"She's a freshman for crying out loud! Have you already given up on sophomores? It's not even November!"

"But she's hot. Can I have the rest of your shepherd's pie, Madison?"

"Sure."

"So you've run through the litter and picked out the runt," Michael said.

"Boy talk! I don't need to hear boy talk. Going to meet us after the soccer game, T.D.?"

"Yeah. That's what I'm saying. I asked Ashley to go."

Chris's attention shifted when Libby and K.J. approached.

"You can't dismiss it. The colonists were outraged by what happened to that girl." Libby parried to K.J.'s thrust, sounding like a defense attorney. Chris recognized her argument: the McCrea incident was significant to the Battle of Saratoga's outcome. "As news spread, people lost faith in British invincibility. There was a dramatic increase in recruits joining the militias."

K.J. shook his head, put his tray down, and went looking for another chair. At the same time, Chris overheard Michael again.

"...doesn't even know what they're talking about. He's such a loser."

T. D. began extending his thumb and forefinger but stopped when he noticed Chris watching him. Just then K.J. returned with his chair.

"You're usually more dramatic, Ms. O'Conner, but check your facts. Bennington was the colonist's real inspiration. Bennington! By the way, were you aware that the battle wasn't even fought in Vermont as some city people tend to believe?"

K.J. pushed his glasses back up his nose and raised his chin. Chris expected him to cross his arms and say, "I guess I told you." But Libby countered before K.J. could advance.

"Walloomsac, N.Y., K.J. And don't forget, you're a flatlander too."

"You two need a break."

Libby rolled her eyes before cracking a smile. K.J. pulled a container of instant noodles out of his lunch bag and walked toward the microwave.

"He's a lot of fun but dead wrong about Bennington," Libby said.

Chris glanced toward her lunch bag. "What's on your training table today, Libby?"

"Humus, macaroni and tuna."

"I'm going to try humus one of these days," Chris said, beginning to smile. "But I already know spaghetti and meatballs tastes better."

"Anything new on Walt?"

Chris told her he'd called the night before, and the message on the answering machine had been changed to his daughter's voice. He'd left a message but no one called back. "If I don't hear this weekend, I'm going up. By the way, this is terrible." He pushed the shepherd's pie around with his fork.

"Want some of this? It's not as bulky as cafeteria food. Even good for you."

Chris wrinkled his nose. "Next thing you'll suggest is I start playing basketball again."

"It wouldn't hurt. But maybe you could start by riding a bike."

"Trying to make me healthy?"

"I'm sorry, but—well, too many fatty foods, all those carbs, and no exer…"

"Yeah. I know!"

"Ok. Touchy subject." Libby looked around. "How did Brent's meeting go?"

"He's after my recertification proposal and wants me to be a more aggressive chairman."

"He may be right. You have a way with people. You bring out their best."

"I don't know," Chris said. "Not sure I want to take this on. I wasn't looking for it."

"Maybe it's an opportunity."

"You've been listening to Dr. George."

"It does sound like him, doesn't it?"

"I've got the years to retire but can't afford it. I'm caught. I'll have to work forever and, hell, I don't even like the kids anymore."

"Neither do I!" K.J. said, sitting back down wearing a wicked smile. "That's what inspires me. Just imagine them squirming during finals. Remember back in the '80s when we could still beat them?"

"Watch what you say," Libby whispered, nodding toward the student section.

"I'm serious," Chris said. "Everything is a struggle. I know how a depressed person must feel."

"Should you see a doctor?"

Chris smiled and shook his head. "I'm not sick. You sound like my sister."

"She must be a smart lady. Seriously, Chris, if I can pick myself back up, you can. I thought I was drowning when my ex and I split. I couldn't focus until I found some help and stood back up."

"You did well, Libby and thanks for the concern, but I'll be OK. I've just got to focus."

"Is there anything I can do?"

"No, thanks. But, well, actually there is."

"Anything!"

"I still don't have a project. Who is your friend over at Weaverton High, the one who does genealogy?"

Libby took out her phone and paged through the address book. She scribbled a name and number on a paper napkin and handed it to Chris. "Claudia Nichols."

"Sounds French and sexy," K.J. said.

"She says the old timers at Weaverton call her Sunflower. I think they're jealous. She's kind of crunchy but has good ideas."

"We veterans hate the young talent. Remember that, Ms. O'Conner," K.J. said.

"I'll give her a call. I've still got some time."

When the metallic horn sounded, K.J. placed the cover back on the rest of his noodles and put the container back in his bag. "I'm on C level. Got to go."

As K.J. left, Libby reached for Chris's arm. "Are you going to be OK?"

"I'll get by, thanks." He folded up the napkin with Claudia's name.

Libby packed up her leftovers as Chris carried his tray to the conveyer belt. They walked out of the cafeteria. When they reached the central artery, Libby said, "I just had an idea for how to get you to like humus."

"How?"

"I'll fix up a few small samples. You know, the really good kinds like pizza humus and chocolate humus. Come over to my place tonight, and I'll serve them with spaghetti and meatballs. I think I have a nice bottle of Chianti in the cupboard."

"That's a great idea, Libby, but some other time. I'm meeting some of the boys in our club tonight."

"Oh! Some other time, then."

When they reached the lobby, Libby turned toward the central stairway, clutching her books to her chest, her eyes down. Chris thought she appeared distant and guessed he'd offended her in some way. He hadn't meant to. Though he wasn't excited about tasting hummus samples and had other plans, the truth may have sounded more callous than courteous. Poor kid. She probably hasn't met many people since moving back. Once you're beyond going out to bars with a crowd, it's harder to meet people. I'll have to be more careful and hope my faux pas will be forgotten. He turned away and started toward the teacher's lounge.

9

It was a mild autumn evening, but Chris draped a red pullover around his shoulders just in case. Flaming leaves hung from the canopy of College Street trees while fallen brown ones lined the curbs and covered the sidewalks, crackling beneath his feet, a sound he loved though it was also a warning of winter. The walk was the elixir Chris needed after the week's discomforts. By the time he reached the edge of the business district, the streetlights illuminated everything. Ahead, Callahan's awaited.

Chris heard Callahan's from nearly a block away. Each time the door swung open, music and conversation flowed out into College Street, warming him like uisce beatha, the water of life itself. The closer he walked, the louder the music. The more he heard, the faster he walked. He felt as if the sirens were calling and couldn't wait to join the sing along.

The townies all told tales about Callahan's. Most had grown over the years depending on the storyteller. Was the original tale true or did it just sound that way? Did the Mighty One Hundred really stand up after each round and throw their empty pilsners into the fireplace? Did the Ponce de Leon Health Club really meet at Callahan's and down pints of Guinness before beating Sigma Kappa in the infamous Mud Bowl? Chris wasn't sure, though he still repeated the stories he thought he remembered whenever he had the chance.

He could attest to one. He'd watched Logan Cassidy carve a poem to Hiram Walker on the men's room door with a can opener one evening during college. The words were still legible but worn down from years of locals slapping them the same way Notre Dame football teams slap the Champion's sign.

Callahan's hadn't changed much over the decades. Inside, pseudo-Irish college kids still crowded around tiny tables. Everyone spoke with a brogue as they ordered drafts and sang songs of rebellion along with the current troubadour who was backed up on to corner platform. Chris recognized a couple of former Academy students who clinked glasses and yelled, "Up the rebel" between songs just as he and his contemporaries had.

He walked passed the dark oak bar polished just like a banker's coffin and given about as much respect. Some townies leaned against it, their feet on the brass rail, talking politics or gossiping with the college kids.

Chris nodded to Julie behind the taps as he continued toward the half dozen tables against the rear wall. They were the treasured few due to their proximity to the fireplace. The fact that they sat beneath a 52-inch wide screen didn't hurt. Those chairs filled up early on autumn football weekends as fans sent someone ahead to reserve a table just as city families did when holding reunions in the park. Jack and Pat Carmichael were talking at the center table. The waitress walked over to Chris as he pulled out chair.

"I'll have a draft, barkeep!"

"Anything for you boys?"

"How about you?" Jack said.

"Down, big fella. It's not good for your heart."

"OK, then—another scotch."

"The usual," Pat said, taking out his wallet and tossing a five on the table. "Any bets on Sunday's game, guys?"

"It isn't worth betting now that Walt's out," Chris said.

Jack smiled. "You always lose anyway."

"How's he doing?" Pat said.

"Anita talked with the family late this afternoon. He recognizes people, can squeeze their hands."

"He's the only one of us who's fit. It doesn't bode well. Excuse me. I've got to visit Hiram." Pat stood and left for the restrooms.

"We didn't think you were going to show."

"It looks like I shouldn't have." Chris glanced toward the empty chairs. "There are only four of us left and one isn't doing so well. We may have to close down the Algonquin Club."

"The Canadiens *scored* on the power play," the TV announcer blared as the waitress futzed with the remote. Players in red-and-white jerseys skated in circles and gave high fives to one another. A defenseman's bruised face flashed above a line of statistics. Up near the front of the bar, the troubadour began singing "Kilgary Mountain" and the crowd joined in.

Jack shuffled the cards before flipping one over and laying six others face down in a row. As he flipped another, Chris said, "I hope he pulls out of this. He should be here instead of in intensive care."

"That's the way they fall."

"Don't be so callous. You can't just pretend it's not happening."

"I'm not. And I'm not moaning either. You do enough for all of us. Of course I'm upset, but I won't dwell on it. There'll always be sick friends…and dead ones, too. Besides, if you run out of friends, you can mope over the stock market or bird flu or some idiot with a gun. Shit, there's enough sorrow around without digesting one person's details until they're meaningless."

The waitress returned. "Here you go, boys."

"Thanks, darling," Jack said.

"This snuck up on us. Remember how we used to joke about getting bald and having big bellies? This is real. Those kids up there, they are us."

Jack placed a red queen on a black king and moved a string of cards over "Pick up your baggage and move on."

"You make everything so simple. Face up or face down." Chris nodded toward the cards. "Pretend whatever's unpleasant doesn't exist. It's not that way for me. I'd love to chuck all the bullshit, but there's always something stopping me. Money, guilt. Shit, I don't know anymore. I can't find a good enough reason to move on. What the hell am I supposed to do?"

"You're asking me! What you've got is an old bartender not a life counselor. I was going to retire by 50. Didn't happen. Not even close. I wouldn't tell you anyway 'cause I don't want to take the blame. But I'll tell you what I'm doing. I'm going to pack up one of these days and head out west to the Rockies or maybe Alaska."

Jack stared toward the fireplace for a second but Chris didn't think Jack noticed what was before him.

"They're always looking for good honyocks up there. I could work on a dude ranch or cook in one of those restaurants where they serve up salmon steaks the size of pigs. I may just paint."

He put the deck down, eased back in the chair, and smiled a little. Jack's plans were always dipped in pure bartender bullshit, but Jack sounded passionate in a way Chris hadn't noticed recently. He'd been so consumed by his own dilemmas he'd noticed fewer and fewer of Jack's.

"Come on. We're too old for that."

The frozen look in Jack's eyes thawed. "No wonder you're unhappy. You've got no vision. Here's what you don't get, Chris. Life goes on. You can get on that merry go round or you can get off. It doesn't matter what the fuck you do, but you've got to do something. Can't hide out forever. If you're too wishy washy to choose, flip a coin."

"You're not serious."

"I'm just repeating what you said to me for Christ's sake. Remember that time you talked all night about Dante? Well, I read over some of his stuff and—like you said— the deepest spots in hell are saved for those who don't act, or some crap like that. All I'm saying is you've got to do something. Anything!"

Jack downed his scotch and stood. It appeared he was walking out until he stopped near the end of the bar and began talking with a chunky brunette. Jack never went looking for Cinderella, just companionship. He whispered in the woman's ear for a while, and she laughed. The more he whispered, the more she smiled. He soon forgot his friends behind him for the brunette soon had Jack beguiled

"Looks like he picked another winner," Pat said, sitting back down. "Probably mess this one up too."

"What are you talking about?"

"Oh! Before you got here, he was telling me about some girl he met last week. She stayed behind after he closed down the Establishment. So he took her home. Said she criticized that painting he's been working on so long, the one of Split Rock. Said she asked him if his nephew did it. It pissed him off so much he threw her out. Typical. Hey, I've got to run."

"So early?"

"My AA meeting up at First Congo started half an hour ago and, besides, this place is getting tempting." Pat downed his club soda and walked toward the door.

Chris sipped on another draft while watching most of the Canadiens' game before giving up. When he pulled the plug, Jack was still hanging out with the brunette. Chris tapped his shoulder as he passed. Jack smiled but was otherwise occupied. The evening had cooled, so Chris pulled on his sweater for the walk back up College Street. It was nearly 10 when he unlocked his apartment door. He winked at Dylan, sat down, and picked up the phone. It rang three times before a sleepy voice answered.

"Hi, Catch."

There was a brief pause. "Catch me if you can!" she said, starting to laugh. "I didn't think you were going to call tonight."

"I met some of the guys over at Callahan's. You OK, sis?"

"I was asleep. No, just dozing. And I'm not OK. I drove up to the cemetery today. I had to see Mike."

"It's his anniversary."

"You remembered."

" Do you want me to call back?"

"Oh, no. No. You're so thoughtful. I should be able to deal with it by now. It's almost 40 years."

"Thirty-six."

"Every time I get close to him, I…I think of all that … Oh, Chris, I just can't let go. Wait a minute." The phone must have tapped against the table. Then, Chris heard,

"Sorry!" followed by the soft sweep of tissues pulled through the cardboard opening. Then, sniffles.

"I'm OK now. We wouldn't have made it without you. We were so deep in debt."

"Let's not worry about that."

"I'm sorry. What about you? And Walt? Any news?"

"He can recognize people but isn't very responsive. I just wish I could do something. I owe him so much. Hell, I wouldn't even be here if he hadn't pulled me out of the water after the accident."

"Oh, Chris. It will be OK. Really, it'll be OK." His sister blew her nose and took a long breath. "Did you meet with Brent? That touchhole!"

"Sis! I'm surprised at your language." He started to laugh.

"No one's going to push my little brother around. I'll take care of you."

"Thanks, but people our ages aren't little brothers or big sisters anymore. We're just old. And, yes, I met with Brent."

"And…"

"He's tightening the screws. I think he's trying to force me out."

"What do you mean, force you out?"

"Now that he's got some time under his belt, he's ready to clean house. Just looking for an excuse. I might be getting paranoid but remember how I said we have to develop our own plans for recertification? That it's a special one-time project? Well, Brent suggested I do a unit on historic preservation in the Old North End, maybe identifying historic houses, that kind of stuff. He said it would be good PR."

"That sounds safe. But?"

"But is right. I think he's setting me up. There was an article in the *GMU Alumni News* saying our board chairman, Regan Andover, just received a grant to identify historic houses in the Old North End. Sound familiar? I'd be cutting into his territory and Regan's already upset with me."

"He is?"

"His son doesn't like my class. So Brent's working that angle, too."

"I told you he was a touchhole."

"I can hang on for a while, keep ahead of Brent, but I'm not sure I even want to keep teaching. Everything's changed. I had my little niche. I'd read all summer and take trips. Walk around Crown Point and try to figure out how Rogers Rangers attacked the French. Or climb Mt. Defiance and see what Johnny Burgoyne saw when he looked down on Ticonderoga."

"What are you talking about?"

"Sorry, I got off on a tangent. I was trying to say I had ways to keep going, to keep interested, but now I don't feel that kind of energy. It's like I'm in one of those shows that plays on Broadway for years and sets a longevity record. I'm doing what I have to, over and over, but I don't have the enthusiasm. It's funny, I used to wake up in the middle of the night to look things up."

"Being a workaholic wasn't always so good either. Maybe you need to go back to the meetings?"

"I never connected with those people."

"It's a process, Chris, not a one-night stand."

"How could I talk about growing up lonely and being afraid of loudmouths when they talked about being beaten up and going hungry? No. I just need a change."

"Well, retire. You're entitled to it."

"I can't afford it. There's just not enough there."

"You saved us. I couldn't have afforded to put the boys through school on my own."

"Besides, Catch, there's still the problem of the carrot."

"Carrot?"

"I haven't left my mark."

"Chris, you've marked a thousand kids. They've written thank you notes. They've called. And the boys! Don't forget them."

"It's not that. I've never taken the lead in anything. I've always stood back in the wings like an understudy. I guess

I was afraid to take a chance. I've always been afraid."

"What are you talking about? Afraid."

"The way we were brought up. We never knew what was going to happen at Uncle Jonathon's. Remember those times he came home early and Aunt Harriet took us away before he got out of control. Or how he'd forget to pick us up from some event. It left us off balance. I went defensive."

"You're talking in circles."

"Think about waking up in the middle of the night because you have to go to the bathroom. You don't want to turn on the light and wake anyone else up, so you try to find your way in the dark. You think you know where things are—a door or a wall. But everything's distorted in the dark. So you stumble. Maybe you fall and get hurt. Sooner or later, you figure out ways to get down the hall. You either take baby steps or crawl. You might even figure it's easier to just not try."

"But look at all you've done."

"I just wrapped myself in history. It was safer to hide in other people's lives. And Walt was such a great leader I did whatever he asked. I didn't mind being in the background. But now— now—there's a chance to leave my mark. That's the carrot. The problem is, I'm tired: tired of Brent's bullshit, tired of spoiled rich kids, tired of Honora's ziti dinners. But the carrot is still there. And I don't feel good."

"Not sleeping again? Call Dennis. He'll order something."

"It's not that. I don't have the energy I used to. I puff when I climb the stairs. I've been having chest pain. My heart pounds."

"Oh, Chris! You've got to call."

"I had a feeling you'd say that. I've got an appointment. It's probably just stress. Doesn't go into my shoulder or jaw. Funny, I used to run that stuff off playing basketball."

"I wish I could still do that. I need to lose 20 pounds."

"Sis, you look great. And don't worry. I'll see Dennis in a few weeks."

"Can you afford to wait?"

"It's nothing. In the meantime, I've got to figure out a way to get through this mess, at least until we know what's going on with Walt," Chris said. "Now, how about the boys?"

"Don't change the subject."

"Really. I haven't heard from Mikey or Jimmy in a while. What are they up to?"

She updated him on Jimmy and said Mikey was traveling a great deal, and she wanted Chris to get an email address because by the time he arrived at his hotels or put his kids down it was usually too late to call. If Chris had an address, he could drop a line whenever he found free time. "Those kids live on their computers and smart phones."

"I'm still behind on that stuff."

"Come up to speed. Even email is becoming old fashioned."

"You sound like Brent and the good doctor. The digital autobahn, blah, blah. Why do I need a cell phone, a computer, and land line? I can only do one thing at a time."

"They may be right. You can't avoid technology forever."

"I've got a new TV."

"But you're still watching *Butch Cassidy* and *Casablanca* on a 20-year-old VCR."

"Tell Mikey I'll send a note on Anita's email. She'll do anything for me. In fact, she'll probably make up the messages and, if she misses me at work, bring the responses to my apartment on her way home."

"Chris, go see Dennis. Please!"

"I will. Soon!"

Chris hung up and looked up at the Dylan poster. "Bob. What am I going to do?"

10

Chris wasted most of Sunday afternoon stretched out on his couch, staring up at his big-screen TV. The Giants' defense had been lucky all day, but when the Redskins' wide receiver pulled in a 40-yard touchdown with 2:30 left, the dam broke. He clicked off the set, tossed the remote on the couch, and headed to the bathroom. There was just enough time for a shower before the 5:15 pm Mass.

He would've stood under the shower forever, but the temperature began falling. After a quick scrub and rinse, he stepped out before the mirror to find a misty, distorted figure looking back. He wiped away the fog. The image he faced was no longer the lean, 5'10" athlete he'd once been but a paunchy timeworn man bent forward like a sailor under the weight of a heavy sea bag. The worst part was he couldn't imagine anything that would improve the apparition.

He dressed, wrote out a check to Saint Isaac's Parish, and hurried down the stairs. Outside, he hesitated by his car as he noticed his neighbor leading his tiny rat-faced dog along the street for a late afternoon walk.

Chris avoided the business section and drove toward the south end of town. Sunday traffic was light as the car coasted around the Wilson Street rotary into Saint Isaac's parking lot. He hurried into the last pew with minutes to spare. As he pulled out his beads, he thought of Aunt Harriet mumbling decades of the Rosary.

Chris recognized the usual supporting cast scattered about the last rows of pews. They wore a day's growth of beards, dungarees, and NASCAR jackets. They wiggled and looked at their watches. They came late and would leave early. They would toss change into the collection basket instead of envelopes or bills. They were a mix of gray-haired worshipers, disinterested ushers, and Sunday-obligation advocates who'd procrastinated until no other alternatives existed. Chris had tried all the excuses himself at one time or another. Either he wanted to sleep late or read the Sunday *Globe*. It was the biggest game of the season. The driveway needed to be shoveled, or he was nursing a cold. Eventually guilt had worked its miracles and he'd drag himself from a warm couch or a good book to face traffic, snow flurries, and an hour of inconvenience because he'd come to understand what the eyes darting about the nave had told him. If he missed Mass, he had sinned.

He started to say a prayer for Walt when everyone rose to greet the celebrant. Chris fumbled through the pages of his missalette, mouthing the responses he'd used since Vatican II. He followed the day's readings until his eyes drifted toward the crumbling plaster above the altar. He couldn't focus on anything but tried again once the homilist reached the lectern. The man's waxy face bore no expression, but his cold piercing eyes reminded the congregation he was zealot.

"My friends in the Spirit…" he began. "Today we have a wonderful announcement. After years of study by a select group of dynamic scholars, and convened at the request of the Pontiff himself, we can finally announce we will have a new missalette at our disposal. Not only will the translation be true to the Aramaic, but it will contain a much clearer presentation of those subtleties that inspire us, some of which have been overlooked through millennia. The text is truly unique, the work of scholars, linguists, and poets, a brief example of the magnificent work…"

Chris took a long slow breath as the homily took on the same monotonous sound as one of Dr. George's talks. He started considering the story in the stained-glass windows that recounted Saint Isaac's capture by the Iroquois.

"As you can see, this minute difference means little to the non-believer but…"

Eventually Chris' attention drifted to the pew beside him. Further down the bench, he noticed the initials JK 46 had been carved into the polished oak seat. He couldn't remember ever seeing them before. The edges of the letters and numbers were worn smooth, rounded not only from the wear of thousands of parishioners' sliding bottoms but also from the attentiveness of the carver. Chris imagined some bored artist taking out a pen knife or a church key and carving initials while periodically glancing about to make sure no one was watching. He couldn't draw his eyes away.

Once the service had concluded, he drove toward the business district and searched the west side for a parking spot and, finding one on lower Main, parked and walked another block to lower College Street where the Cassidy Building stood. It was the last vestige of the Slough area of Queen City and housed a bar called The Establishment. Jack tended bar there when he wasn't off fishing, painting, or playing cards. Chris found a dozen patrons scattered around the tables and bar. Music from WSFT played over the stereo. At the far end of the bar, Jack and a long-haired young man near the waitress's station appeared to be comparing their ponytails. As Jack noticed Chris, he drew a draft and walked over.

"Church call is now officially over. At ease soldier!"

"Looks quiet tonight. You watch the Giants game?"

Jack nodded. "Most of it. It's mandatory in Queen City. My old timers keep telling me how the Giants used to hold their summer camps up at the college. Said the guys watched movies down at the Strong Theatre on Friday night. They were so big they had to sit in every other…" Jack looked down the bar. "Ah, shit. Excuse me a second."

He walked over to the waitress's station and filled her order before coming back. "By the way, you look like shit."

"You know how to say just the right thing."

"It's my job. I'm a trained bartender. Not only can I say stupid stuff but I get paid for it. And people love it!" Jack forced a Cheshire smile and extended his arms for applause while eyeing the bar for empties. An older patron reached out his hand, so Jack drew another draft on his way over. Hits from the '60s played over the speakers above the bar. Chris sipped his draft until Jack returned.

"You've got a bigger crowd than Saint Isaac's."

"I hate to say it, but they're sending me customers. Mine don't even feel they have to go anymore. Not enough big nuns left to guilt 'em into it, I guess. Plus the padres have lost their pizzazz. Robert De Niro instead of Bing Crosby! Scary. They're even afraid to take altar boys on bus trips. Don't want to face the charges. It's like they're trapped in some old holding pattern. Keep repeating the same mistakes. Hell, even honyocks know that if you keep marrying your cousins, sooner or later the kids start looking like chimps."

Chris smiled, knowing that Jack was just getting started.

"So, people come here to complain. They tell sad stories and ask for forgiveness. I listen. I forgive. I pour. I smile. And they give me tips. On top of that, they come back every week and give me more tips. Everybody's happy except the guys running places like Saint Isaac's. They just need a new business model. A good accountant would show 'em that receipts are down. A good pitchman could fire up the crowds, bring back the lost. People need religion, good religion. I used to go to church," Jack said.

"You? When?" Chris said.

"Long time ago! Yup. The family sat together every Sunday cause the old man's philosophy was it's OK to treat us like shit if he dressed everybody up nice and pretty on Sunday, lined us up in the front row, and threw a big check in the basket. I didn't agree so I stopped going. S'cuse me."

Jack stepped off to greet and joke with a petite young woman, then mixed her a daiquiri. He scanned the patrons along the bar as he walked back toward Chris.

"So, Jack, I saw these initials carved in one of the pews. I bet they're as old as I am."

"Wow!" Jack said, raising his eyebrows.

"Thanks a lot. JK 46. I got to thinking about carving initials. Kids do it to prove something or say something like,

'I've been here, or I've accomplished something big.'"

"Dogs piss on fire hydrants."

"It's more than that. People want to be remembered for something. I carved my initials in the gazebo up at Mount Saint Brendan's Cemetery once. I was just a kid, but it was a big thing."

"Yeah, sure."

"Don't you know what I'm saying?"

"Listen. You don't get it. Church goers and initial carvers are all alike. You spend all your time worrying about what to do instead of doing it. You want your name carved on a gazebo or on a stone so that someday maybe people will look at the name and say, 'oh, yeah, I've heard of him. He did the right thing.' Now, how stupid is that?"

"You don't under…"

"Listen." Jack looked up and down the bar. "A few years ago I was out in Chicago visiting some friends. They were artsy-crafty people and for some reason started telling me about this famous cemetery up north. It was called Greenwood or Evergreen or Mount Holier Than Something or Other. Pretty original! Right? Well, they described these big beautiful mausoleums and said all the old beer families were buried up there. Being a bartender as I am, I had to visit. A gorgeous place. Joe Schlitz, the Blatz family, and my personal favorites, the Pabsts, all have big monuments in this one corner of the cemetery. Hell, the Blatz monument looks like a little castle, bigger that the house where I grew up. Further up the drive are the Lunts. The Holden Caulfield Lunts! Everything's beautiful, the stones are great, but I noticed that everybody's dead. They're no better off with their stones and their initials than some schmuck buried in a swamp. That's why I'd rather be right here, rather than in church, carving initials. I'm doing my own carving. I'm carving people's minds." Jack put on a big grin, grabbed a towel, and began wiping down the bar.

"I'm glad you like your work. I'm sure not happy with mine right now."

"Yeah. I know."

"There's so much flying at me. Hell, I'm not sure I even want to do it anymore."

"So quit. Like I told you the other night, just do something. You've got a pension."

"It's not very much. I spent most of it getting Mary Catherine's kids through school. The tough part is now I've got a chance to chair the department. It's being handed to me, but I'm not sure I want to take it."

"Sometimes winning is scary. Picking up the prize on stage can be harder than cleaning the toilets in the basement. I've done both. Excuse me, I'm being summoned." Jack walked off to a ringing phone. "The Establishment," he said.

Chris sipped his beer and watched the crowd. There was a camaraderie among the patrons he hadn't felt at Saint Isaac's. Conversations resonated with warmth. Smiles on the faces of the friends he hadn't met surrounded him. Complete strangers acted as if they'd just arrived home and appeared welcome. There was music. It was like the fraternity.

Jack's face had turned granite gray when he returned. "Bill Hudson called. Walt's dead."

Chris felt the room become quiet. His knee began to ache, so he rubbed it as if the friction would rejuvenate years of worn cartilage. The friends he hadn't met were gone, and the room was filled with strangers. Warm conversations had become cold mumbles. He couldn't see a smile in the place.

"You OK?"

"I..." Chris began but found himself unable to continue because of the pain in his heart.

It wasn't the wound of a single cut or bruise but rather the numbness of having been pummeled by some bruiser in an alley and left disoriented, alone, and cold.

Then the petite girl down the bar waved an empty daiquiri glass, the long-haired man slid an empty glass toward the tap, and the waitress returned to her station holding up an order. Jack sighed but walked away, looking back empty-eyed from the tap.

Chris drained his beer then raised the empty glass toward Jack in salute of something they both felt and understood but couldn't verbalize. Jack nodded.

11

The parking lot outside the First Congregational Church was empty when Chris pulled in. He craved a few minutes alone before Walt's funeral. At the family dinner and wake, friends and family had recalled Walt's escapades and kindnesses so often Chris had felt he'd been bouncing down some back road without brakes. He looked up at the white columns and fortified himself. It's tough to concede someone's life from reality to memory.

Once he felt he could face tomorrow, he walked across the lot to the side door, the same door Uncle Jonathon used when Chris had driven him to his AA meetings. Chris climbed the stairway to the balcony, laid his raincoat across three places, and waited. After a time, students, board members, and Walt's friends began filing in, filling the red-cushioned pews below like checkers on a board. He recognized some prominent community members among the attendees. The Academy's former comptroller folded his walker as he took his seat near the front. Regan Andover and his wife entered, followed by Michael, Madison Amore, and T.D. Glover. Dr. George used a side aisle and proceeded to the vestry. The patchwork of empty places filled in.

Chris moved his raincoat when K.J., Libby, and Anita Small appeared at the top of the stairs.

"Are you OK?" Anita said, squeezing his hand. He nodded.

K.J. and Libby forced smiles when they sat. Libby's was accentuated with tears.

"There's our buddy," K.J. said pointing toward the entrance, where Brent reached out for the hands of everyone he knew and some he didn't.

Dr. George returned from the vestry and joined some board members seated near the front. A moment later the minister entered. Everyone stood. The family followed the coffin down the center aisle as one of the Academy harp-ists played Chopin's Funeral March. Chris thought the student harpist played the dirge with the airy touch of one unaccustomed to grieving. Walt would have laughed. Near the back of the nave, Chris noticed Honora opening her compact mirror as Walt rolled by. She licked her finger then wiped something from her cheek. As she did, Chris glimpsed Jack standing near the rear of the vestibule. He knew Jack would be there.

There was a ceremony and readings. Then the minister came forward. A tall man with soft eyes, he looked kind, though his surplice was starched and cardboard stiff.

"We're on a journey. Travelers all, we find ourselves in a boat filled with fellow voyagers, some supplies, and a simple map. That's all the Father has given us. It sounds like a simple crossing. All we must do is enjoy the passage. But we know that's not the case. Some fellow voyagers frustrate us. We are cast about by turbulent waters. Our boat springs leaks that must be patched. Our supplies run low. We hunger. We lose sight of our destination in storms. Some are even cast into the depths and must be rescued."

Walt's wife took out her handkerchief. Dr. George peeked at his index cards. One of the senior girls began crying. Brent looked down at his smartphone. Jack, in the vestibule, stood still. Chris felt himself struggling to breathe.

"Walt has reached his destination. Safe port. No more storms. No more hunger or thirst. He undertook his voy-age with optimism. He reacted to waves, loss of supplies, turbulence, and led his fellow voyagers against the tem-pest. They are all enriched for his efforts. Will others say the same of us when we disembark?" The minister glanced at notes on the lectern, looked up, and said, "Dr. George Baker will now share a few words of remembrance."

The good doctor walked forward as the minister stepped back. Faculty members shifted in their seats. Jack disappeared.

"Walt came a long way with us, but we still have a long

way to go," Dr. George began.

After the service, the mourners filed from the church to a rousing rendition of "McNamara's Band" played on viola. Some students even clapped in time as the family and close friends filled the cars in the parking lot for the drive to Lakeview Cemetery. Jack was waiting in Chris's car.

The cortege proceeded from the church down Weaverton Avenue and around Bluff's Park. Benny's was closed for the season, but Chris still thought of it and the lake beyond. At the cemetery, the mourners left their cars alongside the narrow drive and walked to the gravesite.

Friends surrounded Walt's family under the canopy, but Chris, Anita, K.J., and Libby joined some of Walt's old TAC brothers behind the family stone. Libby looked like a business professional in her trim gray suit, but she couldn't stop crying. K.J.'s arm was about her shoulders. Angelic Brent clasped his hands at his waist but shattered that image by glancing down at his chronograph all through the committal prayers. Afterward, he hurried off toward his CTS.

Walt's fraternity brothers lingered. After most mourners had walked away, the brothers circled the grave. Someone handed out papers but most folded them or stashed them in their jacket pockets because the years couldn't erase the words. They sang again.

> The minstrel boy to the war is gone,
> In the ranks of death you will find him...

The voices were not as strong as they'd once been, but the emotions were, evoking memories of another funeral. Five decades earlier, they'd sung for Logan Cassidy after he'd perished off the breakwater one August night. Chris wondered if that pain would ever go away.

As the last of the brothers stepped away, Chris, Pat, and Jack continued talking in hushed tones. Chris noticed K.J. opening his car door for Libby. She was still crying. The lake glittered in the distance.

Chris dropped Jack off at The Establishment then

drove Pat back to the church for the dinner. Everyone ate lasagna at long tables with white linen tablecloths and harvest bouquets. Later, Chris and Pat joined a couple of the fraternity brothers they hadn't seen in years and drove over to TAC. They parked in the street out front and retold old stories late into the evening.

"And the Maine game, remember the Maine game?"

"That guy was a bruiser. Anyone remember how many times Walt broke his nose?"

"Too many. I don't think it ever healed."

"Walt knew how to pick a looker, didn't he?" Pat said. "Remember Mini?"

"She could dance. She was a devil in a red dress, red dress, a devil with a red dress on," one brother said, referencing the old tune.

The others laughed.

"You're no Mitch Rider. Or Mitch Miller either," someone said.

"Hey, Chris, the girl you used to date was pretty sharp, too. What ever happened to her?"

"Susan. I lost track of her after college." Chris said, turning toward the window.

"Remember when we rented the camp? Walt could be a little crazy, couldn't he?" Pat said. "Like how he kept short sheeting our beds. I got so pissed, having to get up to remake it while he was laughing from his room."

"Funny that the pastor didn't mention that part," one of the others answered.

"Yeah, that was a mistake," Pat said.

"The club. Remember? We called that camp the club. What was that all about, Chris? I've forgotten," the other brother said.

"It was El's idea," Chris said. "Now Walt's joined El and Logan back at the club."

"We're all going there sooner or later," Pat said. "Closer all the time."

They talked of love and death, foolishness, and hope. Then they said goodbye. Chris dropped Pat off and drove back toward his apartment, but decided against turning into Wells Court and continued down College Street toward The Establishment.

He found a spot at the end of the bar and nursed his beer as Jack kibitzed with his audience. It was nearly 2:30 when he finished hanging the last of the stemware from the racks above the bar. He would've finished earlier but for the two tipsy women.

"Do we have to leave? This's so much fun," one said as Jack announced closing.

"Hell, no!" Jack said and locked the door. He refilled the women's wine glasses.

"This must be a special night for you two lassies to be out and about."

"'Tis. How'd you know?"

"I'm a professional barkeep. I know these kinds of things. I bet I even know what you're doing."

They looked at each other.

"What?" the woman in the brown dress said.

"Either girl's night or book group."

"Book group. That's always our excuse. Book group. How'd you know?'

"It's a trade secret. I bet you're professionals, too."

They both giggled.

"Did you ladies go to GMU?"

"Yes."

"Remember Lit 101?"

"Yeah!"

That was all Jack needed. He started his performance with poetry right out of the old freshman anthologies. First he recited "Terrance This Is Stupid Stuff" and followed up with "Miniver Cheevy." Both renditions drew mild applause. Chris's eyes brightened as he remembered the same poetry.

"I bet you didn't know a honyock could recite pomes" Jack said, pouring still another glass of house red.

"More. More."

"OK. Get ready." Jack cleared his throat and pretended

to roll his sleeves. "That's me favorite," he said after reciting "Stopping by the Woods on a Snowy Evening."

After "Out, Out", he tired of Robert Frost and snuck in a couple of lesser known '60s ballads before making a critical error.

"Wait a minute. That's a Beatles' song. *Revolver*! I think it's on *Revolver*," one of the women said.

"No. *Rubber Soul*. You can do better than The Beatles!" the other woman said.

"Oh. You want the good stuff." Jack shrugged his shoulders.

"Yeah, the good stuff." One woman raised her glass. "The good stuff."

Jack turned to Chris and winked. He cleared his throat before reaching deep into his bartender's repertoire. He closed his eyes. Another world emerged on his face as he began speaking Yeats in a whisper.

> O'Driscoll drove with a song
> The wild duck and the drake
> From the tall and tufted reeds
> Of the drear Hart Lake.
>
> And he saw how the reeds grew dark
> At the coming of evening tide,
> And dreamed of the long dim hair
> Of Bridget his bride.
>
> He heard while he sang and dreamed
> A piper piping away,
> And never was piping so sad,
> And never was piping so gay.

A smile grew across Jack's lips. His voice began to rise.

> And he saw young men and young girls
> Who danced on a level place,
> And Bridget his bride among them,
> With a sad and a gay face.
>
> The dancers crowded about him

And many a sweet thing said,
And a young man brought him red wine
And a young girl white bread.

But Bridget drew him by the sleeve
Away from the merry bands,
To old men playing at cards
With a twinkling of ancient hands.

Chris mouthed the words from yesterday right along with Jack. He imagined Pat, Logan, Walt, Jack, Underwood, and the others singing, arguing, laughing in front of the hallway fireplace. And there was El, sitting off in the corner with her bony legs crossed, cigarette smoke swirling through her hair.

The bread and the wine had a doom,
For these were the host of the air;
He sat and he played in a dream
Of her long dim hair.

He played with the merry old men
And thought not of evil chance,
Until one bore Bridget his bride
Away from the merry dance.

He bore her away in his arms,
The handsomest young man there,
And his neck, and his breast and his arms
Were drowned in her long dim hair.

O'Driscoll scattered the cards...

Jack's booming voice shattered the darkened room. As he swung his arm to demonstrate O'Driscoll's ire, he hit a bottle of Jamieson and knocked it from the shelf. Both the women jumped, awakening Chris from his dream to see Jack stretched out, tiptoeing to rescue the Jamieson bottle before it hit the floor. Chris thought the symbolism appropriate. It had been one of Jack's finest performances but the poem was left incomplete, the brunette became ill, and her friend ushered her into the restroom. When they reappeared, the woman was pale and weak.

"She's got to go to bed. Can you call a cab?" the woman in the blue dress said.

"Only if you promise to come back for a reprise."

"I'd love to hear the rest of the story."

Once the women were in the cab, Jack put on his beret and leather coat, leading Chris outside and locking the door behind. The streets were empty and wet. Chris blew on his hands. Jack dug his stubby fingers deep into his pockets and leaned into the moist air. When they reached Chris's car, he decided against driving and for Jack's couch, so they turned down the hill toward the lake. A few blocks later, they reached the area politicians talked about using words like "urban renewal" and "blight." The sidewalks there stretched from dark-brick windowless walls to the curb. Above them, rusted fire escapes hung in nervous expectation.

"I feel like shit. What about you?"

"It's over. Move on."

Jack let Chris into the apartment and tossed his coat across a worn brown stuffed chair. He cleared some space for Chris on the couch by moving an unfinished canvas, standing it on end against the wall.

"Split Rock?" Chris said, twisting his head to take a closer look.

"Yeah. From Thompson's Point. I'll get it right one of these days."

"What drew you down there?"

"Fishing buddies and the magic fish."

"Magic fish?"

Jack's eyes lit as a little smile formed around his mouth. "Come on, history man, everybody knows its good fishing and the best view on the lake."

Chris covered himself with a blanket and closed his eyes as Jack sipped orange juice and opened a copy of *Scientific American*. The cover listed the main article as "How Meteorologists Use Doppler Radar for Your Forecast." The couch wasn't very comfortable, and the alcohol must have been affecting his REM because instead of unconscious sleep, Chris drifted between being asleep and awake. His thoughts shifted back and forth between black-and-white images of the fraternity and the minister's words: "Will others say the same of us when we disembark?"

Jack appeared consumed by what he was reading, hurrying through the pages until something stopped him. He stood, pacing back and forth before picking up a pencil and a notebook and writing frantically. Chris turned over and covered his head with the blanket as Jack tore sheet after sheet from the notebook and threw them on the floor. A few minutes later, Chris peeked out when he heard Jack laughing.

"C was the speed of light, Chris. It all makes sense."

Chris turned back over and closed his eyes. Later, he heard the door open and glanced at the clock. It was nearly 6:30. Looking up, he caught sight of Jack wearing his leather coat and beret, stepping out and closing the door. Chris lay still for a moment. What's he doing? He wondered. Where the hell is he going at this hour? Since Chris couldn't sleep, he dragged himself out of bed. His head pounded, but he put on his coat and shoes and went outside.

It was that transitional time before dawn. Jack's shadow slid between the vehicles in the parking lot and crossed over the railroad tracks. Sometimes shadows and men look the same. A heavy frost had matted down the grass beyond the Salt Dock parking lot. Jack's tracks on the dew stretched out to the granite blocks that held back the lake.

Not a ripple broke the bay's surface. Not a boat pulled against a mooring. No breeze could be heard.

Two mallards drifted nearby. They noticed Jack standing against the changing sky. They paddled closer, seeking a tourist's handout, circling, and waiting. He paid them no heed. He gazed westward into the dark. The mallards grew tired of waiting and paddled off for more promising sources.

The first rays touched clouds high in the heavens, making them glow purple-red. Soon rays fell upon the crests of distant peaks. The light slid down the high peaks toward the water like an avalanche. The light reflected back across the water, casting Jack as a shadow against the world.

Jack, watching the sky, wiggled his fingers and toes. He loosened his arms and legs, rhythmically moving them one at a time. Though Jack appeared cold, fighting off the frost, Chris wondered if he were actually preparing for some-thing—akin to a runner before the blocks. A few moments later, Jack took off his beret and leather coat and laid them at his feet. Underneath, he wore a white garment, tied with a black belt. He stood alone in his white battle dress, composed himself, and inhaled several deep breaths. Then he drew his feet together. His hands fell to his sides. He bowed, as if honoring the mountains and their herald, the light. He crossed his wrists below his waist and clenched his hands together, forming granite fists. He whirled left and stepped forward into a blocking stance, his left arm ex-tended. He stepped again, gliding into an attack. His right fist flew from his waist.

He spun 180 degrees and executed another block, low and to the right. The movement disintegrated and reap-peared as a thrust toward his unseen opponent's mid-sec-tion. He reeled left. Another block formed, followed by another punch, a step, another block, and then another thrust.

Chris watched Jack's silent ballet from the parking lot. The speed of his dance accelerated with each step he took, with each punch he threw. Jack moved gracefully against the mountains, turning and twisting, blocking and punch-ing through the sequence in a ballet of beauty and skill, a dance of defiance.

Chris couldn't comprehend his place in the drama surrounding him. He'd always played by the rules. When there had been opportunities, he'd chosen the nobler path. Now, near the end of a career, when most look back at their accomplishments and smile, he felt no more settled then during an August night on the lake. He was in wonder of everything but thought it unfair that while his life was in turmoil, his emotions rumbling like a geyser ready to gush, his friend acted out a controlled, restrained performance.

And the only response to his questions was silence.

12

The Academy remained under a pall during the days following Walt's funeral. The halls were unusually quiet between periods as if they too were grieving. Chris struggled through the phase, but, despite feeling intense loss, he managed his schedule, hiding behind reading assignments on Thursday and most of Friday. As the afternoon counted down, he decided to hand back a quiz he'd administered to his seniors.

"I've made notes in the margins where points were taken off. I'll take general questions, but if you want to discuss individual answers and grades, please set up an appointment."

As the students examined their results, Chris picked up his coffee mug, walked to the window, and looked across to the lake. Snow already covered the highest peaks, the veil inching downward day by day. The thought of it reaching Queen City offered no comfort.

The panorama's stillness was broken when Chris noticed movement across the street on the roof of Municipal Auditorium. A maintenance worker was climbing a ladder attached to the side of the cooling tower. When the man reached the mechanical platform, instead of opening the cabinet, he too stared at the mountains across the lake. Chris tried to imagine his perspective. It must have been spectacular, for it was higher. The man turned slowly and looked back at the Academy with its backdrop of autumn foliage and Victorian houses. Chris sipped the last of his coffee, returned to his desk, and locked away his mug for the weekend.

Looking over the top of his reading glasses, Chris noticed T.D. give Michael a thumbs up, but Andover was still absorbed in reading his quiz sheet. Michael's head shook back and forth. Then his hand shot up.

"Yes, Mr. Andover."

"Mr. Martin. This last question. You Vermonters make so much about the Battle of Bennington. There are parades every summer, the banks close, but it's all a sham. I mean, the battle wasn't even fought in Vermont but in some little New York burg. The whole thing was just a side bar to the Revolution."

Madison started to giggle.

"Mr. Andover, Bennington was a significant victory no matter where it was fought. The British were stopped in their tracks. During the following weeks, the Colonial militias recruited hundreds …"

"That's irrelevant, Mr. Martin. The British were delayed because General Burgoyne couldn't make a decision. He was a procras…"

The Academy's metallic horn interrupted Michael but Chris knew the discussion wasn't over when Michael stood, slammed his book closed, and started for the door.

"What was that all about?" Madison said to Michael.

"B+. That man doesn't know his…" Michael said before his voice faded in among other hallway noise.

Chris took several deep breadths before gathering his belongings into his tote bag and started for the door. Just outside, he nearly tripped over Miss Hasan, who was kneeling on the floor, picking up books. As Chris reached down to help, he noticed that her eyes were devoid of expression, lifeless. "Everything OK?" he said. She nodded and hurried off.

After dismissal, Chris stopped by the teacher's lounge to find his mailbox crammed with file folders. Some appeared quite detailed, with references and bibliographies. One contained a single sheet of paper. He stuffed them all into his tote bag for later reading. Nearby, the local section of *The Daily Freeman* lay open on the coffee table. Then Chris noticed the clock.

"Oh, shit!"

"Were you talking to me?" Honora said. She was seated in a chair by the window, reading the latest issue of *Gourmet*.

"Sorry, Honora. I'm late for an appointment."

"Please watch your language in the future. But while you're here, Chris, I was wondering if you've had a chance to look at my proposal?"

"I just picked them up. I'll read them this weekend," he said and left the lounge.

"Chris! Chris!" Libby called as he was starting his car. She ran over from the direction of the girl's locker room. The team was already well into their warm-up routine on the nearby grass.

"One, two, three, VICTORY! One, two, three, VICTORY!" The girls counted.

Libby leaned into his open window. Her face was aglow.

"Hi! How are you feeling? I mean, about Walt."

"I'll be OK. You?"

"Oh, I don't know. It still doesn't seem real." Libby glanced toward the team. "I was wondering if you'd like to talk. I know it's late and silly of me, but I made a big batch of meatballs with the red sauce last night and…"

"I'm Sorry, Libby. I'm tied up. I'm supposed to meet with your friend Claudia Nichols in Weaverton and…" he looked down at his watch. "I'm already late."

"How about Saturday or Sunday?"

He shook his head. "It's just a bad time. I've got to read all the recertification proposals, and I haven't even come up with my own idea."

"Sure. I understand." She stepped away as he started his engine. A passing cloud momentarily blocked the sun and Libby's hand turned over as if questioning rain. The distant cadence of the exercises became louder as she jogged back toward the team. That was considerate Chris thought, but, damn it, I just don't have enough time right now and besides, I don't know if I want to take the risk.

Chris put the car in gear. At the end of the drive, he reached into the glove compartment, found the Isley Brother's cassette, and pushed it into the deck. As he turned up the hill, the drums set the beat, followed by the bass, piano, and guitar.

Two boys tossed a football on GMU's green as Chris drove by. The flag flapped lightly in the breeze. Except for the dying leaves and the calendar, nothing indicated winter was lurking.

Chris turned east at Weaverton Avenue and drove by the new hospital, residences, college dorms, and the entrance to GMU's athletic fields. The street curved slightly by Green Mountain Cemetery and began its long descent toward the Weaverton River and its namesake town.

A century and a half of history lay exposed on the opposite bank. The Weaverton River rushed around the crumbled bricks and mortar remains of massive water intakes that once fed house-sized turbines. Behind them, multi-storied brick skeletons of empty mills jammed the bank. French and Irish migrants had manufactured wool blankets in the 19th century here but now broken glass and empty parking lots flourished. The vacant hulks overshadowed streets with numerous potholes and few businesses.

Chris drove over the bridge and circled the rotary. The center, a cement wasteland, had been the heart of Weaverton until a devastating fire in '48 had destroyed shops, restaurants, and homes. How could Weaverton ever recover from the loss of the mills and the fire? Further up Main, a residential section crested the hill. Many of the original French and Irish family homes now served as residences for 20th-century refugees who dreamed the same dreams as their predecessors but struggled with fewer resources.

There was irony in driving to Weaverton for help. He remembered attending one football game against Weaverton High while still a student at the Academy. A classmate stood in the bleachers and called out for the letters spelling Weaverton. Academy students yelled back each: "W, E, A, V, E, R, T, O, N." Then the loud classmate asked, "What does it spell?" and the crowd yelled, "Nothing!" And Chris's voice blended in. That behavior haunted him as he drove by a bar where he and his fraternity brothers had drunk cheap beer during college.

He turned left at Union Street and began looking for a parking spot close to the high school. The two-story brick building was crammed between apartment houses dating from a time when the mills had been vibrant and cars had been few.

There were no blazers or ties in sight as he climbed the brick steps. New immigrants in their colorful native costumes and head coverings were the norm. He saw no electronic tablets or iPads. They spoke a mixture of broken English and unidentifiable dialects, sounding just as confusing to him as their French and Irish predecessors must have sounded to previous generations. The school secretary looked up when Chris entered the office, but before he could speak, he heard a familiar voice.

"Hey, Chris. What are you doing here?" Rich Hillsborough said, walking out from the principal's office.

Rich was a little shorter than Chris and had a big round face. They'd first met when Chris and Walt had taken some administration courses up at GMU in the late 80s. After that, they'd gone out a few times for beers and conversation. Rich's tie was loosened and his sleeves rolled up.

"Hey, Rich. I'm actually here to see one of your staff."

"Who's that?"

"Claudia Nichols. I asked her for some help with a project. I heard she's used genealogy in her history classes."

"Yeah, she has. You're not trying to recruit her for the Academy, are you? I know that slimeball Brent. He'd do just about anything to steal a good teacher." Chris laughed. "Do I know him or what?"

"Yeah. You do. But I'm really here for help. You know about the recertification reprieve?" Rich nodded. "I'm just looking for ideas."

"Claudia's one of my best. She's probably still in her classroom. 110. Don't be surprised when you meet her."

"What do you mean?"

"She's like we used to be."

Chris became distracted when a tall thin girl in a long red-and-orange dress and head scarf walked into the office. "Hi, Don Mai," Rich said, flashing her a big smile. She smiled back as she walked to a folding table stacked with an array of boxes and cans of food. She took out a list and glanced over it before selecting three cans of vegetables and a cereal box. She stuffed the items into her backpack and walked out. Chris looked at Rich.

"Some of my kids go hungry. Tough to learn if you're hungry. By the way, I call her Sunflower."

"Who?"

"Claudia. You'll see. She drives a '72 microbus. Good to see you, Chris. 110. Right down the hall."

"Thanks, Rich."

Chris found the room, knocked, and entered. He was greeted by large cutout letters above the board painted in psychedelic colors. "We hold these truths!" they screamed. On the opposite wall, a sour-faced King George III scowled back. "Keep the rebels harassed, anxious, and poor!" was printed in large letters beneath his picture. Every inch of wall space was covered. A series of maps documented the boundary changes within North America between the 1500s and the 1800s. A copy of the Declaration of Independence hung on the rear wall beside pictures of the Liberty Bell, Independence Hall, and a large print of the participants at the First Continental Congress. The bulletin board was divided into sections listing lectures up at the college, PBS programs, and a monthly schedule for the History Channel. There was also a strange collage of presidents, which reminded Chris of the *Sergeant Pepper* album cover. A map of the heavens was taped to the ceiling near a cutout half-moon with a lasso around it.

"Hi. I'm Claudia." Claudia was at her desk.

"I'm Chris. A half-moon?"

"My family watches George Bailey every Christmas. We even have a Charleston contest."

Claudia was tall and had light-brown hair parted in the middle and braided long down her back. She wore a dark tie-dyed dress with purple stockings and Birkenstocks. Her youthful face was the image of Vermont wholesomeness.

"Thanks for meeting me. As I said when we talked the other night, Libby O'Connor told me you've used genealogy in your classes. I'm trying to come up with a recertification project and that sounded interesting."

"Have a seat," she said. "I've done different things. My favorite time period is post-Civil War through the Gilded Age. It's a natural for genealogy because there are so many sources. My problem now is that many of my students are new to the states."

"I've got a different kind of student at the Academy."

"Yes, I know. But that shouldn't stop you. You said you just used a text in class. You need to do more. It's not fair to the kids, and if we don't change, we'll lose them. I use genealogy and I try to make it personal. "

"Personal?"

"I want my kids to imagine how their ancestors might've felt or reacted. I have them search out their roots. We use any family information they already have, go to city hall, and look at the records: birth certificates, death certificates, and deeds. They discover where relatives lived, went to school, what church they attended, their jobs. All this affects their decisions, their feelings."

"You have a lot of refugees here."

"That was a problem until I researched about 30 French and Irish families one summer. Some were community leaders, others just ordinary citizens. Now I assign families to the newcomers. It doesn't really matter, since I'm trying to teach skill sets needed for research. Genealogy is just icing on the cake."

Claudia's voice was warm and soothing, making Chris feel relaxed. He loosened his tie and leaned back in his chair. "What about the genealogy part? What activities do you use?"

"We've got some great resources. The County Genealogy Society has space up at the university. I teach kids how to find relatives, parishes, and nationalities using their databases. Kids find other stuff too: deeds on file in city hall, old phone books and newspapers in the library. I show them how to locate the places where their relatives lived, get them to look for family details such as where relatives were baptized, or married, or had their bar or bat mitzvahs. It leads to some great discoveries. For example, did you know in Queen City there were three synagogues within a few blocks of one another?"

"Yeah. I knew some of the old families when I was growing up." Chris was surprised by how quickly he'd been drawn into Claudia's excitement.

"As kids pick up facts, they also pick up on Weaverton's relationship with Queen City. For example, there are a couple of Catholic Churches in Weaverton today, but a 100 years ago, the Catholics went to St. Joseph's or the cathedral in Queen City. They even met in club rooms on Main Street. Their cemetery was in Queen City, too. Mount Saint Brendan's."

The longer Chris listened, the more he understood what Rich meant about Claudia. Her excitement hadn't been hobbled by years of progress reports, state requirements, mandatory courses, and pushy parents. He remembered feeling a similar passion when everything was a first time, when there were bridges not boundaries.

"They discover things like where the original French and Irish sections of town were. I bet you didn't know there's an area called Cork Alley in Weaverton."

"I guess I didn't," Chris said.

"I'm sorry. I get carried away."

"I like what you're saying. You have passion. Teachers need passion."

She shook her head. "There's a lot of educated guessing involved. Students might infer what kind of education their ancestor had from the school's location, the budget that year, the type of texts available, even the teachers' names and backgrounds. They really need to know their relatives to make some of these…" Claudia stopped. "You could do something with cemeteries."

"What?"

"They're filled with details and stories. Places of origin,

epidemics, life spans. All kids have to do is observe, take notes, and discuss what they find. You can graph the results. It would be like putting a puzzle together."

"I used to read the stones as a kid when I mowed lawns at Mount Saint Brendan's."

"I've found lots of great details in cemeteries. People want their stories told so they have them carved on their stones. They list medals awarded, places visited, acts of bravery. I remember finding one tragic story on a gravestone up in St. Albans. It recounts a man's hatred for Abraham Lincoln for not doing more to release his son from Andersonville Prison where the boy died." Claudia's eyes were welling up.

"But that's not real history," Chris said. "It's social history. You're just singling out individuals who may be exceptions. It's chasing social phenomenon. Legends and rumors aren't, I mean…it's like asking someone to watch a CSI episode and then expecting them to understand how the FBI operates."

"My approach isn't everything, but it works for my kids. Language, culture, and complex concepts can create barriers to learning, but who can't comprehend the meaning of a grave?"

They talked, argued, and laughed until Chris noticed the sky outside had turned November black. Claudia noticed, too.

"It's nearly 7:30 and a Friday night. I'm sorry for keeping you so long."

"Oh, no. Thank you. This was wonderful. I haven't had a class this good in years. I'll think over what you've said. I'm still not sure where I'm going with this."

"Call if you need help."

"Claudia, listening to you, I felt some things about teaching I haven't felt in a long time. Thanks." Chris reached out to shake the girl's hand, but she hugged him instead.

As Chris walked passed the principal's office, Rich was standing by the copier holding a stack of papers.

"You're right, Rich. She's like we were."

"People like Claudia reach inside and find things the rest of us don't even know exist. I wish there were more of her. By the way, if you ever want a real job, come back and see me. These kids really need us. It's more about teaching then babysitting."

Chris went out into the cold. He ran his car until the defroster blew warm air across the windows. Through the circular clearing in the frosty glass, he noticed the lights from Claudia's room and the principal's office shining like beacons in the darkness.

13

After sleeping until 9 on Saturday morning, Chris picked up the apartment before running downtown on a couple of errands. When he returned, Bob Dylan peered down from his place in the spotlight. Chris nodded back, placed the mail on the table, and went to the fridge. He moved the milk and some old containers of Chinese around until he discovered a half bowl of his sister's home-made chili under plastic wrap. It smelled OK. He popped it into the microwave, then sat down at the table. The tote bag stared back at him.

After eating, he pulled out each of the certification folders. He held each at arm's length, as if judging their weight meant something. There would only be one issue, he thought.

He opened the top folder but closed it immediately and clicked on his big screen. He found the Notre Dame game on Channel 5, muted the sound, and went over to the stereo. The stack of vinyl albums on the spindle hadn't changed in years. He lifted them off and glanced through the labels. *The Clancy Brothers at Carnegie Hall*, *This Old Heart of Mine*, *Rubber Soul*, *Late Again*, and *Highway 61 Revisited*. The first vinyl dropped. The drums kicked in, the piano joined, and the guitars followed. In seconds, it was summer all over again. He was ready to work.

K.J.'s outline defined a plan to create a database identifying resources from all across the state. The proposal included a list of libraries and historical societies to be contacted. There was also a list of questions that would apply to all sources: hours of operation, chief contact, and email information. K.J. changed the project title to *Combined Historical Information Technology Research*, changing SHITR to CHITR. Chris wondered if Brent or Dr. George would even question the acronym.

He stopped to watch a fourth-and-goal situation. After

Notre Dame scored, he went back to the folders. Libby's outlined a planned senior AP unit. She named movies, docudramas, novels, and nonfiction she'd use to illuminate the changing attitudes of whites toward Native Americans. She'd also included an outline for a second unit, which would investigate regional attitudes toward Vermont's limited African American population and extensive French and Irish populations. It listed works by Robinson, Mosher, Feeney, and Craven as possible resources. The idea was very creative, but Chris had come to expect that from Libby. He noticed she'd scribbled in the margins "54th Mass Unit" and "Slaters" and guessed her idea for this second project came late and may not be complete.

He added another note to the margin alongside Libby's reading list. "*I Will Fight No More Forever* also seems appropriate as General Howard lived out his final years just a few blocks up Main Street from the Academy."

Chris had purposely left Honora's folder until the end. It contained a single sheet of triple-spaced paper with two paragraphs.

Plan for Recertification. That's safe enough, Chris thought, but the fourth sentence bludgeoned his hopes of avoiding another conflict. "The meal will not only help the students gain an appreciation of the time and effort the Pilgrims spent assisting their new neighbors but will also serve as a fundraiser for…" The idea may inspire K.J. to order a loaf of cranberry bread but it did little to sway Chris. He threw the folder on the floor.

"What the hell did I expect?" he said, but Dylan didn't answer.

Peter, Paul, and Mary dropped down on top of the stack, and the stylus arm swung over. Chris grabbed a beer from the fridge, then began flipping channels and watching a PBS documentary. The beer began working its magic, and Chris found his eyes becoming heavy.

It was after 10 when he woke to the rhythmic clicking of the diamond needle against the groove. A pledge break was on the screen. It seemed like a good time to call his sister. It rang a couple of times before she answered.

"Hi, Catch."

"Catch me if you can," she said as the volume on a TV went down. "How you doing?"

"It's been a long week. I'm still dazed."

Catch listened as her brother opened up. Walt's death had left him unsettled, and he found Jack's advice to move on harsh. He talked about the day-to-day grind of classes and departmental responsibilities and his own lack of enthusiasm. He still didn't trust Brent and thought his kids were a pain in the butt, especially Michael Andover. In addition, he wasn't feeling well.

"When's your appointment with Dennis?"

"I knew you'd ask. Couple more weeks."

"Chris!"

"I'll be fine. I promise!"

"OK. I get it. So, ah, have you come up with your own project yet?"

Chris told her about his fallback plan. He knew he could throw together a demography unit using the books K.J. had given him but he'd also been thinking more about doing something with genealogy after meeting with a teacher at Weaverton High.

"Either might work. Before Walt died, this stuff didn't seem important. Now it feels like I have to pick up my game. If I only had something to chase, maybe some family details, it would be more interesting to try the genealogy route."

"Details?"

"I don't know. A family bible with a list of relatives would be a nice start. The teacher I met talked about researching ancestors. Something concrete could put things in focus so I wouldn't have to spin my wheels just to get going. Holding a sword is more exciting than talking about a sword. You know what I mean?"

"I think so. Uncle Jonathon used to say 'the meat and potatoes.'"

"Exactly! Kids might be more interested, too, if I could

show my own results. Takes time."

"And it may be fun."

"Yeah, but there's a lot of planning, too. The unit has to be skills based, and I need to be able to measure results."

Chris gave Catch some examples of teaching students what to look for in newspaper articles or obituaries and then testing them to find similar items in other articles. He explained the long-range goal was for them to make hypotheses based on facts. He hadn't thought it through, but the idea behind the unit was to develop transferable problem-solving skills as well as learn history.

"What do I remember that might help?" Catch said. "You were pretty young when mom and dad died, but I remember Uncle Jonathon and Aunt Harriet saying a few things about mom's family. She and Aunt Harriet were friends. Mom's relatives, the LeClairs, were active in their church. Some uncles were politicians over in Weaverton!"

"I vaguely remember that."

"One of her uncles ran a store. I think Aunt Harriet said it was on Main Street, but I don't know what they sold. She said mom left home early and moved in with her."

"In Weaverton?"

"I think so. But that was all so long ago."

"Are there any records left? Or letters? Did anyone ever do a genealogy?"

"Not that I know of."

"I guess I'd have to start from…"

"Chris, wait! I just thought of something: the soldier in the hallway."

"What are you talking about?"

"The soldier in the hallway. Uncle Jonathon and Aunt Harriet used to take us over to Weaverton to visit Mom's relatives. She had two old maiden cousins, Katie and Elizabeth. They had a seven-toed cat!"

"I remember the cat and Elizabeth, but I don't remember Katie. Wasn't Elizabeth a mousy little lady with curly white hair? She left me a couple hundred dollars in her will."

"She left me some money, too. It was just after Mike died. Anyway, 'the girls,' as Aunt Harriet called them, lived off Main Street in Weaverton near where the roundabout is today. That neighborhood was all torn down in the '80s."

"I drove through there yesterday."

Catch described a yellow two-story house on a side street. There was a wood stove in the kitchen and a big round oak table with a lace tablecloth in the dining room. She told Chris how he'd hid under it as a youngster, but Chris denied it. A long parlor extended from the dining room to the front of the house. There was a wooden Victrola there that had to be wound up with a crank. They'd loved to take out records from the compartment underneath, winding them up and listening to band music from the '20s and '30s. The parlor had heavy dark drapes with lace curtains in the windows, and the shades were always pulled halfway down, giving the room a smoky look.

"Running parallel to the living room, between it and the porch, was a hallway with a stairway to the bedrooms. There was a coat tree near the end of the hall."

"What about the soldier?" Chris said, his voice rising.

"I'm getting to that. Some old uniform hung on that coat tree, and there was a sword. We used to call that uniform the soldier in the hallway."

"What kind of a uniform was it?"

"I don't know. You were only four or five, and the house was pretty dark and spooky. I'd dare you to run down the hallway and touch the sword. I was such a brat."

"You still are."

"Chris! Well, you'd run down the hall and tug on the jacket or tap the sword, then come running back looking like you'd seen a ghost."

"You were so cruel. Do you remember anything about the uniform, the soldier?"

"You were named after him. Christopher Gordon. He was one of Mom's relatives. I think he did something important, but I don't know what."

"Uncle Jonathon said he fought in the Civil War. I was going to look it up but never did."

"Why was that so important?"

"Uncle Jonathon talked about him like he was a hero, and with all the stuff that was happening back then, I guess I'd been looking for a hero—especially a family hero. Remember anything else?"

"No. Yes! There's a letter. After Mike died, I asked Uncle Jonathon about mom's family. He wrote down some information and mailed it to me. It wasn't really a letter—more like a long list of names written in his beautiful script."

"'The Palmer method,' Uncle Jonathon used to call it," Chris said.

"Yes, the Palmer method. I don't know where the letter is, but I'm pretty sure that Christopher Gordon was the soldier in the hallway."

"Try to find it. It could be helpful. If not, I may not have time to use Claudia's ideas."

"Claudia?"

"The teacher over at Weaverton."

"Is she cute?"

"Sis! She's too young for me and besides, I'm a confirmed bachelor. Let's be real. No money, mid-'60s, more than 100,000 miles on my chassis. A 30-ish woman wouldn't even be interested."

"Chris!"

"I'm after recertification not a December-May relationship. Besides, I've got my hands full right now. I'll be spending my weekends getting this project moving until I figure out whether I'm staying another year."

"I'm glad you haven't given up yet. You're so good with kids."

"Always the big sister. Wants her little brother to succeed. Finally."

"You're a success."

"That's what you say. Anyway, look for that letter. I can find anything if I have a map."

"I'll see what I can find."

After Chris hung up, he stared at the images dancing across the soundless television. The shadowy corners of the room appeared and disappeared in sync with the lights flashing on the big screen. On the wall above, Bob Dylan waited for his cue to begin. After a few moments, Chris reached for the remote. His gaze drifted to the empty chili bowl. Good idea, he thought before taking a couple of antacids on his way to the bedroom.

***

Chris tossed about all night before waking Sunday, restless and exhausted. He passed the morning moving from chair to couch and back, trying to read the *Freeman*, and watching TV in an unending circuit of fruitlessness. By noon, he felt overwhelmed. He tried to reason through his emotions. Was he bending under the weight of his new responsibilities? It was a daunting task to try to pick up where Walt left off. Perhaps his old fear of failure was resurfacing. He'd struggled with that for years. It may have been knowing that he'd have to confront Honora now. That would not be pleasant. Whatever the cause, he had to settle himself. Dylan offered nothing. Chris paced the apartment as the TV played in the background until remembering Catch's question about attending the meetings. Could they help? He checked through the old notes on his bulletin board until finding a time and location scribbled on a tiny piece of paper.

College Street was empty. He hurried up the hill and cut behind Waterford Hall, taking a shortcut into the old hospital parking lot. A few cars were scattered about. Outside the side entrance to the old hospital, the yellow light shown like a beacon to a pilot circling homeward.

He walked to the side door and followed the sign down the empty hallway to the conference room. A handsome middle-aged man in a warm red cardigan noticed him and walked over.

"Hi, Chris. It's been a while."

"Yeah, Bob, it has."

"Glad you came. Grab a coffee. We're just getting started."

Chris poured out a cup of rich dark coffee as Bob and the others sat down in the circle of gray metal chairs. Bob spoke as Chris added just a touch of cream. "Hi, I'm Bob, and I'm the adult child of an alcoholic."

Chris knew the faces of the people in the circle not by name but by their stories. Their stories were his. Their pain was his. Their kids went to the Academy. They mowed their lawns and painted their houses. They worked in the banks and shops. And they'd bandaged the same scars he'd bandaged, covering up wounds that didn't show and wouldn't heal. He listened as one after another exhumed their pain. Some voices were loud like storm winds on the lake while others were whispering spring breezes touched with rain. No matter the voice or the wording—no matter the pitch or the plea—each story found a parallel in Chris's heart.

One by one they talked. When a woman named Betty spoke, Chris remembered looking down the lamp-lit street for the headlights of Uncle Jonathon's car.

"I always thought it was my fault. I thought if I just did something, it would be all better," she said. "The later it got, the more worried I'd become. I'd try to study or read or watch TV but couldn't sit still. Finally, the only thing left was to wait at the window in the front hallway, looking up and down the street, as if it would hurry him home. I knew it wouldn't, but that was all I could do. When Daddy finally turned into the driveway, I'd run and tell everyone, 'Daddy's home! Daddy's home!'" The woman lowered her eyes.

"Thanks, Betty. Anyone else want to speak tonight?" Bob said, looking at each of them.

When no one else volunteered, he called for them to hold hands and, bowing his head, he led them. "God grant me the serenity to accept the things I cannot change, courage to change the things I can, and wisdom to know the difference."

As Chris walked down College later that evening, he felt better knowing he was not alone.

***

Monday morning, Chris felt off center the moment he entered the Academy. He walked into the wrong rooms, wrote incorrect assignments on the boards, and spilled his coffee twice.

Despite these problems, he forced a smile as he stopped by the teacher's lounge on his way to the cafeteria, but it dissolved when the restroom door opened, and he found himself facing Honora Webster.

"Hey, Honora, got a minute?"

"I suppose. What is it?"

"It's about your recertification plan."

"Oh! Of course! I'd love to talk."

Chris pointed toward the conference room. The weather headlines in *The Daily Freeman* predicted a cold front the following week. Honora washed her hands, picked up a towel, and followed him in.

"Ah, well, you see, Honora—ah, your proposal isn't going to work."

"Why not? It's just as valid as anyone else's!" she said, her hands fumbling with the towel.

"It doesn't meet the criteria."

"Of course it does! There's research and student involvement. I even listed the skill sets I plan to develop. Let me show you, in case you overlooked them."

She dropped the towel on the conference table and jerked the folder out of Chris's hand.

"It couldn't be clearer, but to satisfy your fussiness, I suppose I can add a few notes and make some changes here and everything …"

"Honora! This is high school! The idea's not appropriate."

She pushed the folder back at Chris before picking the

towel up again and beginning to twist it. "Well, I disagree!" She said, squeezing tighter and tighter.

"The criteria are very defini…"

"You seem to think that unless something's your idea, it isn't any good! You may not know it, but food is the international language. All you have to do is watch Julia Child and Jacques Pepin to understand. Did you ever see their show on crepes?"

"No. I…"

"There's so much history. There's even a national crepe day in France. Le Chandeleur. My point, Chris, is that it's just as appropriate to study and prepare a historical Thanksgiving dinner as it is to—I don't know—read a book."

As Honora spoke, the veins in her hands bulged under the talon-like pressure she exerted on the towel.

"I don't see it that way."

"It's been allowed. Many times! Walt wouldn't have had a problem with it. I know he'd have appreciated the extra effort involved. He was objective!"

Chris's chest tightened as his blood throbbed through his carotids. "Honora, that brings up another point. You have done this before, again and again. According to the guidelines, this project is a once-in-a-lifetime opportunity. Brent and Dr. George, the certification people, expect something unique." He curled his fingers to mimic quotations. "Once in a…"

The blood drained from Honora's lips, the muscles in her face tightened, and her eyes emptied, reminding Chris of the craters on Pluto. He imagined striking a match on her face but, before he could say "lifetime!" Honora exited the room so fast, Chris's quotation floated unclaimed in midair. He took a breath. A victory! He walked back into the lounge where Honora was drying coffee cups and babbling to one of the English literature teachers.

"I suppose I'll just take another silly course and waste another $3600. I was trying to save the Academy some money. But the dinner would've been a lot of effort. More than its worth! Even if Little Honey drove all the way in from Colchester to help! She always helps me out, you know." Each coffee cup she had dried banged as she placed them back in the cabinet. "I've given more than I'll ever get back. It's just not worth it anymore."

"I'm sorry, Honora, but…" Chris began.

Honora's chin rose before she turned and strutted out.

Chris sensed this wasn't over but felt relief knowing Thanksgiving recess was just a few days away. He was trying to stay focused on that when he joined Libby and K.J. in the cafeteria.

"Have you seen a ghost?" K.J. said.

"That bad?"

"I've seen better over at Dowers' Parlor."

"I had to tell Honora about her project."

"Ohhhh!"

"Is there anything I…" Libby began when Nat King Cole's rendition of "The Christmas Song" started playing on her smart phone.

At the surrounding tables, both teachers and students turned to the song.

"Darn! Excuse me," Libby said. She answered. "Hi, Mom. I can't talk right now. I left the ringer on by mistake. What? Not now. Yes, I cooked the red sauce but it didn't work out. I'll text you later. Goodbye. I can't talk. Goodbye." Libby shook her head as she adjusted the ringer.

K.J. looked at them and said, "I hate to say it, but I'm having a great day."

After school, Chris drove directly to Wells Court. Inside his mailbox, he found a faded manila envelope with his name in Mary Catherine's handwriting written on it. He thumbed open the envelope as he climbed the stairs. "Brennan-Gordon-Leclair-Tree" were written across the top of the yellowing first page. "Christopher Farrell married Margaret Nelson, daughter of George Nelson, a native of Ayrshire Scotland," the first paragraph began.

He unlocked his apartment door, dropped his tote bag, and skimmed the first page. On the second, about a quarter of the way down, he saw the name, Christopher Patrick Gordon.

"There he is!" he said to Dylan. "Thank you, Mary Catherine!"

14

Chris loved the way November exposed Queen City. The intermittent rain and cold nights cleared away the showy pretensions of October, offering a palate of muted colors. It also drove away the tourists. He had nothing against them. They filled the restaurants and motels as they searched for the disappearing Vermont landscape of stone walls and quaint barns, but he felt relieved once they were gone. He thought Queen City breathed better after they left, when the college crowd moved inside, when traffic flowed, and the lines to everything shortened. The transitional season also wiped away the trophy sailboats and runabouts from their mantles in the harbor, where most Queen City residents could only watch from the shore, never to be rewarded with so much as a ride. Chris loved best what was left behind. November exposed a stark land of quiet streets, of pervasive grays that hid the mountains for weeks at a time, of tall white pines on the ridgelines, of sleeping gardens and half-painted houses, of unfinished projects. The land held hardy, inspiring people whose roots and traditions had made them tolerant. They did everything they could to help their children stay but knew this place offered little for those who really belonged.

As Thanksgiving approached, Chris adhered to his long-established traditions. A week before the holiday, he picked up a 27-pound Butterball at Cost Plus, along with a few surprises for Catch's family. On Saturday, he drove to her house and dropped off the turkey, two quarts of ice cream, and a quart of maple syrup. Catch had assumed responsibility for cooking the dinner after Aunt Harriet had passed away. She made the holiday her own by preparing the special things her brother, children, and grandchildren loved, but she also continued tradition by mixing up a large batch of dressing using Aunt Harriet's recipe: dried white and dark breads, onions, chicken stock, salt, pepper, more onions, and sage. Lots of sage.

On Thanksgiving morning, Chris picked up his nephews for a local touch football game known as the Turkey Bowl. The bird had already been in the oven for an hour when Chris and the boys left for Smalley Park.

"See you around noon," he called to Mary Catherine as the door closed.

After the game, Chris, his nephews, and some of the former players drove to Pomeroy Park. They stood in a circle where Chris and his friends had played some of the earliest Turkey Bowls. They told stories of former players and games. Then they toasted the deceased, poured beer on the ground, and said their goodbyes for another year.

After returning to Mary Catherine's, everyone helped by following her directions.

"Time to slice the turkey," she said.

"It's my turn," Jimmy said and began assembling the electric knife.

The bird had been resting for nearly an hour when Jimmy went to work. He cut off a few small pieces and handed them to Mikey's teenage girls, saying, "We shouldn't give the kids too much to eat." The girls laughed.

"Uncle Chris," Mikey said, "big turnout for the game today."

"It's nice that those guys come back. It's the only time I see most of them."

"Did you think it would last this long?" Jimmy said.

"No. Just something to do when we were kids."

"Any games you thought were better than others?" Jimmy said.

"Funny, I remember things from 50 years ago but don't always remember where I put my glasses."

"Like what?"

"The first year we played, when I was in college, this girl I was dating invited me to dinner with her family in Orwell, but I turned her down. Some of my frat brothers couldn't go home, so Aunt Harriet let me invite them to dinner. I remember Underwood said he'd bring a pie. It was Walt's idea to play football against guys at Phi Nu Gamma who couldn't get home."

"Who was the girl?" Mikey said. "You've never mentioned anyone."

"It was a long time ago. Her name was Susan."

"Was she upset?"

"I forget. I borrowed Aunt Harriet's car. She had this great old red Dodge Wayfarer. 1949, I think."

"Mom has some pictures," Mikey said.

"I do, too—on my bulletin board. I picked up Jack at his apartment. He was so excited, babbling like a crazy man, punching all the buttons on the radio, looking for football news. He said stuff like, 'It ain't right. No football news on Thanksgiving morning!' He claimed the stations in Port Huron had football news every 10 minutes. 'In between the polka music that is.' He said they were always interviewing guys like Ara Parseghian and Duffy Daugherty, calling them, 'the Kings!' Jack had this silver flask and asked if I wanted some breakfast. Said he was drinking 'wodka' and claiming his ancestors, the 'honyocks,' were smarter than the Irish 'cause the 'Micks' never figured out what to do with potatoes besides grow blight, while his 'honyocks' figured out how to grow 'wodka.'"

"This is good. Great job, mom." Jimmy held up a piece of white meat.

Mary Catherine smiled as she ran the mixer through the potatoes, milk, and butter.

"What about the game, Uncle Chris?"

"We called that one the 'seekers game.'"

"The what?"

Chris started by telling his nephews about the Giants-Bears championship game back in the 1930s. The field had been covered with ice. After one of the players suggested that sneakers would work better than cleats, the coach had sent his assistant over to Manhattan College to see if he could find some sneakers. The assistant had borrowed nine pairs from the basketball team. The Giants had used the sneakers in the second half and had better traction than the Bears and won the game.

"Our game was nothing like it, but the field was pretty sloppy when Phi Nu Gamma…"

"Chris. Can you help with the hot dishes? And boys, get the kids together and come to the table," Mary Catherine said.

Chris and his nephews carried the mashed potatoes, dressing, and a green bean casserole out to the table. Jimmy went back for the turkey. Mikey turned to Chris. "So what happened, Uncle Chris?"

"I'll tell you about the game later, but what I really remember is what happened after at Uncle Jonathon's. You guys were still babies. Before we sat down, Uncle Jonathon took some of the guys to the garage. He probably told them about old Colonel Jackson raising money to build statues of his father-in-law, General Wells, at Gettysburg and Bluffs Park, and about the big scandal when the Queen Brothers built the breakwater. The usual stuff. I know Aunt Harriet kept looking out the window with her lamppost look. When she called for dinner, Uncle Jonathon was already going under. Her face got even tighter. She started to tell him he was drunk but stopped when she noticed you guys watching.

That's when Jack seemed to revive. He told you guys stories about the bubbombinable snow horse and hunting for tree squeaks up in the gores. Everybody was rolling. He kissed Aunt Harriet when she brought out the turkey and gave a blow by blow of the game with his arm around Uncle Jonathon's shoulder. Around desert, Jack's eyes kinda rolled up as his body seemed to deflate. He lowered his head to the table and fell asleep in his mashed potatoes. Everyone just sat there until Uncle Jonathon turned to Aunt Harriet and said, 'Now that's a drunk man!' No one disputed him. And Underwood never brought the pie."

"Chris, will you lead us in grace?" Mary Catherine said as she sat down.

The dinner was a colossal success. After dessert, Mikey's girls cleared the table as Mikey and Jimmy's wives

helped Mary Catherine in the kitchen. Chris and his nephews sat down in the living room.

"Mom said you haven't been feeling good, Uncle
Chris?" Jimmy said.

"There's no pain when you don't play."

"I mean your heart. She said it was bothering you."

"I'll tell you after I see the doctor. Right now, I don't
know what it is."

Jimmy went to his coat and brought back three cigars.
Then Chris and his nephews stepped out onto the deck.
Chris pretended to take a few puffs. He hated smoking but
always joined his nephews because they invited him.

"Did I tell you what we did last summer, Uncle Chris?"
Mikey said.

"No. What?"

"We started going to the track."

"Track! Mikey, can you afford that? What does your
mother think?"

"It's not what you think Uncle Chris. And, yes, Mom
knows. She's planning on coming with us next summer."

"It doesn't seem like a good idea to throw your money
around like that. It's too hard to…"

"Wait a sec. It's not like that, Uncle Chris. Last spring
one of the guys I work with said he was going to the Derby
and invited us along. We packed the kids up and joined a
few other families. Everyone camped out. On race day, we
parked in the infield at the Downs. To tell you the truth,
we couldn't even see the race, but it was such an exciting
atmosphere. It was just a big party with kids playing and
barbeque grills cooking brats.

After we got home, I started reading about horserac-
ing. It's really fascinating stuff. The farms, the breeding,
and who couldn't love the great ones? Man of War, Eddie
Arcaro, Secretariat. It's all pretty exciting. It's like fantasy
but it's history, too."

"Long shots! Just long shots."

"Long shots and millionaires! Uncle Chris," Mikey said
puffing on his cigar. "There's this place near our house, Ar-

lington Park, that caters to families. You know—low prices, picnics, tours of the paddock, meet the horses. It's only 15 bucks for the whole family. So we bring a picnic. You can spend all day Sunday watching races, and you don't even have to place a bet."

"Do you? Bet that is?"

"We give ourselves a limit, Uncle Chris. Ten bucks for the day."

"I'm glad you're not a big spender."

"Uncle Chris. Going to the track is cheaper than going to the zoo and a lot more exciting."

Mary Catherine opened the deck door. "It's time for Monopoly. Are you guys ready to lose your shirts?"

15

Internal Medical Associates occupied a suite of rooms on the sixth floor of the former Queen City General Hospital building. As Chris entered, he realized how little the building resembled the place he'd worked in as a college student. Dr. Rousseau's waiting room occupied space in the middle of the former surgical ICU. Chris hung his coat before going to the desk.

"Dr. Rousseau is running late, Mr. Martin, but we'll get you started shortly."

Chris fingered through old copies of *Cosmopolitan, Yachting, Redbook,* and *The New Diabetes* to pass the time. *The New Diabetes*? Before he found anything interesting, the medical assistant led him to the examining room.

"Take everything off except your socks. And put this on," she said, handing him a johnny.

He changed, then sat on the examining table. The paper sheet covering the table crinkled and cracked as he wiggled his bottom into a comfortable position. The lights were bright, but the air in the sterile white room felt cool. "Clair de Lune" played over the Muzak. Medical offices are so demeaning, he thought as he wiggled to keep his back covered. A moment later, Dr. Rousseau entered. He was younger than Chris, looking boyish despite salt and pepper hair. "You could use some new magazines, Dennis."

"Business manager's job. I'll send her an email, but it won't do any good. It's all about nickels and dimes. How are Mary Catherine and the kids?"

Chris updated his sister's friend. As Chris talked, Dr. Rousseau's eyes darted between Chris and his computer screen. Next Chris answered probes concerning his health as Dr. Rousseau took his blood pressure.

"That's up. We'll take it again later," Dennis said taking a stethoscope from his pocket. He listened to Chris's chest and back.

"Take a deep breath. OK. Let it out. Take another. Let it out."

He asked Chris to observe his finger while moving it back and forth. He rotated Chris's arms and legs and palpated his back all while asking questions and referring back to notes on the screen.

"Let me take that blood pressure again." He put the cuff back on Chris's arm. "That's better. You can put your clothes on. I know how it pisses you off to sit there in your underwear while I talk." Chris smiled, reaching for his pants. "Heart sounds great. Blood pressure, pulse, and respirations are mostly within normal limits. The last EKG we did was normal too, but since you said you've had that chest pain more than once, I'm going to order a stress test."

Chris stopped buttoning his shirt and adjusted himself on the examining table.

"It's pretty benign. Really! Just an EKG while you pedal an exercise bike. Takes about half an hour."

"What if…"

"The cardiac people will send me the results. If there's an issue, we'll discuss the options and develop a plan. For now, just go about things normally. No changes."

Chris finished buttoning his shirt as Dr. Rousseau rolled his chair over to the keyboard and entered more notes into the terminal. The printer spit out sheets of paper.

"Fill out this info sheet with your symptoms and leave it with my scheduler. She'll set up the stress test. And say hi to Mary Catherine." Dr. Rousseau reached for the door.

"Dennis, get a subscription to *National Geographic*."

"I'll bring in my copy the next time you're on the schedule."

Chris filled in the blanks before handing the scheduler his paperwork. She read her monitor, picked up the phone, and made a call. A few moments later, she handed Chris a card. "Your test is December 17th at 3:30. They said to bring sneakers and shorts. Do you need any refills for any prescriptions, Mr. Martin?"

"No thanks. I'm all set."

***

During the second week of December, wreathes appeared in the Academy's lobby and cafeteria. "Holiday Treat" was a listed item on each day's menu. Seasonal music played over the loudspeaker system between class periods. Each morning, sprinkled donuts appeared in the teachers' lounge. The seasonal touches induced a placebo effect on the Academy. Hallway noise appeared softer as students talked of basketball rivalries and clothing choices for the Christmas Ball. If Chris felt any chest discomfort prior to his stress test, he compartmentalized it and filed it away in a drawer marked later. By the time he entered the cardiac lab on the 17th, the test had evolved from a medical necessity to a minor aggravation.

He registered, changed his clothes, and followed the technician to one of three stationary bicycles placed beside desks in a sterile but airy room with many windows. Devices on the desks resembled old Apple IIC computers except for the sets of wires extending between the devices and the bikes. The tech explained that the equipment recorded heart rate and blood pressure while doing an EKG. She said the pedal tension would gradually increase, making the pedaling more difficult, but joked that the hardest part was waiting while she attached the wires.

Chris took off his t-shirt and waited as the technician attached the electrodes. Next, he climbed on the bike and watched a beam of light cross the monitor, jump, and drop in a hypnotic continuum. After the tech placed a blood pressure cuff on his arm, green numbers flashed in a box at the screen's corner. Chris soon tired of the monotony.

"You may begin pedaling."

Beyond the expansive windows lay another cold December sky. The sun balanced on the horizon. It was that nebulous time where light fades imperceptibly into darkness. The hour seemed even later because brooding clouds were moving eastward.

As Chris peddled, the tech noted the BP readings recorded at the top of the screen. She tapped a button on the desk and the pedal pressure increased. She took more readings. On the other side of the room, another man Chris' age removed his shirt and climbed on a test bike.

"How do you feel, Chris?"

"Fine."

The tech tapped the button again and the peddling became still more difficult. Perspiration formed on his forehead and underarms. He anticipated his discomfort would reappear, but it only lurked in his mind. The tech scribbled more notes. After several increases, the pressure against his peddles subsided and with it went any discomfort, real or imagined.

"You may stop."

"How did I do?"

"Dr. Rousseau will contact you with the results."

Though Christmas was only a week away, Chris hadn't begun his shopping. He changed back into his street clothes and drove over to Queen City Mall. Catch, always first on his list, had mentioned one of those single cup coffee brewers, so when Chris noticed one in the window at Champion's Emporium, he went in. Next he headed to The Athlete's Locker for socks. She loved those colored wool ones with the snowflakes and reindeer. Afterwards, he walked to the bookstore for the boys' gifts. He never knew what to buy his nephews' wives or their children, but faced that task with optimism. The attitude paid off because he had most of his presents in the car in a couple of hours. As a reward, he decided to go downtown for a beer and a burger.

He stopped by Wells Court to drop off the presents. He picked up his mail on the way up the stairs but had so many bags he waited until he was inside the apartment before thumbing through the envelopes. Bob Dylan surveyed the presents.

"I'm nearly done. Can you believe it?" Chris said to the

poster.

The message light on the answering machine was flashing, but Chris ignored it. Behind the electric bill was an innocuous postcard signed by the Green Mountain University reunion committee. It mentioned a Memorial Day weekend gathering and suggested viewing the Queen City Marathon as a reunion-week activity. He shoved the card into his pocket and headed back down the stairs.

Chris found a parking spot half a block from the Cassidy Building, threw change in the meter, and walked to The Establishment. Christmas spirit had arrived ahead of him. A handwritten sign on the door listed different drink specials for each of the remaining shopping days. Most of them included something called Reindeer Rum. As Chris opened the door, "Holly Jolly Christmas" blared from the bar's sound system. "Merry Christmas to All" was written in waxy red glitter on the mirror behind the bar. Red candles in hurricane globes dotted the centers of artificial wreathes on the tiny tables and tired garland surrounded the doorways. Rudolph's picture hung on the men's room door, Mrs. Claus' on the ladies' room. The flashing string of red bulbs exuded more the ambience of a brothel than a manger, Chris thought. Jack filled a draft as Chris sat down.

"So, Mr. Grinch, what mischief have the Academy kiddies been up to?"

"It's been quiet, except for Andover. Hey, order a burger for me."

"Sure. What was it this time?"

"We were talking about Jefferson…"

"Hold that thought." Jack reached for a bottle of scotch and walked down the bar to meet a customer's extended glass.

Chris studied an emaciated tree decorating the front window. The scraggly fir had been pulled and tugged so many times the tinsel and garland hung on for dear life. "Little Saint Nick" succeeded "Holly Jolly Christmas" on the sound system. Outside, one of those bell-ringing Santas with dirty hands and baggy clothes walked by.

"She's a beauty!" Chris said, saluting the tree with his glass.

"Ain't she though. I just love how Christmas transforms mankind. She's just a dead bush the boss paid shit for but when you hang cheap lights and garbage on her, she becomes transformed, mystical. Not a retailer in the world that doesn't applaud the symbolism."

"Cynic!"

"Me. That's like the pot calling something something, but I digress. You were talking about the little professor."

"I was trying to explain Jefferson's role at the Second Continental Congress when the kid raised his hand. Everything stops as he begins this monologue about Jefferson and Madison traveling up Lake George and Lake Champlain to study plants. Andover's old man did some research, I guess. The kid had the floor, and his buddies were all taken up with him. He's a little peacock. I don't understand what he or his buddies are up to. It's a battle every day."

Jack shrugged. "You need a hobby to get your mind off that shit. What about that Libby? You talk about her a lot. Maybe you two could go off and tour some old battlefields, search for lost cannons. You could point out important rocks to her. History rocks!"

"Yeah, I suppose that could be fun, but I don't need another relationship."

"Another! Like one girlfriend, 40-plus years ago, qualifies."

"Cut it, Jack! I don't need a hobby or a relationship. I need out, but I'm trapped. I haven't saved a dime."

"I invested my savings in barley, hops, and single-malt scotch," Jack said. "But I've got a plan."

"What is it this time?"

Jack looked down the bar before turning back to Chris. He lowered his voice. "I finally figured it out. I'm sleeping all day and working all night. Got to reverse things. I've got to get out of the bar business and paint full time."

"Same old plan!"

"I'm serious this time. Hold on a second."

Jack walked over to a young couple who were just sitting down. He had them laughing in the time it took to draw a draft and mix a drink. Chris watched him pour gin and grenadine and then add an egg white. After handing it to the girl, he came back wearing a shit-eating grin.

"Pink Lady. Can you believe it? Nobody drinks that shit, but I digress again. I'm as stagnant as you are, and the big guy is catching up." Jack pointed at the clock. "Been reading about Alaska and thinking of going up there to paint. A different mountain every day; nobody's seen most of them. The Hudson River School boys will all jump out of their graves when they see my stuff. That's what I'm going to do."

Chris thought Jack's eyes had a dreamlike glaze over them.

"At your age? What about your bills?"

"Lots of work up in Alaska, all that oil and gas money. I'll find something easy, be a breakfast prep cook in some little truck stop."

"That's a young man's work."

"I'm still strong like bull!" Jack said, raising his arms and flexed his biceps. "How strong do you have to be to scramble eggs? Besides, I'll make so much money, I'll only have to work a few months out of the year, so there'll be plenty of time to paint. And fish. They'll probably call me Sitka Jack. Chris, those mountains are spectacular. Make our little old Adirondacks look like saggy boobs."

Jack left to fill the waitress's order and pick up Chris's burger.

"Been reading lots of stuff, too—Jack London, the gold rush, rafting the Yukon. Not just the touristy shit." Jack was already on autopilot, but something signaled him to shift into overdrive. "Find me a nice Eskimo filly, we'll rub noses and tickle blubber together. When I get sickly, she'll take me out fishing and leave me on the ice with my jig up. I'll die a happy man, frozen solid with a narwhal on the line."

"Jack, I always thought your painting was just a time killer."

"Hell, I'll memorize all of Robert Service's shit. Not just the basics like, 'On the barge with Madame Lafarge' blah, blah, etc., etc., but the fancy stuff like, 'The Shooting of Dan McGrew.'"

"Come on!" Chris said, shaking his head.

"You think it's just another scheme, don't you? Like the farm up in Buels Gore. This is different! Pay attention, Chris. Focus." Jack said, pointing his fingers towards his eyes. "There's a lot you don't notice. People change. Life goes on in spite of us. I've always wanted to paint. I may not get another chance. Look around. Do you think I aspired to this?"

Chris finished his burger, drained his glass, and stood up. "When did you get so serious?"

Jack smiled a big shit-eating grin. "Another for the road, my good man?"

"No. I've got to pick up some wrapping paper. It has to be special for Catch and the kids. Everything has to be special. It's Christmas!"

"Yeah. I get it. I see the trees through the windows."

Chris reached into his coat pocket for his gloves and found the reunion postcard. "Did you get one of these?" He handed the postcard to Jack. "Some of the old gang may be there. Underwood, Susan Boisvert. It might be fun to see them again"

Jack shook his head. "You forget I didn't graduate. In fact, I didn't even attend. I just look brilliant."

When Chris reached the door, he looked back. Jack was near the far end of the bar, reaching for the scotch. Alvin and the Chipmunks were harmonizing in the background. The room was bathed in a brothel's red glow. Everything seemed appropriate.

The flashing red light on Chris's answering machine caught his eye as soon as he opened the apartment. He turned on the lights, placed the wrapping paper on the table, and hit the play button.

"Chris, this is Dennis. They found some abnormalities in your test results. It's probably nothing more than an equipment malfunction, but just to be safe, I'm scheduling another test. It's called a Cardiolite stress test. They inject some radioactive dye into your veins and have you run on a treadmill. After, they take pictures of the dye so we can assess how the blood pumps through your heart. Call tomorrow for the test's date and time. In the meantime, no strenuous activity! Catch up on some of that reading you're always planning to do. No strenuous activity! Merry…"

The tape ran out before Dennis could finish. Chris sat down and looked up at Bob Dylan. "Merry Christmas!"

16

The furniture in the cardiac department's waiting room was standard issue Swedish modern—uncomfortable, encouraging Chris to pace. Where the hell is she? he thought just before he noticed through the glass door his sister hurrying toward the waiting room, stuffing her keys into her purse. He reached for her hand as the door opened.

"I've been driving round for 10 minutes. There aren't enough spaces in that lot."

Chris didn't hear what Catch said after that. His stomach was jumping around so much he could only concentrate on pulling her down the corridor toward another set of swinging doors.

"We have to get to the lab."

"Lab?"

"That's where they do the test."

They pushed through the double doors and stopped before a young clerk at a computer. She asked a few questions and looked at the screen.

"Put this on over your shorts. Wear your running shoes," she said, handing Chris a johnny and pointing toward a changing room. "Someone will be out for you."

Catch flipped through the local section of *The Daily Freeman* while Chris was in the dressing room. As soon as he returned, a nurse arrived, led him to a cardiac chair, asked his name, and inserted an IV portal into his arm. Then a radiology tech arrived as if on cue. The woman introduced herself and spoke about isotopes while opening a metal box. From it, she injected a liquid into Chris's IV. His arm warmed and he began feeling faint. "Just sit here a few moments," she said. Catch sat down beside him and squeezed his other hand.

"You OK?"

Chris shrugged and grimaced. "Catch, this doesn't make any sense. When did we become the old people we used to laugh about? Aren't I stylish?" He stood and turned a mock pirouette while holding the johnny wrapped around his back. "This isn't me. This is some old guy who snuck into my body when I wasn't looking. I've become Uncle Jonathon or Aunt Harriet or mom's old cousin in Weaverton, the one who patted her cat."

"Elizabeth," Mary Catherine said with the hint of a smile.

"I want the other me back—the one who water skied and played touch football at Pomeroy Park. The one who hung out all night at Benny's. Where the hell is he?"

A passerby went far around the seating area as Chris's voice rose in some desperate crescendo. His sister took his hand as he sat back down and rubbed his forearm.

"It's OK to be nervous, Chris. It's probably nothing."

"I'm not nervous. I'm scared. Look what happened to Walt!" He looked away. "Catch, when we were kids, I wanted to get beyond curfews and for Christmas to come early. I wanted that first kiss, and my driver's license, and to vote. I prayed for things to speed up, to get the hell away from Aunt Harriet and Uncle Jonathon. But once that started, it was already too late. Now I feel like a kid, trapped in an old man's body."

"I know. I know." Catch rubbed his arm.

"I got distracted preparing tests and paying bills, waiting for the car to be fixed. All that time, the clock was ticking. It was like falling asleep at the drive in. The movie kept playing. Now I know I've been asleep but the movie is almost over. I wanted to be 16, Catch, not 67!"

Instead of defending the indefensible, Catch reached into her purse and took out an envelope. "I told the kids last week. Jimmy said to wish you luck. Mikey sent this."

The envelope was addressed to "Uncle Chris" at his sister's address. He fingered it with both hands before ripping off one end. Two handwritten pages were folded inside.

Dear Uncle Chris,

Mom told us you are going to have some heart tests, so I thought I'd drop you a line and wish you luck. I know you won't need it, but I offer it anyway.

When we were growing up, you were always there, putting yourself out for Mom and Jimmy and me. After Dad died, you stepped right in. You taught us to play baseball and took us fishing. (Remember when Jimmy fell in the Brown's River?) You attended our games, our plays, and our graduations. You called to check up on our grades and, as if you weren't running hard enough, you bought the groceries mom couldn't afford, paid our tuition bills, and got us through college. You even bought us new cars before you bought yourself one.

At Thanksgiving, I watched you with my daughters. You still have a big heart.

That brings me to what I really want to say.

Remember how I said I've been going to the track? The guy who invited us to the Derby gave me a book about Secretariat. It's a wonderful story. It has all the stuff about long shots (and millionaires) and hard work, but there is something else. Did you know that when Secretariat won the Derby, he ran each successive quarter mile faster? In fact, the horse continued to accelerate through the entire race. He was still accelerating when he crossed the finish line. That's amazing, simply amazing.

After Secretariat died, they did an autopsy and found his heart was gigantic. It was nearly three times larger than a normal horse's heart. The doctors were astounded. It made me think of you continuing to push yourself for us. I guess that what I'm trying to say is that there's nothing wrong with your heart, Uncle Chris. It's just too big for the doctors to figure out.

Love,

Mikey

Chris closed his eyes as a gusher of warmth erupted inside him, forcing its way from deep within his heart up through his throat toward the blackness behind his eyelids. It tried to burst out in a hundred places but he struggled and swallowed, clenching his fists, grinding his teeth, using all his inner power to wrestle the force back into reluctant submission.

"Mr. Martin." A voice called from the doorway. Chris stood, handed the letter to Catch, and followed the nurse down the hall.

The testing room was crammed with equipment. A treadmill stood in the center, surrounded by shelves, stacked with multiple pieces of electronics. There were lights, switches, and wires everywhere. The only instrument Chris recognized was a monitor, which was mounted before the treadmill. There was more electronic equipment in an observation room off to the right, behind a thick glass window. It reminded Chris of pictures he'd seen of NASA centers during the shuttle program.

A tech with a shaved head and dressed in light-green scrubs watched one of those screens as Mario Brothers figures danced across it. When he noticed Chris, he turned off the game, picked up a clipboard, and walked over to greet him. "Hi, Mr. Martin."

The man introduced himself and said the test consisted of making Chris run in place on the treadmill and recording his heart's activity. He said they'd increase the speed at regular intervals, but warned him that if he felt sick to tell them immediately. The tech turned to his clipboard. "Now, just to verify a few things: What is your name?"

"Christopher Gordon Martin."

The tech also verified his birthday—7/8/44—and his doctor. He looked at Chris's bracelet. Then he checked off some boxes and smiled as if Chris had already passed the test. A wave of melancholy flowed through Chris's veins. This is my life and someone's reading me a fucking script, he thought.

The tech instructed Chris to remove his shirt and began

attaching leads to his chest as others entered the room. A nurse walked behind Chris to the observation room and paged through a chart. A man and a woman, dressed in scrubs, entered and stood behind him, speaking in low tones. He thought he heard the woman say "…possible coronary artery…" just as the door opened again and three men, wearing white lab coats, proceeded to the observation room without acknowledging Chris's existence. The nurse handed one, a bald fellow with a goatee, a chart then leaned into a microphone.

"Hello, Chris! We'll begin in just a moment," the nurse said from the control room before turning back to the three doctors.

The tech told Chris they were going to record a baseline for a few minutes before increasing the speed. "I'll tell you each time it's about to change. At the end of the test, I'll also raise the track's angle. You know 'Heartbreak Hill?' The Boston Mar…"

"I get it."

"Sorry. Looks like you're in good shape, so this'll be a breeze. We see some doozies in here," the tech said, putting on a set of headphones.

"Go ahead," the nurse said into the microphone.

The tech flashed another empty smile before flipping the switch on the treadmill. Chris stepped on and walked to the motor's low whine while the goateed man pointed to something in the chart. The reflection in the observation-room glass showed the two people in scrubs talking.

"How do you feel, Chris?" the nurse said.

"OK."

"I'm going to increase the speed," the tech said.

Walking became uncomfortable at the faster pace, so Chris shifted to a slow jog. The light trail on the monitor sped up.

"How do you feel?" the nurse said.

"OK."

Chris thought the man with the goatee appeared to be giving a lecture, shaking his finger in the air each time he made a point.

The whine increased a few decibels as the speed increased. Chris leaned forward to keep up, swinging his arms faster; the wires dangling from his chest bounced from side to side. The monitor's light trail took off. Chris's breathing became more labored. Sweat poured from his temples, and he gasped for air. He swung his arms with determination. The goateed man squinted at one of the monitors, the people in the reflection inched closer, and the tech's head bounced to the rhythm of some invisible tom-tom.

"You OK?" the tech said.

Chris nodded and the speed increased again. The routine was repeated four times before the tech finally said, "This is it. You're at 'Firehouse Corner'. Here comes Heartbreak Hill."

The treadmill tilted upward before the tread accelerated to a lightning pace. Chris dug inside himself for the strength to keep from being swept away. He leaned even further forward. His jaw tightened. His lungs were on fire. He promised to begin a regular exercise program if he completed the test. Everyone was watching, waiting. Chris gasped for air, then gasped again. And then he felt it. A second wind. New strength. A breakthrough.

"We're slowing down," the tech said.

The whine faded immediately as the treadmill slowed and the angle dropped. When the treadmill halted, Chris stood with his hands on his hips, taking deep breadths, listening to the blood pounding through his carotids.

The three men in the observation room left as hastily as they'd arrived. Chris heard the goateed man mention "a normal QRS complex" as he pointed his preaching finger skyward. One of the people behind Chris checked a beeper, then walked out, while the other picked up *The Daily Freeman* from a nearby chair.

A moment later, a radiology tech entered the room with a wheelchair, read Chris's bracelet — following another script, no doubt — and began wheeling Chris away when the treadmill tech held up his thumb up to Chris. "One hundred and forty percent, man! Who knew?"

The radiology tech whisked Chris down the hall to a darkened radiology room. As his eyes adapted, Chris noticed a white metal table inserted into a large white donut-shaped piece of equipment that purred like a Saturn 5 on its launch pad. He thought he heard an announcer on WSFT FM mumbling about traffic along Route 7 as a tiny man in a lab coat and wire-rimmed glasses walked over.

"I want you to lie on the table while I take some images of your heart. I'll turn up the music to muffle the noise once the test begins."

Chris stretched out on the cold metal before the man operated some controls from a console, making the table inch inside the donut. The space was confining, and the humming noise so obnoxious he closed his eyes and tried remembering what Mikey's letter said. His breathing slowed though his heart still pounded. The humming disappeared beneath the radio's volume. Chris's breathing was nearly normal when he heard familiar drumbeats and piano strains introducing Rod Stewart singing "This Old Heart of Mine."

Chris closed his eyes as they filled with tears.

***

After the test, Mary Catherine followed Chris to Wells Court where he'd parked his car and got in with her. She drove down College before finding a space outside her favorite bistro.

They sat near the front window. As Chris read his menu, he felt his hand rising to his chest as if pulled by some phantom. Catch noticed and leaned forward.

"You OK?"

"Yeah. Oh, I'm sorry," he said, lowering it. "I was just thinking that a few weeks ago, I had indigestion or a muscle pull or something benign. Then Dennis saw a blip on a graph. Now, everything's off balance. I'm afraid to order the Eggs Benedict, for Christ's sake, because of the cholesterol. And I can't think of anything else. Hell, even my arm's worried, I guess."

Catch smiled.

"Catch, if it wasn't so scary, I'd think it funny how quickly life changes. First Walt. Next, it could be me. What happens if this is really serious?"

"Oh, Chris."

"I mean it. Will my life ever be the same? Will I ever not worry?"

"Chris, you're getting way ahead of yourself. You don't even know if there's a problem."

"It doesn't matter. Everything's changed."

Catch reached over and rubbed Chris's arm. He smiled back. When she finally dropped him off, he kissed her on the cheek. "Thanks, Catch. Always the big sister."

As he reached into his mailbox, he noticed his nosy neighbor and his dog returning from a walk. The man appeared to be staring at him, making Chris wonder if he was somehow marked. His phone was ringing as he unlocked his apartment. He hurried to catch it.

"Chris. It's Dennis."

"What's going on? Have you heard anything?"

"Yeah. You're all set, Chris."

"All set? What do you mean, all set?"

"Everything's OK! The test was negative."

"Negative! I don't get it. How can it be negative? I heard them say something about an abnormal carotid artery."

"That's what they suspected before the Cardiolite test, but it proved that the problem was with the original test equipment, not you. There must have been a bad electrode. Power issue maybe. Who knows? But the test confirmed your heart is OK."

"But what was the problem? Why do I have the chest pain?"

"It was probably all the coffee! On your questionnaire, you said you drink six to seven cups a day. That would cause the symptoms: chest discomfort, anxiety, insomnia, rapid heart rate. I'm surprised you don't have an ulcer. Cut back to two cups of decaf a day. It'll all go away. I'll follow up with you next visit."

"That's it?"

"That's it."

"Are you sure?"

"Yes. I'm sure. Forget it!"

"But Dennis, you don't just forget something like that."

"Chris, you're the only one who can work that out, but there's nothing there. You're OK."

"Ok, I guess. Thanks, Dennis."

"You're welcome. By the way, I didn't finish your exam the other day because of your heart issues, so I've scheduled another appointment. Someone cancelled Christmas Eve at 4 pm so you're my last patient."

"Do I have to? I'm all right, aren't I?"

"You're fine. It's just that I didn't finish your physical. I need to review your lab work and check you're prostate, so if you bring your prostate, I'll be sure to bring my finger and some rubber gloves."

"I bet you say that to every guy over 50."

"I do. And I also tell them I have lots of tissues so they can dry their bottoms. And their tears."

He imagined Dennis smiling as the line went dead but he didn't think it was funny. As he returned the phone to its cradle, he lifted his hand to his chest, wondering what was really happening to him.

17

Everyone at the Academy understood the phrase "day before vacation" was crammed with contradictions. Students intuitively knew the words meant a warm-up to vacation, thus they chose to exert little or no effort, saving their energy for vacation. The teachers' contracts, however, called the day "mandatory," which forced them to follow the syllabus. For Chris, the rhythm of the day usually became a chess match of moves and counter moves.

Students wiggled in their seats, coughed, passed notes, dropped pencils, and created dozens of distractions prior to the 2 pm holiday assembly. In response, Chris feigned interest in the subject matter, forced smiles and nods, asked easy questions, avoided conflicts, gazed at Lake Champlain, and eyed the clock at every opportunity. The members of the choral society and the holiday strings were especially prone to restlessness as the hands of the clock moved at an infinitesimal speed. A rumor had circulated that music directors from various New England colleges would attend this concert to search for scholarship candidates for their institutions. Mr. Villemarie, the Academy's music director, told Chris that these kinds of rumors could get his students to work their hardest with the limited practice time available. He'd also told Chris he circulated variations of this rumor each December both to enrich the performances and to combat student apathy.

When Anita Small called for the choral society and holiday strings ensemble to proceed to the gym, Chris was relieved. He was battling the early symptoms of a cold and didn't know if he could take the punishment much longer. He sat at his desk and told his American Heritage class, "It's OK to do what you want until the assembly!"

A few moments later, Anita notified the rest of the student body to report to the auditorium. The hallways instantaneously filled with noise, crowding, anticipation, and relieved teachers. Chris followed his seniors down to the auditorium, trying not to stay too close. He even waited outside the double doors while his students scattered throughout the auditorium. His responsibilities were over. K.J., Libby, Honora, and others waited in the auditorium's lobby before taking seats a few rows inside the door.

"Are you leaving tomorrow?" Chris said to Libby as they sat down.

"Car's packed. I'll be in Jersey between 10 and 11 tonight!"

"You must be excited, seeing the family and all."

"Mixed blessing. I love them but after about five days of 'When are you moving home?' I know it's time to get back to work."

The curtain opened, exposing the choral society lined up on the stage's left, standing on a three-tiered platform. The holiday string ensemble was on the right. Mr. Villemarie, a tall matchstick of a man, came forward, bowed to the applause, and welcomed everyone. Almost immediately, he turned and coaxed the chorus through a series of holiday favorites: "Jingle Bells," "God Rest Ye Merry Gentlemen," and "O Tannenbaum." His sinewy conducting was as entertaining as the choral arrangements. After more bows and smiles, he turned to the holiday strings and again raised his white-gloved hands. They worked their magic, beginning with David Rose's "Holiday for Strings" and selections from sources as varied as *Peter and the Wolf* and *Messiah*. The performance was exciting and varied, culminating with "The Carol of the Bells." Chris sniffled through most of the numbers before deciding to slip out into the auditorium lobby to blow his nose. He returned to his seat as the choral society was taking its final bow, and the auditorium doors on the opposite side of the room were already swinging back and forth. "Wonderful! Wonderful! Bellissimo!" Honora trumpeted, kissing her fingertips and saluting the performers.

Once the applause died down, the seats began to empty. Chris followed Libby and K.J. through the swinging doors into the auditorium's lobby when Chris noticed a draft coming from the door to the parking lot.

"That's funny," K.J. said. "It doesn't usually get cold in here until they turn down the thermostat after dismissal." The comment activated something in Libby. She glanced around the lobby and, noticing some students going out the open exit, started toward it as if there were an emergency. K.J. appeared lost but as more students hurried toward the door, his eyes lit up. "Must be a fight," he said and ran after Libby with Chris a step behind.

Chris reached the parking lot and saw a circle of boys gathered. Some were yelling, "Hit him! Hit him!" Libby broke through their ranks, pushing and pulling students out of the way while barking, "Open up! Out of the way! Open up!"

Chris could see Michael Andover and Basil Hasan facing each other. Their blazers were off, their fists raised. Libby reached them and stepped between Andover and Hasan.

"Hands down!" she yelled as Chris reached the circle. Hasan stepped back, but Michael's focus was unbroken. Libby stepped toward him. "You heard me, Andover! Now!" Michael's trance broke. By the time Chris reached the circle's interior, the boy's fists had begun to drop.

"OK, it's all over! Inside, boys! Inside!" K.J. shouted, pushing and pulling the others back towards the door.

"What the hell's going on?" Libby yelled at Andover. He stepped back. "What happened here? Who started this?" Libby said, glancing back and forth. "I said, what happened?"

Hasan spoke. "He pulled my sister's hijab."

"I did not!" Michael yelled, stepping forward.

"Well, somebody did. And you were right behind her."

"Listen, you son of…"

"This ends now!" Libby said, reaching out and pointing her finger at Michael's face.

Brent's voice rose above Libby's as he hurried toward the gathering. "Andover! Hasan! Go to my office! I'll take care of this, Libby. Now the rest of you, get to your home rooms for dismissal. The buses will be here in a few minutes, so hurry up! Hurry up!"

Andover and Hasan's emotions were still smoldering as they picked up their blazers and strutted toward the door with Brent right behind them.

"Good catch, Libby!" K.J. said.

She took a deep breath. "Whenever there's movement like that, it's usually a fight."

"Or a fire drill," K.J. said.

"You OK?" Chris said.

She smiled. "Yeah! But I'm pumped now. I don't think I'll need any coffee for the drive to Jersey. Guess I'd better get going while I've got this high because there's going to be a hell of a letdown in about six hours."

"Merry Christmas," Chris said. "And nice job! That was really gutsy."

"Thanks," she said before turning toward the lobby.

Chris watched her for a moment. She was his mentee, a fellow teacher, someone he ate lunch with, yet he'd never suspected she had such spirit. She'd been friendly, inviting him to dinner, and he knew she was intelligent, and a great coach, but beyond the daily obvious, he didn't know much about her. And he began wondering why he hadn't invested the time to find out.

**

Chris's nephew Jimmy and his wife had invited the entire family to New Haven for Christmas week. They planned to attend church and open gifts on Christmas morning, see the Rockettes at Radio City, and eat Italian down on 40th Street near Times Square. If time, visit the Met. Chris felt terrible that he had to call to cancel two days before Christmas. "I've caught a terrible cold and don't want to spread it around."

He stopped by Catch's house and dropped off presents for everyone just before she left.

"I hate to see you alone on Christmas. Maybe I should stay."

"No! I'll be in bed or on the couch. If I get sick of watching Bowl games, I can always work on my recertification project."

"Call me Christmas night."

"Sure. Tell the kids I love them."

Chris settled in on the couch and turned on his big screen. For the next few days, he slept whenever he wasn't drinking hot bouillon or ginger ale. When he checked his mailbox on Christmas Eve, he noticed his neighbor's little rat-faced dog sniffing the tires on his car. There were numerous advertisements among the bills. Why did they always arrive when the sales were already over? He threw out the circulars then laid the bills on the kitchen table where he'd already propped his reunion postcard against an empty glass. Unexpectedly, his thoughts danced over previous Christmases. He remembered listening to St. Issac's choir sing carols before midnight Mass and decorating a large evergreen with Catch in Uncle Jonathon's living room. Aunt Harriet became upset later that night when Uncle Jonathon stumbled and knocked it over. And he remembered the time Susan Boisvert invited him to her home in Orwell during their junior year at GMU.

***

After leaving her family's Christmas Eve party, they sat in the old Dodge as its engine purred. He kissed her. Her lips tasted sweet as a sugar cookie.

"Don't go, Chris," she said. "After we've opened the gifts, we'll go to midnight Mass then eat a big turkey dinner. And besides, my parents really like you."

"I promised my sister I'd be back when the kids woke up. And I told the guys staying behind at TAC I might stop by."

She turned away.

"What is it?"

"Chris, you're wasting your time with those guys."

"What do you mean?"

"They're, I don't know, reckless. I just think…"

"I know you don't like the fooling around but they've expanded my world. At Uncle Jonathon's we never discussed Norman Mailer, or the IRA, or the church. Hell, the Red Sox was the only safe topic. At TAC, I can have a beer and talk about whatever I want without fear of Aunt Harriet or Uncle Jonathon shushing me. And besides, I can handle it."

"I understand, I guess. It's just that it's Christmas, and I want you to be with me."

"We'll have plenty of time together once we get through school."

They kissed again before she got out and walked around the Dodge to the driver's side. He rolled down the window and held her hand until he began backing down the driveway. She was still in his rearview mirror when his headlights turned north on Route 22A and the silent snowflakes filled in his tracks.

***

Chris returned to the couch, poured out two capfuls of cold suppressant, and switched channels. The opening credits of *It's a Wonderful Life* filled the screen, so he pulled the comforter Catch had made for him around his neck and turned the volume down. Outside, snow began falling, covering the world in a pure white silence.

He tossed and turned as George Bailey's story unfolded until finally drifting into an unsettled sleep. Suddenly, he found himself sitting on the edge of his bed. The room was dark. In the distance, he heard singing and a fire crackling. He stood, feeling confused and dizzy, and went toward where he thought the doorway should be. He felt his way along a corridor, keeping his hands against the wall for balance. The music was familiar and grew louder. When he reached the top of the stairs, he noticed the smell of smoke and noticed diffuse light below. He started down.

The stairway opened into a large room with a fireplace and doorways leading in different directions. The room was smoky and disheveled. A Christmas tree lay on its side atop presents and an old portable television with a bent coat hanger for an antenna. Uncle Jonathon was sitting before the fireplace wearing a double-breasted suit. His eyes were closed but he was singing. An empty quart of Ballantine's sat on the table beside him. Sparks from the fireplace were spitting out toward old newspapers and photographs scattered across the floor. One photo was of boys in uniforms; another showed a pretty young girl wearing a halter top and cut off dungarees. Her hand was reaching toward something when sparks landed on the photo and the paper began to burn. When Chris saw the sparks, he hurried forward. "Uncle Jonathon, wake up!" But the man didn't move. Chris reached for the photo but the flames were so hot he dropped the picture and it crinkled on the floor.

Uncle Jonathon's eyes remained closed. "The minstrel boy to the war is gone, in the ranks of death you will find him," he sang. Chris felt a chill and turned. In the darkened doorway, he saw Walt and Logan Cassidy watching him. He blinked, and when he reopened his eyes, he found himself on the couch, under Catch's comforter in a feverish sweat. The television showed a voiceless man cutting pennies with a long, slim carving knife as a sign flashed across the screen: $39.99 for two complete sets.

***

Chris remained in bed most of Christmas day. That evening, he called his sister.

"It just wasn't the same without you, Chris. Are you sure you're OK?"

"Don't worry. It's just a cold."

After two more days of old movies, the Mormon Tabernacle Choir, and college football, Chris became restless. He called Pizza King to order their special, and as he waited for the delivery, he noticed the demography books K.J. had lent him. He thumbed through the tables of contents and index pages and decided to start his project. After a slice of pizza, he gathered some pencils and a notepad, muted the volume on the big screen, and went to work.

"Can you believe it, Bob? I'm working during vacation. I must be getting old."

The reading was slow at first. Chris never cared for statistics but found that the concepts were explained well. He thought of other resources available. The Academy's library held copies of census data and GMU's library was just up the hill. If he had time, he could explore the County Genealogy Society. He sketched an outline, but it didn't feel right. If his efforts this school year were indicative of what to expect, the unit would just be a continuation of terrible. He had to do better but couldn't imagine how, so he called Claudia Nichols.

Claudia offered different suggestions but stressed keeping kids involved by making the work personal. "Take them out of their element. Anyone can go to the library and read a book. To make statistical data interesting, you'll have to challenge students to discover something like their relationships to other larger groups."

"Seems like a lot of effort."

"People don't grow unless they step out of their comfort zone."

Chris fine-tuned his outline over the next few days, but he still hadn't figured out how to use genealogical information when his flu-like symptoms reoccurred. He felt so weak on New Year's Day he turned off the Rose Bowl in the second quarter, took an analgesic, and went back to bed. Early the next morning, he called the Academy absence line and left a message. "Anita, this is Chris. My cold just won't give up. I've spent my vacation in bed. Can you find a sub for me? And just to be safe, get someone who can cover both tomorrow and Friday. If I rest all weekend, maybe it'll all go away. See you Monday."

He pulled the blankets over his head and drifted off to

sleep. By Friday he was out of bouillon but found a few cans of turkey noodle soup in the kitchen closet and added extra water to stretch them. By Saturday afternoon, he was feeling better and got out of bed. After scanning the sports pages, he noticed the envelope Catch had dropped off with Uncle Jonathon's information.

The brownish-gray envelope Uncle Jonathon had given to Catch years before reminded Chris of old houses with too much cigarette smoke. The postmark said September 1988. Inside were five sheets of paper, each the same brownish gray. After glancing through the pages, Chris guessed the letter was a copy because the pages were so formal, so precise. Notes had been added to the margins in different scripts and ink colors, as if others had added notations after the original was complete.

The letter began with BRENNAN-GORDON-LE-CLAIR TREE written across the top of the first page. Chris felt something magical in this and held the letter at arm's length. The fading sheets, the Palmer script, and the dates from nearly two centuries earlier all deepened his fascination. He began reading.

> Christopher Brennan married Margaret Nelson, daughter of George Nelson, a native of Ayrshire, Scotland. Died March 21, 1849 at 80. Margaret Nelson Gordon died December 25, 1843 at 54. Christopher Brennan died at Weaverton on August 24, 1858 at 55 years. Jane??? Nelson wife of George Nelson died on June 7, 189? age 53 years. Margaret Catherine Brennan, sister of Christopher Brennan, married a Mr. Gordon first name unknown and emigrated to Black Rock, Quebec, Canada.

Everything he saw was new. Who were the Brennans and Nelsons? He'd never heard of Black Rock, Quebec either. He lay the papers down and from his bookcase retrieved a map of Quebec. He searched through the index of localities. Black Rock was not listed.

At Black Rock, three children were born to the couple.

> Christopher Patrick on June 17, 1831. He served in the
> First VT. Cavalry as a farrier in the Civil War. On No-
> vember 26, 1866 he was married to Ann Daugherty,
> born Oct. 27, 1848. Christopher Gordon died in Weav-
> erton, Mar. 22, 1889? Christopher and Ann are buried
> in Green Mt. Cemetery in Queen City. Graves are, I be-
> lieve, north side of cemetery.

Chris had always assumed—based on his father's
name, Martin, and his mother's name, LeClair—that all his
ancestors had come from France. The first page shattered
this idea. Already he'd found Scotch and Irish mixed in.

"I've already come this far, Bob. I guess I'll have to continue."

> Catherine Cecelia Gordon, your grandmother, was
> born in Black Rock, Quebec, Canada on 14 Mar, 1837.
> She married Francis E. LeClair on July 5, 1854. She died
> in Black Rock, Canada on Dec. 14, 1884, aged 47. Fran-
> cis E. LeClair died in Weaverton on 17 Feb. 1896, aged
> 68 years. Children none.

"That doesn't make any sense, Bob. My grandparents
must've had children. Was Uncle Jonathon confused or am
I?"

Despite the letter stating his grandmother had "Children none," six were listed a few lines later. "Louis P.
LeClair" was circled in red ink with "your grandfather"
written in above it. He was "...born on Mar 15, 1870, died
in Weaverton on Mar. 17, 1936."

Chris found his mother, Marjorie LeClair (Martin), listed on the third page. More pages and more names indicated other family branches. "Moved to Fond Du Lac in
Wisconsin" was written near one. A note beside another
said "died in North Hoosick, NY."

After rereading the pages numerous times, he still
found the relationships too cloudy to picture, so he decided to simplify things by placing the data into a family
tree. He placed Catch's children, Catch, and himself at the
bottom of the tree and worked upwards. His grandparents
and great grandparents' generations followed. Once he'd

listed everyone, he reread the chart. Because he only had a few months to complete his project, he erased names of relatives not in a direct line, as well as those too far back to find easily. The soldier in the hallway, Christopher Gordon, and his sister, Catherine Cecelia Gordon, sat at the top of the tree.

***

Chris called his sister the evening she returned from New Haven.

"We had a great time. And we saw the *Man of La Mancha* revival."

When he heard the title, he broke into a dramatic recitation. "Hey, Sancho, give me a sword 'cause I'm Don Quixote, man of…"

"Enough! Richard Kiley you're not. Sounds like you feel better. What did you do last week to get so much better?"

"Worked on my recertification and looked through the letter Uncle Jonathon sent. Did you ever investigate the details?"

"There was no time. Little League and soccer took precedence. I just filed it away."

"I drew out a family tree from it. Hope to work my way up it. Funny, but the letter doesn't sound like Uncle Jonathon. Once he started talking, he was like a kid with a secret. This letter sounds too restrained, too factual for him."

"Aunt Harriet died about that time, and Uncle Jonathon was drinking a lot."

"I know. I drove him to AA meetings more times than I can count."

"You were always the care giver. I don't know where his information came from, but it's all we have."

After Mary Catherine hung up, Chris sat back and thought about what he had for family data. He'd have to be skeptical. There was no one to vouch for the information and no one to follow up with because anyone who'd ever known the details was dead.

18

Years of observation had taught Chris that students' tendencies toward mischief lessened with falling temperatures and rising snow. So, during January, he channeled his students' energy by assigning research papers. The routine, though productive, was demanding. Each day he dashed between his classrooms and the library, where he assisted students with their research questions. Near the end of one sixth period European Traditions class, he was assisting one of his juniors when Brent appeared, hurrying toward the library's large conference room. His arms were filled with binders. "I'm glad I ran into you, Chris."

"What's up?"

"Alumni council meeting," Brent said, nodding his head toward the conference room. "Then Sheriff Flannigan is stopping by to discuss safety protocol. Did you see my memo?"

"It wasn't in my mailbox."

"You've got to read your email! I wondered why you hadn't answered." Brent took a deep breath. "I need updates on your department's projects. The state's been calling. You're the only chair I haven't heard from. This isn't a free ride, you know."

"Take it easy. I've been sick. And everyone is working on them except Honora. She's taking a class this semester."

"What about K.J.? You can't keep protecting him, you know. He's not up to anything inappropriate, is he?"

"K.J.'s on track."

"He'd better be. What about you? Have you even started?" The binders in Brent's arms shifted. He rebalanced them, then glanced toward the conference room. Every chair was filled.

"I've started."

"There's a lot at stake. You have to…"

Honora Webster hurried by. "There are some chocolate

chip cookies on your desk, Brent. Little Honey just baked them."

"Oh, thanks, Honora," Brent said, rolling his eyes as she walked away. "So kind of you."

"I've outlined a demography unit to fit in the freshmen curriculum. Building it from scratch. It's all hands on stuff. Gathering data, making hypo…"

"Brent! It's time!" Dr. George called from the conference room doorway.

"Yes, Dr. George. Be right there," Brent said before turning back to Chris. "What did you say?"

"I'm building a demography unit. Data gathering and analysis."

"Sounds kind of dry. Is that all you could come with?"

"I may inject some genealogy, but I still need an angle. Still lots of work to do."

The binder atop Brent's pile slid off, crashing to the floor, leaving Brent juggling the others. Members of the alumni council in the conference room looked up. Chris picked up the binder and placed it back on top.

"Thanks. Anything else? The council's waiting."

"I discovered a relative who may have fought with the First Vermont Cavalry during the Civil War. It was a prestigious unit."

The top binder remained unstable. As it shifted again, Brent swiveled his hips and elbows like a tight rope walker twisting himself into balance. "Jeez! What'd you say?"

"The First Vermont. They fought at Gettysburg and in the Valley. I think I read once where General Custer led them, but I don't remember any details. I've got to check them out."

"So your relative fought for Custer. Interesting!"

"Maybe."

"Brent. We're waiting!" Dr. George called.

"Keep digging. You can't afford mistakes," Brent said, nodding toward the conference room.

He started backing away when Chris called to him. "Brent, what did you do about that fight between Andover and Hasan before vacation?"

"Nothing there! I spoke with Andover's old man. Boys will be boys."

Chris shook his head as Brent went into his meeting. After answering a few student questions, Chris returned to C level, where K.J. was just closing his door as Chris hurried by.

"Hey! What's up?"

"Brent's feathers are ruffled," Chris whispered. "Did something happen between you two today?"

"I told him his tie didn't match the jacket. And those socks!"

"He's paranoid enough without you messing with his head. Watch yourself!"

K.J. nodded before closing his door. The metallic horn sounded as Chris entered C44. He went to his desk to unlock the drawer for his coffee mug when a bent paper-clip fell from the lock. The drawer was still locked, so he opened it. His mug and grade book were both in place. No problem, he thought, and called Madison to take attendance. As soon as she punched in the all-present code, Michael Andover's hand shot into the air.

"Yes, Mr. Andover?" Chris said, smiling as he waited for the first salvo.

***

Weaverton City Hall was located a block off Main Street in the basement of the former United Methodist Church. As the Methodist's congregation grew older and their ranks thinned, the remaining parishioners faced higher costs, forcing them to make a deal with the city. In return for the periodic use of municipal space for church activities, the church members donated the church to the community. The city pulled out the pews, installed a basketball court that doubled as the city council chambers, and moved their offices and records from rented space into the basement. "Win, win," the council had said. "Lose, win," the church had said.

Chris parked in a visitor space behind the building. It was 8:42 on a late January morning, time for attendance in his freshman World Outlook class. He wiggled about the way one does before giving a speech or lining up for a race. Years of routine had conditioned him to feel guilty about missing a school day even though his contract allowed professional days and demanded recertification. After justifying his actions to himself once again, he descended the steps into the rear of the city building.

"Hi, I'm doing some research into my family history. I'd like to look at the birth and death records. "

Weaverton's clerk led Chris past desks stacked with town reports, green statute books, and piles of property-assessment forms. Two signs were taped to the wall outside the vault. One listed the hourly charge for records research and the other warned not to use the copier without permission.

There were no windows inside the stainless-steel door. Four milky bulbs enclosed in protective metal cages provided the only light: a yellow sepulchral glow. The first row of metal shelves held large leather-bound books. Land Records was printed in elegant script on each of their brown bindings, making Chris imagine candle light and quill pens.

"These are the birth and death records, Mr. Martin," the woman said, pointing down the second row, where squat volumes, bound in rich black leather, sat.

The other shelves appeared less organized. Large and small volumes stood alongside stacks of spiraled notebooks, dusty rolled-up maps, and sealed cardboard boxes. Green file cabinets lined the room's outer walls. More boxes sat atop them, along with other maps, and miscellaneous stacks of paper. At the vault's far end, a collapsible table, surrounded by various chairs, sat on a faded Persian rug. The table was cluttered with stacks of file folders and a partially wrapped half-eaten tomato sandwich.

"If you use a volume, any volume, leave it on the table.

Do not reshelf it!" Chris nodded. He turned, hearing voices back in the office, and noticed two men in sweatshirts. "Call me if you have any questions."

They both looked at the sandwich. The woman folded the wax paper around it and carried it away. Chris tossed his coat on a chair then sat down. He reached into his tote bag for his index cards, pen, and Uncle Jonathon's letter. He reread it until he found, "Louis P. LeClair was born on March 15, 1870. Died in Weaverton on March 17, 1936."

Next he retrieved the black-leather book he sought. Death Records: 1932–1937. He methodically fingered the pages. Each was an original death certificate, completed by former clerks, and filed in chronological order. The entry spaces on the forms were filled in with bold fluid script.

His grandfather's certificate listed the following:

Date of Death	March 17, 1936
Name	Louis Patrick LeClair
Place of Death	Dunbar Hospital
Residence	94 Maple Street
Date of Birth	March 15, 1870
Occupation	Janitor, Weaverton Public Schools
Widowed	Agnes Shannon (Husband of)
Father	Francis E. LeClair
Place of Birth	Weaverton
Mother	Cecelia Gordon
Place of Birth	Black Rock, P.Q.
Buried	Mount Saint Brendan's Cemetery

There were other facts: his illness, its duration, the undertaker's name.

Chris had concrete data, accurate data—the stuff historians search endlessly for. The possibilities overwhelmed his imagination, making him blink as if facing high beams coming round a curve. These were threads leading who knows where: unknown names, dates, and places pointing in different directions. There were so many new paths to choose from, he began discussing his options as if Bob Dylan were listening.

"I can search the cemetery to see if there's a stone. Maybe it lists other relatives. And there's an address. I can check the land records for details about the family homestead. There could also be hospital records or the undertaker's. I think that place is still in business."

He pulled out the diagram he'd made of the Brennan-Gordon-LeClair tree from his tote bag. "I've got actual proof of the thread to Cecelia and Christopher Gordon. Now it's a physical trail not just hearsay. Where should I go?"

"Excuse me, Mr. Martin!" the clerk said from the vault doorway. "Did you call me? I heard talking."

"No. I'm sorry."

Once the clerk left, Chris leaned back and looked up toward the milky light. He began laughing, wondering if he talked to himself whenever he was alone. Up above, Chris heard running footsteps and felt the pounding of a dribbling basketball.

After returning to his apartment, Chris called the offices of the Catholic Diocese of Vermont. The receptionist transferred him to the archivist.

"Frank Gadue."

Chris introduced himself and said he was doing some family research. "Can you help me find the location for a grave in Mount Saint Brendan's Cemetery?"

"Sure. Who is the deceased, and do you know when they died?"

After Chris told Mr. Gadue what he knew of Louis Patrick LeClair, the man put him on hold. Chris paced as Dylan eyed him suspiciously in the fading afternoon light. Chris turned on a floor lamp before straying to the window. Down the street, one neighbor shoveled the snow off his bushes and tossed it into the street. Then the man started his car and drove back and forth over the snow.

His nosy neighbor walked his tiny rat-faced dog along the sidewalk. After the dog defecated on a tiny patch of open grass beside Chris's car, the man glanced in both directions, kicked snow over the dog poop, and yanked the little dog on, leaving a steaming pile of snow.

"I knew it was him," Chris mumbled.

"Did you say something, Mr. Martin?" the archivist said over the phone line.

"No. I'm sorry."

"OK, I found what you wanted. Louis is buried in Section B, Lot 74."

Mr. Gadue told Chris to drive up Archer Street hill and turn in at the third drive. The LeClair lot is on the right, or east, side about three quarters of the way down the drive. There was a Brennan lot behind the LeClair lot and two other Brennan lots across the drive.

"If you can't find it, list the names off prominent stones in the area and call back tomorrow—ah, Monday. We're closed on the weekend. I'll point you to the LeClair lot from anything you can identify. If that fails, you can always look at the map."

It was too dark to drive over to Mount Saint Brendan's, so Chris decided to wait. He opened the local section of *The Daily Freeman*, glancing over local articles but lingering over the obituaries. His foray into family genealogy had heightened his awareness, so he read each name and date, searching for those tiny, specific words writers use to encapsulate the vast human experience into an inch-and-a-half by eight-inch column. He wondered if he'd ever find any more than that level of detail about family members who had died long before he was born.

***

On Saturday morning, Chris drove up Archer Street and parked near the third drive into Mount Saint Brendan's Cemetery. A sign on the fence warned "NO DOGS ALLOWED IN THE CEMETERY." He smiled, thinking

K.J. would say most pooches, like his sophomores, don't read; and most people who walk dogs in the Old North End don't pay attention to signs. The drive hadn't been plowed so Chris trudged northward through boot-deep fluff.

Queen City residents barely noticed Mount Saint Brendan's as they hurried up Archer Street, but if they stopped or even slowed down they'd realize what a treasure it was. The area's once prominent Irish Catholic families slept in a beautiful, if neglected, spot near the intersection of the Hill section and the Old North End. The cemetery sloped down gently from east to west through scattered oak, locust, ash, and cedar until finally facing off against the crumbling tenements across Wilson Avenue. Chris could see the Adirondacks by looking west over the roof of the Ahavath Gerim synagogue. The mountains appeared close enough to touch.

Mount Saint Brendan's north side hugged the bluffs that rose above River Bend Road. From there, he could glimpse the rich bottom lands of the Intervale and the rolling hills beyond. He could also see the dead factories crowding Weaverton Falls.

Chris remembered, as a child, peddling up to those bluffs and daydreaming. He had wondered what it was like to work in the factories or if he had anything in common with the people who did. He'd planned to hike down the bluffs one day, cross the Blue Bridge trestle into Weaverton, and climb to the top of Water Tower Hill. He never did.

He walked slowly, passing large granite monuments he knew from his time mowing lawns and from Uncle Jonathon's stories. The gravestones for Fitzsimons, McMahon, Casey, Finnigan, Logan, Shea, Cassidy, and others vied for his attention. He finally stopped about half way down the drive. He'd expected the LeClair stone would be easy to spot, but the windblown snow disguised everything, reminding him of snow sculptures. He retraced his own footprints before turning again and walking further north up the drive. Then, off to the east, he spotted LeClair carved in bold roman letters on a waist-high granite stone. He stood still. His fingertips tingled. He rubbed them together. It wasn't the cold. He stepped closer. And stopped. Then he inched around the stone. Letters and dates were carved on the back.

1870	Louis P. LeClair	1936
	His wife	
1876	Kathryn L. (Harrigan)	1924
	His wife	
1878	Agnes L. (Shannon)	1928

Another discovery. His mother had had a stepmother. Though Chris had a few details—a death certificate and a single gravesite—he knew nothing substantial and wondered what other surprises awaited. A small commuter plane's engine distracted him as it approached the airport over the Old North End. The tiny craft floated down its glide path before disappearing beyond the trees. Then he heard the sound of reversing props.

19

"What does he want?" Chris said, holding up Brent's note.

"He didn't say, but it must be important. Dr. George is with him." Anita rolled her eyes. "They stop talking every time I enter. And Brent keeps moving things around his desk."

Chris shrugged, went to Brent's door, and knocked.

"Come in!" Dr. George was sitting in a winged-back chair, his eyes closed, his arms extended over his knees in a jury-rigged lotus position. He unfolded his legs and slipped his loafers back on as Chris closed the door. Brent, who was pacing behind his desk, wolf like, stopped, placed his hands on his desk, and leaned forward.

"Who did you piss off?"

"What are you talking about?"

"We received this from the Education Department," Dr. George said, handing a letter over to Chris. "It's a complaint against you."

The document was addressed to Dr. George on the commissioner's personal letterhead. After opening with a friendly greeting, the letter went on:

> We are in receipt of an informal inquiry from an anonymous source concerning Queen City Academy's new history department chairman, Mr. Christopher Martin. The complainant states that Mr. Martin lacks the proper credentials, qualifications, and certification to hold such an important position in the state, and at an institution of such high esteem as Queen City Academy. Further, it states Mr. Martin uses antiquated and inappropriate teaching methods in his classroom.
>
> Please respond within 10 days, stating Mr. Martin's qualifications, including appropriate courses or experience, as well as the status of his state certification.

Our office will review any information presented and determine whether further action is required.

The commissioner's signature completed the page. Chris sat down.

"What's this all about, Martin?" Brent said.

"You tell me!"

"Gentlemen! Gentlemen, please. We don't need fisticuffs," Dr. George said, raising one hand. "It's all very simple. It appears some 'do-gooder'..."

"Coward!" Brent said.

"'Do gooder' has taken it upon himself to solve, or perhaps create, a problem. Nothing more, nothing less."

"I don't get it."

"You screwed up!" Brent said, his face turning a fiery red.

Dr. George's glare held Brent in check before he turned back to Chris. "Who knows? Could be something serious, but more than likely it's just an angry parent who's upset with his child's grade. Remember, seniors are starting to hear back about their college applications. That always stirs up the hive."

Chris thought Dr. George looked like he was inflating as he talked.

"It doesn't really matter. What matters is the response. We must fight fire with fire. Strike while the iron is hot. Chris!"

"Yes, sir. What do you want me to do?"

"Have Anita copy this letter. Take it home and write a response tonight. Fill it with applicable details: years of service, education, degrees, professional and fraternal organizations, conferences attended, your current certification and special endorsements, offices held—all the usual resume stuff. Don't forget any administrative courses you've taken. Check your transcripts and identify the courses by name and number. But make it look like a job application not a confession. Don't mention your GPA unless it's over 3.0. No, 3.5. Was it over 3.5?"

"Yes, sir."

"Good. Put it all in memo format and—for God's sakes—mention the accelerated-portfolio project you're working on. It shows initiative. But don't provide any details. We don't want to poke cane holes in a cow turd as we say back in the Granite state. Have it on Brent's desk tomorrow. Any questions?"

Chris had many. He wanted to know who was attacking him and why; he wanted to know what he could do to resolve the problem without too much effort; he wanted to know how to make it all go away.

"No, sir."

"Brent, I want you to take Chris's letter and embrace it."

Brent's face compressed as if he'd just bitten into a sour dill.

"Couldn't we just avoid all this by saying Chris's position is temporary? It would take the heat off. I could mention we're screening other candidates."

"We're not going down that road, Brent. This is war. Speak with authority. Seize the opportunity. Attack! You take Chris's memo and add some crap about losing Walt. Then—here's the key—mention the terms of the hard-fought union agreement. Emphasize Chris's seniority, experience, all the fluff. Were you teacher of the year?"

"Yes, sir."

"Put that in, too, address it to me, and sign it."

"But…"

"You're the middle man, Brent. Do it!"

"Yes, Dr. George."

"I want it on my desk by Thursday noon. I'll drop by the commissioner's office on Friday and schmooze him. He understands. He's been there. He and I will put this baby to bed. Keep it hush, hush. Can't let the alumni council find out."

Chris said, "Why would they be involved? The state looks into complaints all the time."

"That would screw up everything," Brent said.

"What are you talking about?"

Dr. George looked at Brent. Their silence sounded like a cannon inside a castle. Finally Dr. George said, "Tell him."

Brent's face tightened even more, looking as if he were going to pop.

"Tell him!"

"We've been working through the alumni council to soften up a big donor for new electronics, tablets. They think they have a mark. Jim Essex—you know, Catamount Coffee—has expressed interest but wants everything hush, hush. If anything blows, it might scare him off."

"Math and science already has tablets," Chris said.

"For everyone! For everything!" Brent screamed. "We're going totally digital next year and everyone needs tablets."

"I don't get it. What are you talking about?"

"Chris we're taking the big step." Dr. George stood, stroking his beard. "It's coming eventually, so we want to be ahead of the curve."

"Should you be telling him?"

"Shut up, Brent. Chris, the Academy's going to a tablet-based learning-module curriculum next year. PBR. Performance Based Recitation. All students will follow assigned readings, then be tested. They'll need to demonstrate what they've learned before moving forward. It's all about test results. Data bases and digits."

"But that means teachers will be nothing more that test monitors," Chris said.

"That's for us to worry about! Just answer the complaint," Brent screamed.

"Are you going to tell the teachers?" Chris said.

"In good time."

"That will drive out…"

"In good time." Dr. George looked off into the clouds. "That's why we have to think outside the box. It's not rocket science to know that the best defense is a good offense. Consider the time-honored words of Godlewski: 'Knead the dough. The bread will rise.'"

An evil little smile spread across the good doctor's

face. Chris had no idea what Dr. George meant, but he did know that if the tablet plan went through, teaching as he knew it could change forever. He imagined that under Dr. George and Brent's direction, his profession could degenerate into handing out computer assignments and electronically collecting them at the end of class. No individual imagination. No need for enthusiasm. It seemed so sterile, a place where creativity and initiative would fall second to following the dotted lines. Chris thought it ironic that he even felt such emotion given how his own initiative and enthusiasm had waned.

"Are you OK, Chris?" Anita said when he came out of Brent's office. "You look like you've been punched."

"I'm OK. But I need your help."

"Sure. Anything."

"I need a copy of this. And do you have a list of contacts over at the Department of Education? Someone over there owes me a favor, and I'm going to try to collect."

Anita swiveled toward her PC and reached for the mouse. A few clicks later a page popped out of her printer.

"These are Brent's regular contacts. Does it help?"

"It sure does. Thanks. By the way, how's your brother?"

She shook her head. "Too weak for a transplant. They're going to try some new meds. Thanks for asking."

No one was in the teacher's lounge. Chris added water to the tea pot and turned on the stove before rereading the letter. "Anonymous source" emitted a unique smell. He didn't know who or what he was up against. The worst part was the accuser didn't have to prove anything, just question. He dropped a lemon zinger decaf bag into his coffee mug and sipped it on his way to the conference room. The list Anita provided was comprehensive, but he was only after one name. When he found it, he picked up the phone. A few rings later a familiar voice answered.

"Hi, Mini, this is Chris Martin. Yeah, it has been a while. Years! Hey, I wondered if you've heard about Walt."

They talked about their friend for nearly an hour. Mini

giggled when Chris reminded her of Walt's invisible dog, Spot, but she cried out with laughter when he retold how Walt and Logan tried to build a skating rink by flooding the fraternity's front lawn. "Logan 'borrowed' a GMU plow and cleared the lawn. Walt thought the water would just freeze over the snow so he left the hose on all night. The next morning the police were at the door. The water had run down the sidewalk and frozen, turning Weaverton Avenue into a bobsled run all the way to the business district. The cops made him spread salt all the way down the hill." Eventually, the conversation shifted toward other old friends. She and Chris laughed over some memories but others weren't as pleasant. As Chris felt the conversation begin to struggle, he mentioned the anonymous letter. "Mini, I could really use your help."

"I still owe you one."

"Thanks. Here's my number. Let me know what you find."

It was nearly 5 pm when he hung up. He finished his cold tea, took out his notebook, and began outlining his response to the commissioner's letter, wondering who was behind the anonymous letter. Two hours later, he had a complete draft. As he reread it one final time, he felt a vague uneasiness rising somewhere deep inside himself. He took a deep breath, wondering again whether the daily grind was beginning to wear on him or if Dennis had overlooked something in his diagnosis.

***

The next morning, Chris brought the response to Anita between first and second periods.

"How's he doing today, Anita?"

"Not good, Chris. The meds aren't working yet. Say a prayer."

He reached across her desk to squeeze her hand. "I will. I hate to bother you, but could you type this up when you get a chance?"

"Brent said it was coming."

"I'll be back to sign it during lunch break."

When he returned after fourth period, Honora was leaving Brent's office, carrying an empty plate.

"Hello, Honora."

"Oh! Hello," she said, hurrying out the door.

After Chris proofed the letter, he signed it, and knocked on Brent's door. Brent was nibbling on a large peanut-butter cookie. He immediately wiped his hands before taking out a paper towel and spray bottle and cleaning his desk's glass top. "You've got a 91 Endorsement?" Brent said, reading the second paragraph.

"I thought I wanted to be a principal when I grew up."

"I'm impressed. This should work." Brent carried the letter and a folder out to Anita. "Blend these together here and here." He pointed to different lines. "And watch out for this. It has to be over at Dr. George's office this afternoon."

Chris hurried to the cafeteria, where he joined K.J. and Libby for an abbreviated lunch. Afterward, he conducted his European Traditions class before returning to C44 for his seniors' American Heritage, his last class of the day.

Halfway down the corridor, Chris could hear chatter inside C44. Like truckers on CB, classroom noise can be informative or just noise. There were still a few moments before the period horn, so Chris went to the window. The lake was beautiful. He glanced around, trying to decipher any undertones, and noticed some of the athletes were dressed in their letter sweaters. Pom-poms lay on the books beneath Madison's desk. Books crashed on desks as students prepared. Michael Andover had begun another snowboarder and was adding the flames behind it. T.D. was doodling. Another student had written what looked like a score. QCA 100, W 75 followed by sketches of basketballs and backboards with hoops. Intercity rivalry, Chris thought.

The metallic horn sounded and attendance was taken.

"Our history is filled with larger than life characters.

Today we're going to discuss one of the more important, Henry Clay. In 1819, Missouri applied for statehood…" Chris talked for nearly 15 minutes before dropping pencils, passed notes, and wiggling tissues distracted him too much to continue. He walked over to the board and wrote down a number of pages from the text.

"Tonight's reading. Get it done now, and go support the team tonight."

The classroom atmosphere changed instantly as the seniors opened their texts. Most settled into the reading. Chris walked over to the window with his mug of tea. He looked across the frozen lake. Yesterday's expanse of icy-blue choppy water had solidified, creating a vast mirror wasteland from Queen City's salt dock to the base of the Adirondacks. As the clock ticked down, Chris circled the room. He stopped by T.D. Glover's desk, noticing block letters on his notepad. T.D. looked up. His eyes screamed, "What the hell do you want?"

Row after row of BEAT WEEVERTON covered T.D.'s notepad. Chris leaned across the desk, picked up T.D.'s pencil, crossed out the EE, and wrote EA above it. T.D. turned a shade of very ripe tomato and appeared ready to scream just as the metallic-sounding horn signaled the period's end. With 20 pair of eyes upon him, the skinny athlete stood and pushed his way toward the hallway, leaving a trail of misaligned desks and chairs. As he left the room, T.D.'s hand formed an L by his side. Michael Andover looked at Chris and shook his head.

Once the students were gone, Chris gathered his belongings and turned out the lights. He was happy to leave the dysfunction of the Academy behind.

20

GMU's campus grew eastward from Waterford Hall after Chris's undergraduate days. The library expanded. The bookstore, ice cream bar, and Ag building were long gone, replaced by a large student center locals referred to as "the Taj." New health-science, agriculture, and chemistry facilities filled in the spaces around the library where basketball courts, cow pens, and storage barns once cluttered the landscape. Outside the library, a prominent vestige of Chris's college era, the Hand of Knowledge, still welcomed students. University websites and brochures described its dirty bronze metal fingers as probing skyward to "pluck dreams from the cosmos." That artistic imagery clashed with Chris's memory of Logan Cassidy sleeping off a hangover 10 feet up in the sculpture's palm.

Walking through slushy snow, Chris approached the library with the same skepticism he viewed the Hand of Knowledge. Though the campus appeared different, he wondered if the students were. Those exiting the library wore denim jeans and cowboy boots instead of Pendleton skirts and dirty bucks. They carried backpacks. Most stared into tiny handheld screens instead of their contemporaries' faces. But had they changed?

He walked through the lobby where students in cubicles searched for information from laptops. Gone were the easy chairs. Gone were the rows of maple card catalogues. The index cards in Chris's tote bag were as out of place as he was.

He followed the reference librarian's directions to the far end of the second floor. Everyone he walked by in the open stairway was talking on smart phones, though numerous signs indicated "Quiet Area."

"I'm looking for back copies of *The Daily Freeman*," he told the pocked-face young man, sitting at the help desk laptop.

The youth led him to a metal frame with hanging files attached, opened a file drawer, and pointed toward small graying cardboard boxes. "Each of these holds a reel of microfiche. Dinosaurs! They'll all disappear once the fiche to disc project is complete."

The young man rattled off a list of operating instructions for the fiche readers before leaving Chris to experiment. He fumbled, inserting the film from the 1936 box before playing with the controls until a page came into focus. *The Daily Freeman*'s early 20th-century editions had narrow columns printed in a tiny 5.5-point type. There were few photos, and those were black and whites. Advertisements, consisting of catch phrases in differing type sizes, fonts, and styles—some with drawings, some without—surrounded the news items. He noticed an ad for Bailey's Music Rooms on Center Street and remembered previewing new 45 records there in the sound-proof booths. W.G. Reynolds Company's advertisement pictured handdrawn, stylish bedroom furniture behind a woman in a ball gown.

He searched the edition for March 18th, the day after his grandfather's death. Finding no obituary, he scrolled forward to the 19th, where a brief article on page four, under the headline Weaverton News, added details to facts he'd already discovered.

> Louis P. LeClair of this city died at Dunbar Hospital yesterday morning at about 11:30. Mr. LeClair was the fifth son of the late Francis M. LeClair of Weaverton and Cecelia Gordon LeClair of Black Rock, Quebec.
>
> He was born in Weaverton, March 15, 1870. On September 10, 1903 he married Miss Kathryn Harrigan of Hoosick Falls, New York, whom he survived. To this union were born…

The additional data plugged gaps in Uncle Jonathon's letter, and the town clerk's records. The article mentioned organizations Chris's grandfather had belonged to and offices he'd held as well as people who'd attended the service. Again, Black Rock, Quebec appeared. Chris noted the new facts on his index cards.

Queen City's past distracted Chris from his search. It always did. *The Freeman*'s pages were packed with a mixture of news and gossip listed under titles like "Social Events" or "Town Notes." One Queen City Town Notes article mentioned a gubernatorial fundraiser for Col. H. Nelson Jackson. Another announced plans for a new bandstand in Bluff's park. And a third was a sympathy note addressed to the family of one Kathleen Cassidy, whom the note called "a spirited lady." This was quaint small-town stuff, he thought and continued reading until some nearby students, closing down their laptops, reminding him of his morning classes. He returned the microfiche to their files, gathered his belongings, and hurried out of the building.

The red light on his answering machine was flashing when he returned to his apartment. He walked by Dylan's gaze and hit playback.

"Hi, Chris. This is Mini. I have some information for you. Give me a call."

***

Chris called Mini numerous times over the following few days. Each time, she was either on her phone or away from her desk.

***

No one was at the help desk when Chris returned to the fiche readers later in the week. He opened Uncle Jonathon's letter and ran his finger down the page, searching for specific names. He thought gathering information on his grandfather's brothers might provide alternatives if data became scarce in his search for Christopher Gordon. He struggled to read the cursive in the letter because it grew smaller and smaller as it progressed across the page until finally disintegrating into a bumpy line. After closer examination, he deciphered some names and dates and looked for the appropriate microfiche. He searched through the 1912 roll until he found information on one of his grandfather's brother in the February 8th edition.

> G. Fredrick LeClair, Assistant Postmaster, passed away at his home on East Center Street of consumption after several days of illness.

The machine wouldn't remain focused despite Chris's attempts to adjust the lens. Finding the other readers all in use, he gathered his belongings and went to the basement to visit special collections, hoping to look through the city directories. He'd once used them for a local history course and thought they might list where his relatives had lived in Weaverton, and perhaps their occupations.

"I'm sorry. I've already locked up the files and turned down the terminals." The special collections librarian said.

The sign behind her noted closing time at 10 pm. Frustrated again, Chris walked up to the lobby and sat in one of the easy chairs. He opened the letter again, this time searching for Christopher Gordon's name.

> Christopher and his wife Ann Daugherty Gordon are buried in Green Mt. Cemetery on Weaverton Ave. Graves are, I believe, on north side of cemetery.

He had decided to search for their graves over the weekend when he noticed Claudia Nichols walking by the checkout desk. He hurried over to catch her just as she reached the door. She said she'd been doing research on her recertification project, a study of how immigrant Irish built the railroad through the center of Weaverton, then asked how his project was coming.

"I've been reading obituaries."

"Sounds like you really know how to have a good time."

Chris laughed, told her about his demography unit, then showed her Uncle Jonathon's letter. He said he'd begun searching for details of his family history just as she had done with Weaverton residents. Then he mentioned

Christopher Gordon. "I've really just started but it's so time consuming. And the further back I go, the less I find. Any thoughts?"

"You've got lots of options. You can keep working backwards. The newspapers and town clerks have lots of data. Weaverton has a historical society over in the Mill office building. I know they have old photos of athletic teams, some businesses, even pictures of the downtown area. You may find something there. But I think this Gordon, the one in the Cavalry, may be hard to trace. There aren't many pictures of the First Vermont, and the ones I've seen don't identify the troopers. And unless he was wounded or got a medal, there may not be much. Do you have any of his correspondence or a diary?"

"Nothing and no relatives to follow up with."

"That's not all bad. At least there aren't any biases or misinformation."

"I'm not even sure about this letter," Chris said, holding up the yellowing pages.

Claudia looked it over. "Interesting. It looks like 19th-century style, but you say it was written about 30 years ago?" Chris shook his head. "Consider it a primary source but verify the facts. It's better than nothing."

"There's not much time left. Where would you go from here?"

"You could try the county genealogical society. They've got all kinds of resources. Check *Vermont in the Civil War*. It's a great website. And special collections has city directories, letters, diaries, military information on the First Vermont."

"I just went down there, but they closed."

"The quickest thing would be to keep reading the newspapers."

"You would?"

"The old *Freeman* was filled with news from the front. The paper was a lot folksier in the late 19th and early 20th centuries. No wire services, so newspapers gathered information from anywhere they could. They used military

telegraph reports, casualty lists, even letters sent home by
the troops. Not unusual to find quotes right out of some
trooper's letter to ma about a battle or the lousy food. They
weren't always accurate, but Christopher Gordon's name
might pop up and lead somewhere else. Queen City and
Weaverton were small towns; everyone knew everyone
else or knew a family member. You're bound to find details that don't appear in the records, and they're already
organized by date. You can follow the First Vermont right
through the war, day by day. If you don't come up with
anything on him, you'll learn about others in his unit and
can make assumptions. For the time you have, you'll learn
more reading the old *Freeman* than from anything else."

"Thanks, Claudia."

"I just thought of something else."

"What's that?"

"The pension records. The government kept a file on
every soldier. They're stored at the National Archives. I've
retrieved a few. Let me check with the archives for you and
see what I can find?"

Chris gave Claudia the information she needed,
thanked her, and walked back home to Wells Court.

***

Late Saturday morning, Chris drove along Weaverton
Avenue to Green Mountain Cemetery. It lay atop the hill
where the avenue began its descent toward the Weaverton River. He drove through the iron gate and parked beside the flagpole. Chris was looking for a lost grave in the
same cemetery where a 40-foot granite column proclaimed
Ethan Allen's grave, yet, no one knew for sure where Allen
was buried. Chris didn't care though.

The letter said the Gordons' graves were on the cemetery's north side. Chris zipped his coat and walked
through spring patches of snow. He passed tall white pines
whose trunks had grown so large they tipped some of the
19th-century granite monuments to awkward angles. A

rusting metal fence lined the cemetery's north boundary right at the crest of the hill where the Queen Family's dead looked down upon Weaverton.

He began walking the rows of markers. Tiny sandstone, limestone, and granite monuments marked the graves of early citizens. Some markers were squat. Some tilted. Some were cracked or broken off. Weather had worn away carvings—especially on the limestone markers—forcing Chris to kneel and run his fingers through the grooves as he tried to distinguish letters and dates. Some told simple stories. Ireland, The Great Famine, Queenstown, Montreal, Captain, Colonel, Farmer, Gettysburg, 1830–1896 they said.

Time moved on with each new section he walked. Blocks replaced single stones and grew larger. Squared blocks, chipped blocks, blocks topping other blocks. Bronze plates appeared. Obelisks appeared and grew. Some stood upon bare ground, others on blocks, others on blocks on mounds, always upward, always bigger. They were rough. They were polished. Sometimes alone, sometimes in clusters, were family plots surrounded by individual markers for children. They told their stories. Newspaper publisher, hospital founder, Chateau Thierry, Belleau Wood, Medal of Honor, Pastor, Partner, Explorer were words from that generation.

Chris plodded back and forth, row after row, reading abbreviated, disjointed histories of hardships and heroism, love and death. He stopped wherever he thought he'd found a clue to the Gordon story—his story—but the clues continued to lead nowhere.

He reread the letter again and again, looking back across ground he'd walked. He was searching, hoping, questioning. So many stories were waiting to be told but he was the only one reading. Didn't anyone care enough to come and learn?

A warming south wind melted the snow around the bases of the white pines.

***

Saturday evening Mass at St. Isaac's was already underway when Chris sat in the last pew. JK 46 was waiting there along with two disinterested ushers. Chris watched as the pasty-faced preacher climbed the pulpit and picked up a sheet of paper.

"Today we have a letter from the bishop: 'Dear Diocesan Brothers and Sisters, I wish to formally announce the completion of the sale of the Diocesan office complex and grounds in Queen City. The property consists of four buildings and nearly 40 acres…'"

More distraction, Chris thought. Jack was right. They needed a new business model.

He lowered his head and closed his eyes. Instead of solace, he found more agitation. Everything during the last months had been like that—a swirling, frenetic voyage through melancholy and frustration.

At least one aspect of his life felt under control. His recertification project, a sterile conglomeration of numbers and populations and history, was complete. It sat on his desk, backed by methods, ratios, and equations. But reading the gravestones still enticed him. Could he use that somehow or was it just a meaningless distraction? Another reading assignment? Did the stones have more to offer? When he'd mowed around them as a youth, he hadn't understood what they said. He hadn't noticed how much they told. Now he was beginning to see that their words recounted stories and paraphrased history. They painted pictures of Queen City—its citizens and the country—that history books only hinted at. He couldn't just put them aside. There was so much detailed, information on those gravestones. He had to find a way to entwine what he was learning into his work.

"The nearly $15 million will be used in the following ways. First…"

This isn't helping me, Chris thought. He slid to the end of the bench and walked out.

21

Chris listened to each of those around him. He knew them now. Not every detail—like the kind of cake they liked or their dogs' names, but he knew what they'd endured, what they were made of. He knew how they'd fought back and how they'd moved forward. And he felt they wanted to know him too. He took a deep breath. "Hi. I'm Chris. And, I'm an adult child of an alcoholic, though my family was a little confusing. Listening to your stories, I've realized they're my stories, too. I've lived them. I was afraid and lonely. I didn't know who I was. I put myself down. I didn't know we had so many similarities. I didn't ask to be this way. It just came with the territory. I always felt something was different when I was growing up and thought I'd done something wrong, needed to change somehow. So I ran away. It wasn't very far—from my aunt and uncle's house to my fraternity—and it seemed like a good idea at the time. At first, everything was different, exciting. What I didn't know was that some of my brothers were just like me—no more prepared to live in one place than the other. All I was doing was changing ponies.

A lot has happened this year, some of it reminding me of that old stuff. Parts of it were messy. I'd stuffed a lot of it away, but I'm finding it never really goes away, does it? Eventually, it finds a way back. I've only told a few people what happened to me. I was embarrassed and afraid. But I want to tell you because I need to put it behind me forever, because if I don't fix it now, I may not have another chance.

After my junior year in college, some of my fraternity brothers and I rented a camp out on Lone Tree Point for the summer," Chris said and began revealing his distant past in the precise delivery of an historian.

***

One of Chris's fraternity brothers, Jim Underwood, had made a deal to scrape and paint an old camp for reduced rent. It was a tiny box near the end of the dunes that had suffered years of summer people and little maintenance. The others—Jack, Pat, Walt, and Logan—didn't mind. They liked the location and, besides, there was an upright piano and a fireplace. When they moved in, the place was filthy. The wind whipped sand from the dunes through the cracks and screens, leaving a trail of crunch that remained the rest of the summer. "Nice touch," Jack said. "We should call it Dragonwych."

The rental agreement became less important as the temperature rose. The brothers gave up sweaty scraping for beers and the beach. Jim wasn't around whenever there was work to do, but reappeared after Pat's father lent his son the family boat, a sleek red-and-white Glastron with a big Merc 85. The guys built a water-ski course from plastic milk jugs tied to bricks, and they skied or lay on the beach most days while Bob Dylan, Ray Charles, or Dick Dale and the Del-Tones blasted from Walt's speakers, propped in the front window.

In the evenings, the brothers went on boat rides around Rensselaer Island or over to Kannada Lodge to eat pizza, listen to the bands, and try to meet Trinity College girls who would ride the ferry across Lake Champlain to drink beer and dance. Sometimes they piled in Aunt Harriet's old Dodge and drove to Benny's for fries. Jack liked to choose the late-night routes back to camp, often directing Chris through one of the college's old farm barns or across the football field, while leading everyone in singing "Johnson's Motor Car" or the Weaverton High fight song. He especially liked the chorus, always yelling out, "Weaverton High! Fight, team, fight!" while shaking his fist in the air.

Chris thought it all harmless, and he enjoyed his new freedom.

El visited on Memorial Day, wearing her old WAC uniform. She'd attended the annual VFW service by General Well's statue in Bluff's park. While following Jack around, she noticed copies of *Peyton Place, Valley of the Dolls,* and a stack of *Playboy* magazines. "What the hell's this, troop?" she said. Jack told her it was their reading corner and tried dishing some crap about keeping abreast of current events. Jack pointed to one issue and said, "There's an interview with Dr. King in this one." El responded, "Great. This is a regular Algonquin Club!"

Susan worked in the Adirondacks but came over on July 4th. Ray Charles was scheduled to play at Bayside Skating Rink so everyone piled into the old Dodge and drove over. When they discovered the concert was sold out, Jack and Logan discussed ways of sneaking in and meeting the Raelettes, but Chris and Susan decided to stroll down to the beach, where the sand was still warm, and the music, having worked its way through the gaps in the old skating-rink walls, floated over the water. Chris took Susan's hand and led her into the shallow water, and they danced barefoot to "Georgia on My Mind." Susan's white summer dress swayed against the backdrop of the black lake.

The camp was still only half painted when Susan returned on Labor Day weekend. After she skied, it was Jack's turn. Chris steered through the course but instead of circling back kept heading south. Susan slid across the seat, and they talked above the hum of the Merc. She told him Dylan was coming to the gym in October.

"I know. We've been listening to him all summer."

"I don't like his new sound. You know, he was booed at Newport."

"He's just evolving."

Jack continued cutting back and forth on some phantom slalom course until the boat whizzed by Rocky Point, but, by then, his movements lost their precision. He slipped one arm through the tow rope handle and began waving the other. When North End Beach came into view, Chris turned to Susan and pointed. "Aunt Harriet brought Catch and me here when we were kids. She didn't want us around the house when Uncle Jonathon was drinking. It was just a little thing, but I'll always have it. When the sun set, she'd take us to Benny's."

Jack struggled to stay up but finally let go. Chris pulled the throttle back and the Glastron rose up on its own wake. Thunder Rock lay off the port bow. It was perfect. Blue sky. A fresh, southerly breeze kissed the surface, leaving ripples here and there for miles. There was a light scent of gasoline. Jack treaded water behind the boat. Ahead, the Adirondacks, summer green, formed a jagged line 50 miles south along the western shore.

Chris turned to Susan. Everything seemed perfect. "This was a great summer except that you weren't around."

She kissed him then told him she worried about him. "You can't tell what Jack, Logan, and Pat are going to do. I've heard those guys can be reckless."

"I can take care of myself."

Jack yelled, "Cut the kissy-face huggy-bear shit and get me out of the water! My appendages are shriveling up. All of them! And the horse under me needs some air." As he climbed onto the transom, the sublime panorama appeared to hypnotize him.

Back at camp, Jack and Chris walked the boat in while Susan dashed ahead, telling Chris to close his eyes and wait. He sat in the sand, hearing children's voices down the beach before a car door slammed. Susan returned and handed him a long rolled-up cardboard tube. "What's this?" Chris said and drew out a large poster of a curly-haired Bob Dylan wearing a guitar and harmonica, leaning into a microphone.

"I pulled it off a telephone pole up near GMU. They're all over town."

Chris drew her close and kissed her before she dove into the August lake. He followed and they floated side by side as the sun inched its way behind the mountains. After drying, they walked toward the camp. Susan went to the wood box while Chris stepped inside. Jack, Logan, Pat, and Walt were seated around the table with beer glasses before them. Jim and Walt's girlfriend, Mini, looked through the stack of LPs by the stereo.

"Cardinal Puff shall now take his first drink of the evening," Jack said, picking up his glass with his thumb and forefinger, the other fingers extended.

"Good form," Pat said.

Chris found hot dogs and rolls in the fridge, picked up paper plates and plastic utensils from the breakfast bar, and an old copy of the *Freeman* to start a fire.

"Cardinal Puff shall now take his third drink of the…"

"You blew it! Third and FINAL!" Walt shouted. "YOU GOTTA CHUG!"

Chris went back outside as Jack lifted his glass. After starting a fire and roasting hot dogs, they talked in whispers. The fire cast crackling sparks against the sky. Susan leaned her head on his shoulder, and they listened to the laughter riding on the music. Later they walked in the shallows as the ripples from some distant breeze touched the shore. Chris gathered more driftwood but when he noticed goose bumps on Susan's legs, he ran inside for a blanket.

Jack was leaning against the breakfast bar, holding the receiver of a disconnected wall phone. "I need a speak to Her Majesty. Hi, Bess! I was callin' about that outfit you wore ta Berlin! It wasn't your color. You ever thought 'bout periwinkle?"

In the corner, Mini was sitting on Walt's lap. The two were laughing so hard, tears ran down their faces. Even Underwood smiled.

Back outside, Chris covered Susan's shoulders, and she snuggled closer. The music inside grew louder, flooding the night. As they watched the moon rise, Chris listened to Susan's breathing and felt her warmth. He kissed her and began caressing her. She lay back on the sand, and he leaned over and kissed her again. Then a panic-filled scream rang out from the darkness.

Chris dashed toward the camp with Susan right behind him when a second scream sounded from behind the camp. It came from where the cars were parked. Running passed the kitchen window, Chris noticed the brothers playing Cardinal Puff. The music shielded them. Ahead, Chris saw Mini struggling with Underwood behind Aunt Harriet's car. Her hair was disheveled.

Chris grabbed Underwood and pushed him away. "She came on to me!" Jim said.

"Liar! He came up behind me when I was getting my sweater from the car."

Underwood stepped up to Chris. "You don't believe that little tramp, do you? She'd say anything to…"

Chris clenched his fist and took a wild swing. The punch grazed off Underwood's cheek below his left eye but was solid enough to bounce him back against the Dodge. It did little more than enrage Jim. He started toward Chris but stopped when the floodlight above the camp flicked on and the screen door opened.

"What the hell's going on?" Walt yelled.

Everyone stood still except Mini, who ran to Chris and threw her arms around his neck. "Thanks. I owe you." Then she took Walt's hand. "It's nothing. Let's walk, and I'll tell you everything." Walt started toward Underwood but Mini pulled on his arm. "Please!"

Underwood went inside and slammed the door.

Susan turned to Chris. "This is out of control. I've got to leave."

"But …"

"It's 80 miles to Mt. Marcy, and I'm working the rest of the weekend."

Chris walked her to her car. She put her arms around Chris's neck. "I told you about those guys."

"I'll take care of them"

"Don't be reckless!" She kissed him goodbye. "See you back in school."

When Chris reentered the camp, Pat and Logan were arguing about the Red Sox and Jack's head was in the refrigerator. Logan went to turn up the stereo. Underwood, looking pissed, turned it back down. "You guys think you know what happened. But you don't get it, 'cause you're drunk."

"We're certainly not pregnant, asshole," Logan said.

Underwood said to Chris, "Whenever they're drunk, they don't listen."

"Shut up, asshole," Walt said, walking in as Mini's car pulled away.

"You're all out of control," Underwood said before walking out.

Walt started to go after Underwood but Chris pulled him back. Just then Jack began laughing. "I love it!" he said.

"What's so funny?" Pat said.

"He's right. Underwood's right, for a change. We don't get it."

"What're you talking about?"

"This!" Jack said, extending his arms. "All this. This is the American dream, brother! This is what everybody wants. Live on a beach, sleep late, have toddies with your buddies. We're doing it! And we're only in our 20s. People work their whole lives for this shit and never get it."

Logan raised his shoulders. The others had blank faces.

Jack laughed again. "I'm only 23, and I got the American dream. Sit by the water. Not a fucking care! Sip toddies all day. And more. Fights! Just like Madison Square Garden. It's only 10 o'clock, and we already had a couple." He looked around. "Pretty sad, huh? Never really get it, do we?"

Everyone was quiet until Pat spoke up. "Let's go for a boat ride."

"I don't think we..." Chris began

"It's OK. It's OK. You drive. You!" Jack said, pointing into Chris's face. "You're not drinking. Logical."

Chris thought he'd made a mistake but didn't want to argue, didn't want to stand up to all those guys. He thought he could just go along and take care of them all.

The sand was still warm as they pushed off the beach. Pat caught up, carrying a six pack. Walt dropped the motor as Pat climbed in, and Chris started the engine. Pat stretched out on the rear seat beside Walt. Logan sat up front between Jack and Chris. When Chris forced the throttle down, the boat leapt forward.

A yellow crescent floated above Whiteface Mountain, coating the Adirondacks in gold. The Glastron sprinted over the glass water, shattering ripples into shards that flew off and disappeared in the dark. They ran south until the lights from Queen City Bay appeared on the portside. Chris steered out toward Rensselaer Island. The warm air caressed their faces as the boat moved over the water.

Pat opened two beers. He passed one to Jack but Chris shook his head. Logan's eyes were closed, his head down. Walt took the beer and stared off. They circled Rensselaer Island but as Chris wheeled back toward the camp, Pat tapped his shoulder. "Go through the harbor and stop at the Salt Dock. Benny's is still open."

Jack nodded, so Chris aimed for the south end of the breakwater.

"Faster. It's really smooth tonight. Nobody's out," Pat yelled.

"It's wide open."

"This baby's got some guts. She'll do 38."

It was too dark to see the speedometer but Chris thought he felt the speed inch up as he leaned into the throttle and held it.

"There's the breakwater. Not too close," Jack said.

Chris began a sweeping turn around the south end just as the light on the south tower came around, blinding him for an instant. Logan stood up. "What the hell's that?" He pointed into the darkness.

When Chris refocused, he saw a white dinghy floating less than 20 yards ahead. It must have broken loose from one of the sailboats moored inside the breakwater. He wheeled left. As he did Logan's hand slipped from the windshield, and he lost his balance, falling on top of Chris just as Chris noticed the breakwater straight ahead. He pushed Logan aside, pulled back the throttle, and wheeled right. The sharp turn avoided a direct hit to the breakwater but the boat's momentum swung the stern around and into the Redstones. It was as if the rocks themselves had reached out for the brothers.

There was a loud crunching noise and then some-one screamed. Bodies flew out of the cockpit. Chris felt a sharp blow to his shoulder before losing consciousness. He woke as he rolled downward, hitting the water. He couldn't move. Gasping for air, he slid below the surface, surrounded by liquid darkness. He couldn't determine up or down. He wanted to swim, but neither his arms nor his legs responded. The warm water was soothing like a pool's shallow end on a hot day. The moonlight above faded, and he closed his eyes, feeling sleepy, when a hand grabbed his collar and jerked him toward the surface. When he broke through, he began coughing and felt himself being dragged backward as he looked at the Milky Way. Water rushed around his ears. He gasped. Then he felt himself pushed face first against the cold Redstones.

"Hang on!" Walt said before moving back into the darkness.

Chris grabbed something sharp and held on. The wa-ter lapped against his face. Queen City's lights shown above the distant shore but Chris couldn't make out any-thing nearby until the light on south tower rotated around again. The boat lay upside down with its propeller at a halfcocked angle toward Queen City. A life preserver and a paddle were floating beyond it. Ten yards to his left, Pat was floating face down.

Chris's arms and shoulders were numb but he began swimming. When he reached Pat, he turned him over, cra-dled his neck, and pinched his nose as best he could. He took a deep breath and was about to cover Pat's lips with his own when Pat began coughing. Pat opened his eyes and a faint smile appeared. Chris grabbed his collar and kicked a spastic sidestroke toward the breakwater. Pat was more responsive when they reached the rocks, so Chris pushed him up against it. "Grab something!" He turned to look for others. "Anybody there? Jack! Walt! Logan!"

"Here!" Jack's voice called.

Chris saw a shadow clinging to the side of the over-turned Glastron. Then Walt called out of the darkness, "I can't find Logan."

The windows at the Coast Guard station near the Salt Dock were all illuminated, and a siren rang out in the distance. A searchlight flashed across the surface of the bay.

***

Chris stood beside the brothers in Dower's Parlor over the next two days, shaking hands, hugging friends, promising to get together. At the cemetery, he listened as the minister promised eternity but couldn't comprehend any of it as he stared down at Logan's coffin, laying on a synthetic green rug, stacked with vases of dead gladiolas.

After the burial, the brothers gathered round the Cassidy grave. El, wearing her uniform, stood at attention and saluted before laying some coins atop the stone. "From the cup," she said. The brothers sang "Minstrel Boy." When it was over, everyone looked around as if something else was supposed to happen.

Walt told them it was just an accident. "No one knew the dinghy was there. We didn't want it to happen. It just got away from us. But we can't forget. We've got to do something to make things better."

Everyone shook their heads in agreement but Jack. "Move on," he said.

Chris and Susan walked toward the Dodge. When they stopped, she broke the silence. "I need some time to think about things, Chris. I'm going home for a few days."

"What do you mean 'time?'"

"Everything's so confusing right now. It was out of hand. I don't understand any of it. If everyone weren't…"

"I wasn't out of hand. It was an accident."

"I'm not explaining myself. I just know it doesn't make sense. I need to think." Susan brushed her lips against his cheek before hurrying along the line of cars where Jim Underwood stood, holding a door open.

Chris moved back into Aunt Harriet and Uncle Jonathon's house. Aunt Harriet hugged him after he placed his bags in his room. He slept, he ate. And after retreating for a few days, his healing began. Late that week, he crossed the street to the park and kicked a football up and down the field. The fall semester had commenced and Chris returned to classes. Jack had disappeared and the rest of his friends were laying low. Susan didn't return his calls. When he wandered through the fraternity during the Homecoming party, looking for familiar faces, he saw few so he listened to the Mentionings bang through a couple of covers before finding El in the kitchen. She hugged him.

"I don't have anything left to give, El."

"There's always something left, Chrissy Chris."

He buried himself in his studies seeking a new normality. He'd forgotten about the Dylan concert until a Saturday in October when he noticed a poster on his way into the library. After finding a cubby upstairs and opening his books, he struggled with his assignment, but by 7, it had become so quiet he couldn't concentrate. Losing all resolve, he left around 8 and noticed another Dylan poster as he cut across the green toward the hospital lot where the old red Dodge was parked. The night was summer mild. The sky dotted with stars. Nothing but the calendar mentioned the season.

He drove toward Bluffs Park and the lake beyond but the summer crowds had vanished from Benny's, so he parked right beside the bus.

"A quart of fries, Benny."

"This is the end of 'em, kid. Eat up," Benny said, checking off items on a list.

"You closing?"

"Business is slow. See you next season."

Chris sat at a picnic table and picked through the crunchy fries. The trees about the park wore brilliant colors but fallen leaves dotted the walkways. He couldn't see the lake through the darkness. Then Benny's lights flipped off.

He started the old Dodge and drove down Bluff's before turning up Main Street hill. No buses were parked outside the bus station. None of the usual students were out—neither early movie viewers returning to the dorms nor early bar hoppers skipping down toward Center Street. They must be at the Dylan concert, he thought. He clicked on the radio and punched D for WDOT. The Four Tops were belting out "Sugar Pie." Chris tapped the wheel to the beat and inched down on the accelerator. A little further up Main, the library lights bathed the library's marble steps in a spectral glow. The Hand of Knowledge bore an eerie Halloween-like look.

He turned right off Main before nosing the old car toward the gym entrance. Bob Dylan was in there, and Chris decided to sneak in to see him. His heart started to race. Instead of parking in the lower lot, he drove up to the roundabout outside the lobby. Feeling emboldened by the green doors propped open and the lack of security officers, he drove up over the curb and parked on the lawn opposite the main door. A couple walked out as Chris reached the doors. "I didn't like the electric," Chris heard the girl say.

The lobby was empty and the doors to the gym closed. Everything was quiet as he hurried toward the gym doors on the right. One swung open when a couple walked out, and Chris caught it, walking into the darkened gymnasium. He leaned against the back wall and waited for his eyes to adjust.

A few people sat in the bleachers but most were stretched out on a patchwork of blankets spread across the basketball court. The room was less than half full.

He peered over the crowd toward the stage where the curly-haired singer stood in a spotlight, talking with band members behind him. One hand covered the microphone, the other clung to the neck of his guitar. Some of the band tuned their instruments. Others fingered cords beyond the reach of the sound system. Their laughing and bits of conversations flitted about like shadows.

Dylan turned and faced the crowd. Conversations faded or broke off mid-sentence. Chris thought the musician was looking for someone in the audience so when his gaze reached Chris's side of the gym, Chris imagined Dylan had been looking for him. The singer nodded to his band and there was a snap of the snare drum, a beat of the base followed by the organ, which was responding with the same abrupt, circuitous melody that had blared across Lone Tree Point all summer. Dylan began singing "Rolling Stone" with the whisper of a tambourine in the background.

Chris had arrived in time. Just in time. He mouthed the words, felt the notes, and was drawn into the rapture.

The performance was more than Chris could have imagined and hoped for but many weren't as enamored as he was. Between him and the stage, people picked up their belongings and tiptoed out. One couple in front of Chris stood and folded their blanket. They blocked his view of Dylan temporarily, so he moved to the right. Someone else opened the lobby door, allowing a long thin beam of light to pierce the darkness, revealing the couple as they moved through the crowd. It was Susan and Jim.

Everything else around Chris disappeared. The music continued but he couldn't hear it until the couple had nearly reached the door when, Susan's eyes met Chris's. He froze. She forced a smile before turning away. Jim noticed too and lowered his head. And the lobby door closed behind them.

The brief paralysis Chris endured ended abruptly. He started for the door but when he banged through into the lobby, Jim and Susan had nearly reached the outer doors. He took a few hurried steps before stopping, no longer driven—without passion, without emotion. The couple opened the outer door and the music returned. As they began vanishing into the night, Susan turned back, her eyes opaque, her face devoid of emotion. Chris understood what Dylan was trying to tell him.

***

"After I graduated, one of the guys, Walt, helped me

find a job. I liked history, so it was easy to bury myself in it. I spent a lot of time with my sister's family and taking care of my uncle. I did what I had to. I know none of it was my fault but for years I've wondered how my life would've been different if I hadn't been raised the way I was. I can't change any of that, but I can change how I go on."

"Thanks for sharing, Chris. Does anyone else want to share?" said Bob. "OK, let's join hands."

22

The following Sunday, when Chris entered the library, two sleepy students sitting behind the circulation desk reading were the only people in sight. The fiche room was dark, the desk empty. Chris tripped the light switch and placed his tote bag by a reader. Uncle Jonathon's letter told him he wanted the fiche for 1889. He found it and began searching through the columns for Christopher Gordon's obituary. On page two of *The Daily Freeman* for March 23rd, he discovered a brief note midway down the page.

> Christopher Gordon of Weaverton died of consumption yesterday. At the time of his death, he was Postmaster of Weaverton. He was an honored veteran, having served in Co. A, First Vt. Cavalry.

A notice on the 24th announced the funeral time at St. Brendan's Church in Weaverton on the 25th. On the 26th, another announcement said members of the Stannard Post of the GAR, Grand Army of the Republic, a veteran's organization, attended the funeral. It named the bearers and said Christopher Gordon was laid to rest in Mount Saint Brendan's cemetery.

Chris sat back. No wonder he couldn't find his relative's grave in Green Mountain Cemetery. Uncle Jonathon's letter was wrong.

He read through several more days newspapers, but his hope of discovering any substantial information about Christopher Gordon faded the further he moved beyond the date of the man's death. As with many people, his mark disappeared with his passing. If Chris hoped to uncover more details, he'd have to follow Claudia's advice and continue reading Civil War era newspapers. He put that thought aside when he remembered Libby had invited him and K.J. for dinner. In 15 minutes, he would be late.

Chris followed Weaverton Ave. back into the center of

town and turned at Elm Street, driving a half block further before parking in the city lot. The three-story structure on the corner had always been white with green shutters. He remembered being young and watching painters stretched out like aerialists across the front of that building, reaching to cover as much surface as possible from the tops of their 30-foot ladders.

Some late-spring flakes danced on the light breeze between the stones in Elmwood Burying Ground across the street. There were no footprints. There were no plowed paths. The gates were locked. Chris entered Libby's apartment house, climbed to the second floor and knocked on 2B's door.

"Hi. I'm glad you could get away." She said, letting him into a bright living room that smelled of mushrooms and onions. "Let me take that. And have a seat. "

Chris handed her his coat, which she brought to the bedroom and laid down across the soft pillow. She paused before her mirror and adjusted the thin gold chain about her neck. She ran her hands down the sides of her slacks. Not a wrinkle. "Can I get you something to drink?"

The tail of her cat clock ticked back and forth as she moved through the living room toward the kitchen.

"Sure."

She lifted the cover off the mashed potatoes, examined them with a chef's eye before fluffing them and adjusting the burner.

"I hope you don't mind that I added some onions to the potatoes. I love them," she said, adding another pat of butter and setting the timer.

"I do too. Hey, you're right across the street from the cemetery."

"It's always very quiet here." She laughed. "That was poor. Do you want a glass of wine or a beer?"

"Beer if you've got it. Besides, you said the steak was going to be smothered in wine." He loosened his tie.

"I guess I did."

"No need to dirty one of those," Chris said, watching

Libby reach for a glass.

"K.J. called. He said he and the wife can't make it. Said something about relatives showing up late last night."

"Oh!"

"By the way, does she have a name? He always calls her the wife or 'my other half.'"

"I think it's Rocinante or Glumdiclitch. You know, like one of Frodo's friends."

"Chris!"

Libby handed him a beer, then went back to the fridge. She placed a plate on the coffee table with thin strips of green peppers, carrots, slices of zucchini, and a few bright-red cherry tomatoes surrounding a bowl of dip. Chris eyed the plate cautiously.

"Mystery dip?"

"Ranch."

"Not humus?"

"It's Sunday." She raised her glass.

"I didn't think you were supposed to drink when you trained for a marathon."

"Training holiday. I have a few weak points, you know." Libby smiled. "Speaking of weak points, K.J. said you had a stress test a while back. You didn't mention anything."

"I had some symptoms, chest pain."

"And?"

"I took some tests. The doctor says it's nothing, so I guess I'm OK."

"I'm not surprised with Brent all over you and all that extra work. It's enough to make anyone sick."

"Thanks for noticing."

Chris looked out the window across the street. Sunlight poked through holes in the cloud bank, letting circles of sunlight dot the cemetery. "Pretty."

"I walk there sometimes. It's like an oasis—"

"I bet you're going to say something about a lot of interesting history too."

She smiled and picked up her merlot. "Well there is! I

was reading about General Stannard."

Libby seemed to brighten as she told Chris she'd discovered that the Civil War general once lived near the cemetery. He'd been buried there, but the GAR paid to move his body to Lakeside Cemetery in order to honor him with a more prominent gravesite and monument.

"I know, I know," Chris said, laughing. "You never get away from it, do you, Libby?"

"I guess there are other things. How's your project coming? I haven't seen you much." Libby ran her finger around the edge of her wine glass.

"I thought I was done, but I keep finding little things and getting ideas. The main part is complete, but I've started researching some of my relatives. Claudia suggested it. In case I ever teach the unit."

"In case?" Libby said, her voice sounding softer than Chris remembered from school.

"If I can put up with Brent and that Andover kid until June, I'll have a chance to breathe."

Libby inhaled the fragrance of her wine taking a small sip before leaning back and curling her legs up under herself like a cat. When she pushed her hair back behind her ear, Chris noticed the freckles on her neck. They were usually hidden behind her hair. "I'm glad you came. There's never enough time at work to get to know people. All we do is rush around, but Sundays are for relaxing. What do you usually do on weekends?"

"Right now, it's recertification but over the years I spent most of my spare time with my sister's kids. Her husband died young. Now the boys are all grown up. Sometimes I hang out with the old fraternity crew. Watch games, play cards. You know, guy stuff."

"Yeah, guy stuff. Do you have anyone—I mean anyone besides your family?"

"No. I never found the right girl. There was this one. We dated while we were in college, but she took off with another guy. I haven't seen her since." Chris hesitated before saying, "What about you?"

Libby picked up a slice of green pepper and dipped it in the dressing.

"I thought I'd found the right one, too. But it didn't work."

"I'm sorry."

"It all started off so well." Libby looked into her glass. "We met late in the '80s, at GMU. I was a city kid who came here to ski. I joined Tri Delta and did all the right things. Bart and I met at one of those big house parties up on Main Street."

"A college romance!"

"Yes, but it continued after school. I followed him to New York. He did Wall Street while I subbed at a few schools up in New Rochelle. When he made VP in his firm, we married and bought a home in Westchester."

"Wow!"

"Yeah, we hit the jackpot. Except he was also hitting the jackpot with every new intern who wiggled into his firm. I can't believe I'm telling you this. No one here knows. He lied to me. I didn't know for months. When I found out, I came apart. I ran away for a while and did some awful things. Then I moved back in with my parents. I was 33, and I had to move back in with my parents! That was a long time ago and now—well, it's all behind me." Libby took a deep breath and closed her eyes.

"I'm really sorry, Libby. I suspected something, but I guess we just talk about school when we're at school. I didn't know."

"It's really nice of you to care. I know you hurt some-times, too, and I'm sorry."

Libby reached over and squeezed his hand. The next thing he knew, she leaned forward and kissed his cheek. The moment was electric. Chris sat still. Something in the touch of her hair on his shoulder and her sweet scent ig-nited flames inside him that had lain dormant. He felt his breathing deepen. His fingertips sensed each fiber on the couch's arm. He held his breath.

Libby must have sensed the change because she sat

back. She looked into his eyes. "I'm sorry, Chris. I got carried away. You were so nice to listen."

"That's OK. That's OK."

He stood and brought his beer with him to the window. He took a long swig then looked back at her. And his watch.

"I've got to go, Libby."

"But—"

"I've got to do some more research. Everything is starting to close in on me. And the library is only open until 5 on Sundays."

"Chris. I wasn't …I mean…I don't know what got into me. I guess it was the wine. I'm not used to …You know. It's Sunday."

"That's OK. Hey, where's my coat?"

"Sure. Sure."

Libby returned from the bedroom carrying his coat. He took it, leaving her nothing to hold on to.

"I'm really sorry if I…"

"You didn't do anything wrong, Libby. It's me. Thanks. I've got to go."

As he buttoned his coat out in the hallway, Chris thought he heard a glass break. Then the kitchen timer went off. The buzzing continued as he walked down the stair and out into the street. He knew he had overreacted to her kiss. It was only a thank you, a kindness from a kind person, yet he'd recoiled as if some incision had been palpated. Was he afraid of being hurt again? He reached his hand up toward his chest.

***

The rest of the afternoon, Chris sat in front of the fiche reader without seeing a page. After the library closed, he went home and flipped channels. That night he couldn't sleep and tossed about. His emotions preoccupied him so much he barely noticed the early morning commotion in the hallway. A gentle knock on the door appeared to him dreamlike, distant, but once it turned to pounding, Chris snapped out of his slumber. He flipped on the light, picked up the Louisville Slugger he kept by his bed, and tiptoed across the dark living room. "Who is it?"

"Iss me. Jack."

"Jack?"

"Ya!"

He opened the door to find his friend leaning against the jamb wearing his beret and a shit-eating grin.

"What the hell are you doing? It's nearly three o'clock."

"Chrisss. I won. I won big. Big!"

He took Jack's arm and led him to an easy chair. "What are you talking about?"

Jack's hand searched for his jacket pocket, finally reaching inside and pulling out a wad of cash. Chris saw twenties and fifties.

"Look. I won big! Won big! Nine seveny fi."

"Where did you get it?"

"I won. I won big. Game at Lakeside, St. John Club. Evyweek. You take it. Don gif it back if I'm drunk. Promise!" Jack shook his finger in Chris's face.

"I promise. Now, let me get you a blanket. You can stretch out …"

"No. I gotta go. Gotta go." Jack struggled to his feet. He bumped into the pole lamp beside the chair but caught it before it fell.

"'Scuse me, sir," he said and grinned again. He grabbed the door knob for support and turned back. "I won big, Chris. Really. Don't gif it to me if I'm drunk! I need la'er." Jack held his finger to his lips. "Shhh. I won big. Shhh."

Jack descended the stairs and stepped back out into the night.

23

Mrs. Parker's mac and cheese was the lead item on the cafeteria menu, dictating Chris's choice without him reading the rest of the list. K.J. was already eating his when Chris sat down at the teacher's table.

"Looks like those extra pounds aren't as important as they used to be."

"There are exceptions to every rule."

"What do we do with our projects, boss? I'll be done in a couple days."

"Let me check with Brent. Not sure how that was resolved. It's been back and forth."

"How about yours?"

"Doing a lot of reading. Started the genealogical stuff. You'll get a kick out of this. I've been walking around cemeteries."

"Now this is interesting!" K.J. said, rubbing his hands together. "You know, once there's a body…"

"You've seen too many crime-scene shows, K.J." Libby said, placing her tray on the table. "May I join you?"

"Sure," Chris said without looking up. "Seriously, K.J., I've walked Green Mountain Cemetery and have been reading old copies of the *Freeman* up at GMU."

"You OK?" Libby asked Chris.

"Yeah! Sure! The reporting style is really different from today's news. It's almost sing-song, full of pleasantries."

"Ooh. What am I missing here?" K.J. said, looking back and forth at the two.

Libby broke the brief silence. "I burned the steak!"

"Burned the steak? I don't get it. Oh! Right. Sorry, Libby. I didn't plan on guests.

"Not a problem. We'll do it again, sometime."

Chris glanced toward Libby. She covered me, he thought. He continued describing the *Freeman*'s old format, its advertisements and artistry. He talked about the different styles of grave stones he'd seen at Green Mountain Cemetery and recounted some of the stories he'd discovered reading them. K.J. and Libby seemed drawn under his spell until the crash of some falling dinnerware at a nearby table broke it. Then K.J.'s smart phone announced a text. He glanced at it, then slipped the device back in his pocket.

"Home. Checking up on me."

"What's her name, K.J?" Libby said.

K.J. eyes expanded behind his glasses. "Who?"

"Your wife. Your 'other,' as you say. I still don't know her name."

"Oh! It's Lu." K.J. turned back to Chris. "So, where to now?"

"I'm not sure. Everything in the letter is suspect. My primary source was an alcoholic octogenarian who had me looking in the wrong cemetery."

"Excuse me. I've papers to check before class." K.J. picked up his lunch tray and hurried toward the tray's conveyor belt.

"What's with him?" Libby said.

"What?"

"His wife. He doesn't want to talk about her. I've asked before."

"He's gay, Libby."

"So!"

"He's old school. Comes from one of those families with its own pew in some church. When he came out last summer, they backed off. And worse, Brent found out. Talk about old school. He can be harsh. K.J.'s a very private person. Give him some time."

When K.J. returned for his books, Chris reached into his tote bag and lifted out the thick stack of index cards he'd accumulated, showing them to K.J."

"This is my problem right now. Any ideas?"

K.J. eyed the cards before picking one out and reading it. "Easy. Meet me during 8th period tomorrow. I'll give you some ideas. Got to go," K.J. said and hurried away.

"Easy for him to say."

"Stick with it, Chris," Libby said as she stood. "You looked lost for a while but now it seems like you're headed in the right direction. Enjoy. The race is in the running. Not the finish line."

"This about running, Libby? The journey?"

"Yeah, it is. Everything is."

Chris took one last bite of mac and cheese before placing his utensils on the tray.

***

The answering set's light was flashing when Chris entered his apartment. "This is Mini. I saw the letter. The writer's been in your classroom or knows someone who has. He mentions boring reading assignments, superficial discussions, and stuff like that. Doesn't sound like the Chris I knew. The writer didn't ask for a response, and there was no name or return address. The only clue is the postmark. Colchester. I'm off to the Tri-State conference for a few days. Leave me a message if you need anything else. I'll be checking."

Chris made a peanut-butter-and-jelly sandwich and watched the weather on his big screen while eating. The temperature was rising along with the barometer. After finishing his milk, he grabbed his tote bag and headed out. The library lobby was nearly empty. He walked down the staircase to special collections and stopped at the help desk.

"I'm looking for the Queen City and Weaverton city directories," he said and was directed to the third aisle. The directories, which were more like magazines than books, were arranged by years. Chris checked the bindings for the 1920s and '30s editions and brought them to one of the long work tables. Over the next few hours, he filled out dozens of index cards with notes. Afterward, he sorted them by individual, then by year. The data he'd collected would allow him to follow where each of his relatives had lived and worked through the decades.

After special collections closed, Chris returned to the microfiche readers. The 1st Vermont Cavalry formed during the fall of 1861 so he decided to start looking through the 1861 microfiche. If he wished to follow that unit through the war's duration, he had four years of papers to read, so he began skimming the columns for headlines, hoping to spot relevant information.

He found lots of distractions in the *Freeman*. There were advertisements for businesses in Queen City that Chris had heard of, such as the Howard Opera House, along with contradictory headlines about whether or not Jefferson Davis was dead. He was lucky to have noticed a tiny piece at the bottom of a September issue, which said, "L.B. Platt of Weaverton has been commissioned to a raise cavalry regiment in this state."

He raised his finger to the screen, mouthing the words. More diversion followed. One article announced plans for a strawberries-and-cream festival the following year; another reported the jury selection in the trial of Ryan Cassidy, who'd been accused of stealing Redstone from the Queen Brothers' quarry. Each new edition teased him with potential leads, but he found nothing substantial. It was nearly 11 pm when he noticed an ad for a store named Jewett's announcing, "Men's Calf Brogans for $1." Just below the ad, a byline caught his eye, "Vermont Cavalry Regiment." It noted an announcement by Col. Lemuel B. Platt:

> To my fellow citizens—being directed by the lion, Simon Cameron, Secretary of War, to enlist and organize a regiment of cavalry in the State of Vermont, I shall establish recruiting offices in 10 different localities of the state where I am satisfied a company will immediately enlist…

***

"You won't believe what I'm finding, Catch," Chris told his sister later. "I've found where some of mom's relatives lived and their occupations. I even started following the Civil War in the papers—just like a Queen City resident would have. It's making me wonder about things I'd never cared about. When we were living with Uncle Jonathon and Aunt Harriet, the present was so screwed up, I just wanted to get away from the past. Now, I can't ask enough questions. I feel like I'm on the verge of finding something. It's pretty exciting."

"What are you going to do with it all?"

"I don't know, but there's a lot more out there. I've just begun reading Civil War newspapers, so I'm going to keep looking. Catch, I have to."

"I suppose you do."

***

Chris met K.J. in the teachers' lounge the following afternoon and gave him his index cards. K.J. read through a few of them. "Are these representative of the data you've collected?

"Yeah."

"Then it's simple. All you need is a database!"

"That would make Dr. George pretty happy, but I've never done that."

"This is the perfect application, and I'll make it easier. All you'll have to do is type. Just pretend the PC is an old IBM Selectric. You've got the data. You know how to type. Just enter and hit save."

"I learned all the theory behind computers in school but got bogged down by DOS. Those first programs were so hard to use, I just backed away. By the time the software became friendly, I was over 50 and had lost interest. Heck, Anita still writes my emails and fills out my forms. You sure I can do this?"

"This will be a piece of pie, a slice of heaven," K.J. said, looking at an index card. "Anita can help. The blind see when Anita speaks. She's taught rocks how to use a PC, although, speaking of rocks, Brent still makes her print out his emails and dictates responses for her to type."

"Thanks for the comparison!"

K.J. opened his laptop and began asking questions. By the end of eighth period, he'd designed a basic form, saved it to a file titled LeClairHistory, and printed out a copy of the disc.

Chris returned to his classroom and prepared a quiz for his World Outlook freshmen, then locked his desk, grabbed his tote bag, and left for Anita's office. There was an odor of fresh paint in the hallway, and it became stronger when he entered the central stairway and started down the stairs. On B level landing, he met Barney, the custodian, who was folding up a drop cloth. A brush and a can of institutional beige were nearby. Chris nodded toward the paint. "Problem?"

"Kid stuff. Just kid stuff."

Anita was hanging up the phone when Chris opened the principal's office door.

"Good bye, sheriff. Oh, hi Chris."

"Sheriff?"

"The natives are restless. Did you see the central stairway?"

"Yeah. What's that about?"

"Someone spray painted a big red Z on the wall with flames streaming behind it. I guess Zorro's back for his diploma. But it's got Brent nervous. He has a 'feeling,'" Anita said, raising her fingers in quotes. "So he wants Sheriff Flanagan to discuss ways of discouraging our budding artist. I don't think it'll work. Someone's been painting trolls on the back wall of Municipal Auditorium for months and the sheriff hasn't deterred them a bit. You know, I actually like the big troll under the mushroom. Hope the artist doesn't get caught," she said with an impish smile.

"This is Queen City Academy, Anita! Trolls aren't welcome here."

"I guess. Now, what can I do for you? You look like you're after something."

He showed Anita the disc and told her about his index

cards and the file. She directed him to the chair beside hers, turned her laptop towards him, and began a tutorial. Most points made sense. There were a few constants within the Academy. Anita knew how to run an office and use a PC. Brittany knew how to count change and dress well. Brent didn't know the difference.

"Take my laptop for the weekend and try it yourself. Call me if you get stuck."

"Thanks, Anita. Now, I need one more favor."

"Anything, Chris."

"Take a look at the substitute list. I need to know who covered for me when I was out after Christmas. And who covered when I took my professional day."

"That's easy." Anita said and opened a file on her PC.

She looked up the dates and found the same person listed as substitute each time.

"It was Little Honey!"

"Thanks, Anita," he said, picking up her laptop.

I wonder if she wrote the letter, he thought. If she did, what does she have against me?

Dylan's gaze seemed to scrutinize the laptop Chris carried into the apartment.

"I've got some work to do this weekend."

On Saturday morning, Dylan watched Chris clear the kitchen table and sort through his index cards. He turned on the PC and inserted the disc. He ran into problems immediately and called Anita, who listened as he talked his way through the dilemma.

"That's it. I didn't look under CD drive for the file. Thanks, Anita."

He'd crossed out dozens of cards by the time he quit, but to be safe, he wrapped rubber bands around them and placed them in a shoe box on the bookcase.

After a sandwich, Chris called the diocese to ask for directions to Christopher Gordon's gravesite, but they were closed on weekends and no one answered. The day was warm and buds were trying to pop so he left anyway for Mount Saint Brendan's Cemetery. He rolled down his window, letting all the sweet spring smells fill the car. He turned north at the top of College and followed Pinnacle Street. He tooted his horn as he passed TAC, where some pledges were raking leaves. They waved back. Other than a few people on bicycles, the rest of Hill Section seemed abandoned.

Chris parked outside Mount Saint Brendan's and began walking along the fourth drive at the top of the cemetery. He stopped at nearly every gravestone, but his luck was no better than it had been at Green Mountain Cemetery. After searching for over an hour, he became convinced there was no use looking for Christopher Gordon's grave until the diocese could provide some directions. He returned to his car and drove to Weaverton.

It was midafternoon when he parked outside the Mill office building. The sign said the historical society was in the basement so he followed the arrows to the former machine room. It was filled with mementoes of Weaverton's late-19th and early 20th-century past. He wandered through, looking at old advertisements, photos, trophies, the flotsam of Weaverton's history. In a bookcase near the east wall, he discovered several metal-jacketed photo albums. He thumbed through each one. Pictures of children lined up outside schools were mixed with ball teams and parades. On the backside of one picture, he noticed "F.E. LeClair Clothier, Main Street" written in pencil.

The faded black-and-white framed men in starchy white shirts and wide ties who looked back at the camera from behind a glass display counter filled with belts and handkerchiefs. A rack of double-breasted suits hung behind them. One tall, balding man wore wire-rimmed glasses, a vest, and a hardened stare. A tape measure hung around another man's neck.

There were several picture frames on the wall above the bookcase. One showed an elm-lined park filled with people dressed in summer clothes. Children ate hot dogs, men wore bowlers and a black mutt sat alone near the frame's edge. Another large frame held individual photos in oval cutouts. "Weaverton School Officials 1924" appeared in fanciful script. Above the name Louis LeClair, the stern-faced man from the clothing-store picture wore a straw hat and frosty, dark eyes. Chris tried to see inside his ancestor but couldn't.

***

Jack was flirting with a gray-haired woman in a brown pantsuit when Chris entered The Establishment. Cinco de Mayo was in the air even though remnants of the St. Patrick's Day brouhaha still littered the bar. A torn shamrock was taped to the mirror and a green cardboard leprechaun's hat rested atop a half bottle of Powers.

"Hey, bud. Draft?"

Jack poured a draft as Chris found an empty stool.

"Yeah. You know, I've still got some money of yours."

"'Hold 'em till you need 'em,' is my motto. I don't need 'em yet. Long time no see, history man. What's up?"

"Just little stuff. I've been collecting data, reading old newspapers."

"Sounds exciting!"

"Cut it out. We historians like this stuff. Articles about local politics and city events. Some of it reads more like gossip columns than what we call news. I've found some great articles about the Civil War while looking for tidbits about the Vermont Cavalry. I'm starting to get a real picture of life in Queen City and Weaverton during the 19th and early 20th-century.

"You picked off an interception."

"What?"

"Your momentum's changing. It's nice to see you when you're not complaining."

"Touché," Chris said, raising his glass.

"Sorry, bud," Jack said when he noticed an empty beer glass down the bar. He returned a few minutes later. "The twit?"

"Quiet. I hope he stays that way. I'm trying something

different in that class. I've assigned some outside readings on the Civil War instead of using the text."

"*The Red Badge of Courage*, no doubt. At least in my day."

"Nowadays it's *Killer Angels*. It does real justice to Gettysburg."

"That's a new twist to your repertoire. I liked the movie. Excuse me." Jack hurried off toward his waitress. He came back after mixing two drinks.

"How's the painting? Still working on Split Rock?"

"I can't get the blues right. The water changes every time I go down there. Because of the wind, I guess. It—oh sorry, I'll be back. One of those days."

Chris ordered a second draft, then a burger. The bar kept filling and Jack kept moving, so after finishing his fries, Chris waved to Jack and left cash on the bar. Jack barely noticed. As Chris reached for the door handle, Libby came in.

"Oh, hi."

"Hi," he said, stepping back and feeling awkward.

Then, both of them began speaking at the same time.

"I was just…"

"I was getting bored." She laughed. "And decided to take a walk. Spring is really here. Want to join me?"

In the background, Chris heard the sound of ice crinkling in a glass and rolling around and around followed by a cork popping from a bottle and liquid dropping on to ice.

"Thanks, but I've still got some stuff… "

"I get it, Chris," she said. "You need your space."

"I guess I still do."

Libby walked down the bar to the seat he'd just vacated. As Chris left, he heard her say, "Merlot."

Chris, starting up College Street, noticed a couple up ahead, holding hands and whispering. When the girl laughed softly, he sensed the link between them and wondered whether he'd ever find such a relationship again. Libby was offering him openings, but he wasn't sure of his feelings. There were only so many times she'd understand. Relationships meant risks, and he was closer to taking risks than he'd been in years. But before he dared to venture further with Libby, there were still obstacles to face. He had to prove to himself that he could lead the department. He had to face his past. And then, he had to put it behind him. He crossed to the other side of the street when the Wells Court signpost came into view.

24

The morning air had already warmed to shorts and t-shirts temperature when Chris drove into the lot behind the Academy. He parked, grabbed his tote back, and started for the cafeteria lobby door.

The lobby was empty but for one student, Miss Hasan, who was kneeling outside the girls' lavatory, gathering up books and pencils and binders which lay scattered across the floor. Chris hurried over to help her. As he handed her some pencils, she tried to smile.

"Thank you, Mr. Martin."

"No problem," he said before noticing there were tears on her cheeks. "Everything OK?" She nodded and started to turn away. "What is it? Did someone do this? Did someone say something to you?"

"They don't say anything. They don't have to. But you know you're not welcome." She said before turning and hrrying into the girls' room.

Chris heard laughter down the central artery. At the other end stood Madison Amore, just inside where the artery entered into the main lobby, holding what appeared to be a can of spray paint. She stepped out of sight as Chris approached. When he reached the lobby, he found Madison along with the other cheerleaders looking at a new banner draped from one side of the lobby to the other.

Seniors, it's almost here!
Class Pictures, May 15 — Gown Fitting, May 18 — Prom, May 23
Graduation, June 6!!!!!

"Hi, Mr. Martin. Like our banner?"

"Nice job, ladies."

The girls were all smiles until Chris asked, "Any idea what happened to Miss Hasan?" They looked at each other with blank stares. Madison shook her head but didn't answer.

Chris continued toward the principal's office. "Thanks for letting me use your laptop, Anita."

"Any problems?"

"I didn't set any speed records. Would you copy this and run off a paper copy?" He handed her a disc. "I don't want to lose all my work." Anita agreed then said Brent wanted to see him. "What now?"

"I'm not sure, but he's jittery. He been on the phone with Dr. George since I arrived. Maybe about our budding Rembrandt. He struck again over the weekend. Barney found it and called Brent at home. A flaming E in the third floor hallway near C26. Brent had him repaint the entire wall.

"I thought I smelled paint this morning."

Anita picked up the phone. "Chris is here. Yes, right away."

She nodded toward Brent's door. Chris gave her a high five, knocked, and entered. The principal's hands were already extended across his desk as Chris opened the door. "How are you, Chris?"

As Chris sat in a Cardiff House wingback, he noticed the picture of Brent and Dr. George at the Catamount Invitational lay face down on the bookcase. "Great. What's going on?"

"Oh, same old, same old, buddy," Brent said, fidgeting with the paper weight on his desk. "Fifth hole at Catamount Valley is still soggy; graduation is in sight. But we have some real issues to deal with. Dr. George is playing hard ball these days, and you've probably heard that another letter appeared on the third floor. The purity of the temple is compromised, Chris."

"What?"

"Never mind. Did I mention the commissioner told Dr. George he's satisfied with our response about the anonymous letter complaint?"

"No. When did you hear?"

"Couple of weeks ago."

"You've known for weeks?"

"That's not the point." Brent stood and looked out the window. "The board got wind of it. They want a full-blown presentation on your department's projects before they'll offer you a new contract. It's scheduled the last day of school."

Chris took a deep breath. "OK."

"And Doctor George just got off the phone. He's meeting with Myra Spelling today and wants to know what's going on in the History Department."

"Everything's on track, Brent."

"Details! What about K.J.?"

When Brent raised his voice, Chris retreated into a defensive posture. "I've told you everything. K.J. has done his homework. He's got all the data he needs. IT built a database, and the kids are populating it. It'll be ready any day now."

"Keep an eye on him."

"He does good work."

"That's not the point. We have to watch his kind."

"What? Brent, he's a real asset…"

"Never mind. What about the others?"

Chris told Brent that Libby had contacted historians around New England for more insight into their work. One even volunteered to visit the Academy and speak. He mentioned Honora's course on dietary requirements for school-lunch programs when Brent interrupted.

"I know. I know. What about you?"

"I'm putting the finishing touches on my demography unit. Still doing some family research to familiarize myself with other resources, but I don't need that now."

"What did you find out about your Civil War hero? It's important."

"Hero?"

"Yes, your relative. You said he fought with General Custer's cavalry at Gettysburg and Cedar Woods."

"Cedar Creek!"

"Whatever. When I told Regan Andover, he got really excited. He's written papers on the Vermont Cavalry but said he'd never heard of this guy Gordon."

"I don't know if he was a hero or a goat, for that matter. All I know is he was in the Vermont Cavalry at some point."

"Well you'd better dig up something. Dr. George and Regan Andover are expecting it."

"That's not the way it works, Brent. I can't just make stuff up.

"You'd better find something! You see where I'm going here, Chris! You see where I'm going?"

"I didn't tell them anything about heroes."

"This is about playing ball with the team, Chris. And while we're talking about Regan, his kid's been complaining about you again. He told his old man you insulted him in front of everyone in class."

"The little shit didn't do his assignment. All I said was 'anyone who didn't complete their assignments would get a lower grade.' That's an insult? Those are the rules. Besides, he's been insulting every one of his teachers since he was waitlisted at Dartmouth. "

"Doesn't matter, Chris. Play ball or everything evaporates. If I screw up, you cover. If you screw up, I cover. That's how it works. I can't recommend anyone who doesn't run with the Gipper. Now find a hero!"

"I'll keep looking for facts, Brent, but I'm not promising anything but facts."

Brent's hands-free intercom went off.

"Brent!"

"Yes Anita."

"Sheriff Flannigan is on line two."

"Thanks. And, Anita, I'll be in conference after the call." Brent said while dismissing Chris with a sweep of his hand and punching line two.

"Yes, sheriff. I was just thinking about you, old buddy. We have to get...excuse me a second." Brent covered the mouthpiece.

"Find a hero!" he said before removing his hand. "Now, sheriff, about this painting issue. This is the second instance. What do you think we should…"

Anita looked up at Chris as he closed Brent's door behind him. "You OK?"

"You know how he is."

Anita started to hand Chris the lottery list from the *Freeman* but Chris raised his hand.

"I didn't buy a ticket."

"What?"

"Never mind," Chris said, reaching for the door knob.

Anita looked confused but refocused when the door swung open and Brittany Newport walked in carrying a stack of requisitions.

"Hi, sugar," Brittany said, walking past Chris. "Anita, is Brent free?"

Chris walked to the teacher's lounge and headed for the hot water and tea bags. After refilling his mug, he returned to C level, where a faint smell of paint still lingered. The morning flew by with the promise of sloppy Joes for lunch. Libby never showed, but while they ate, Chris told K.J. he was apprehensive about how his seniors would respond to his new approach to the Civil War. He said they seemed to like *The Killer Angels*, but it wasn't finished yet.

As soon as the mechanical horn sounded the end of seventh period, Chris started to the principal's office to pick up the things Anita was copying. Passing the teachers' lounge, Honora Webster charged out the door, nearly barreling him over. He stepped back.

"Hi, Honora."

Her head snapped away as if Chris weren't even there. In the past, he'd justify such behavior, thinking she meant no harm or her parents hadn't spent enough time on manners, but this time he felt as if some moron driver had just cut him off in traffic. "Honora, we need to talk." He said, pointing toward the conference room.

"I've got things to do."

"Now!"

"What is it?" Her head tilting backward, which made her look as if she were staring down from a pedestal.

"Now!"

She strutted into the conference room with Chris right behind. He slammed the door so hard Chris worried he'd broken the latch.

Honora's face stiffened and her spine arched. "Well?"

"I learned something interesting, Honora. It seems a complaint was lodged against me with the Education Department." Honora's eyes widened and she glanced toward the door. "Yeah. They received it shortly after your niece, Little Honey, substituted for me. Isn't that strange?" Honora inhaled. Chris placed his hands on the conference table and leaned forward. "That person also thinks I'm not qualified to be chairman of the History Department. My teaching methods are in dispute, too. Do you happen to know anything about that?"

Honora shook her head just as a red blush appeared at her turtleneck and began climbing her neck. Her eyes darted from door to window.

"The postmark on the letter was from Colchester. Isn't that where Little Honey lives?" Honora nodded. "What are the chances of someone living in Colchester knowing about my classroom and registering a complaint?" The maroon tint hit Honora's chin and moved toward her ears like a lava flow on Krakatoa. "But that's not what I wanted to talk to you about."

Honora began to exhale.

"I wanted to let you know, in case you talk with anyone from Colchester who asks, I have a double certification. High school history and administration." Chris said, now beginning to smile. "A few years ago, Walt and I took the concentrated Admin./Certification program up at GMU. Twenty credits. He was hesitant about accepting the department chairmanship—after I turned it down—so I promised to take all the courses with him if he took the job. It was kind of fun to study with him again, just like we did in college. Did you know I took those courses, Honora?"

She shook her head but it looked more robotic than real. "Now, I've got some things to do. Any questions?"

"No" formed on her lips though there wasn't a sound.

He gestured toward the door. As she reached for the knob, he said, "Say hi to Little Honey for me."

Honora started to cry. She sobbed so hard Chris felt he had to do something, so he offered his handkerchief. She took it and wiped her eyes. She appeared to recover, though her shoulders still rose and fell in spasms. "I'd do anything for her, Chris. Anything! You know how it is. It wasn't easy to help with those boys. I watched you. After Little Honey's parents…oh never mind. You acted like you were on your way out, thinking of leaving. I just thought I'd help you decide. But it was wrong. I'm, I'm… sorry." Her words faded into a whisper. Chris waited for a moment after Honora left and breathed in his small victory. She was a proud woman, and he imagined how difficult it must have been for her to apologize. But he'd done nothing to deserve her treachery. He'd merely accepted what the contract offered, carrying on where his friend had left off. Further, he knew he'd have to remain vigilant, not knowing what else he'd have to face.

That evening Chris returned to the fiche readers in the GMU library, where he read articles from the spring and summer of 1862. He followed the First Vermont's movements from a graveyard near Annapolis, MD, into the Shenandoah Valley where they camped near Harper's Ferry. The cavalry clashed with the Confederates at Mt. Jackson, where the Rebels made a stand. Other articles reported movements by an 80,000-man Confederate force under General Stonewall Jackson moving toward Sharpsburg. When lists of the wounded began trickling into the paper after the Battle of Antietam, Chris searched for Christopher Gordon's name. Nothing. He continued until, on the next page, he came across a printed roster of the First Vermont Cavalry listing Christopher Gordon as a member of Company A.

He felt a smile growing inside himself at his discovery, but when he looked around to tell someone what he'd found, he discovered a room full of strangers: people who didn't care, people doing their own thing. Their faces bore the same expressions his students wore. They told him he'd been failing them, that he hadn't presented ideas in ways that would challenge or excite them. He knew he hadn't done enough, hadn't taken advantage of their learning styles or even bothered to tell them the back stories of history—the human stories Uncle Jonathon used to tell about people like Colonel Jackson sitting on their front porches, or Calvin Coolidge riding in a bootlegger's car. Or Mick Finnigan knowing all the bootleggers. Those were the things that made Chris first love history. What did he love now? What excited him? What could he do to inspire others once again?

He leaned back from the screen and remembered that when he first fell in love with history, there were drumbeats pounding deep inside his chest.

It happened during the early 1950s. He had been riding in the back seat of Aunt Harriet's red Dodge Wayfarer and, as he'd watched Addison County's green waist-high corn speed past, his sister was reading *A Tree Grows in Brooklyn*. Up in front, Uncle Jonathon had been rambling on about Sir Jeffrey Amherst and Roger's Rangers while Aunt Harriet fingered her rosary, silent lips moving, eyes closed, beads of sweat dotting her forehead.

As the Dodge climbed the Champlain Bridge, Chris had leaned forward and grasped the front seat. Far below, intense blue waters. Ahead, emerald mountains.

"There it is! Crown Point," Uncle Jonathon said.

The fortress's gray stone chimneys loomed beyond the dusty parking lot. Faint drumbeats rode the breeze. Uncle Jonathon loosened his tie, rolled his white sleeves up, locked the car, and stepped off. "Hurry!"

As Aunt Harriet pulled Chris forward, the walls rose higher and higher and the drum beats became clear. He ran to keep up but everyone had longer legs. Then, standing at the edge of a crowd, half hidden behind Uncle Jonathon's leg, shaking, he'd seen men in tri-cornered hats, white gaiters, and long blue coats march into view. A fife played and an electric chill climbed his spine. The marchers stepped closer. The drum beat louder. He felt his hair stand on end. He could hardly breathe. He'd squeezed Aunt Harriet's hand and the drumbeats rattled deep inside his soul.

If only he could make his students feel the drumbeats.

25

The long evenings at the library were taking their toll on Chris. His energy levels seemed to drop especially later in the day. He was also sweating more than usual and his eyes were constantly red, so he tried to counteract his fatigue by taking short naps before returning to the library. The increased chatter during seventh period told him some of his seniors noticed his lack of energy but seemed to misinterpret what they were seeing. He heard whispers mentioning bloodshot eyes and REM sleep. Looming graduation, warming weather, and senior privileges must have been contributing factors to their misunderstanding. No one cared much or questioned. They had finished reading *The Killer Angels* and expected a quiz, so they were more attentive than usual as Chris took his coffee mug from the desk and swirled the cold decaf. T.D. winked at Michael. Madison wiggled her tissue after sitting back down.

"Today we're going to conclude our discussion of Mr. Shaara's book, *The Killer Angels*."

The students reached for their copies but Chris raised his hand. "Put those away! Let's just talk about what we've read."

The students looked at each other as Chris walked to the board. He drew what appeared to be a backwards question mark then added a sunburst of lines above it.

"This is a rough drawing of the battle lines in the Gettysburg area," he said in a slow monotone.

"Very rough," Michael whispered to T.D.

Chris smiled at the remark. "These are the roads. Here is the center of town. Cemetery Ridge, the Round Tops are here." He drew an X at each of the different places he'd mentioned.

"Make sense?"

A few students shook their heads.

"Let's talk about the first day. The Confederates met

by the Union Cavalry here. Who was their commander?"

A few hands went up. Most faces were blank. T.D.'s elbow went down on the desk and he planted is chin on it.

"Miss Amore."

"General Buford."

"That's correct, Miss Amore," Chris said while noticing more inattentiveness than usual. He glanced out at the lake, wondering how he could make this better. Then he was inspired.

"Instead of a quiz, we're going to review the entire book," Chris said, looking at his watch, "in the next 30 minutes. If we do it, no reading assignments for a week. Miss Amore, keep time."

His students began looking at each other as if they were in the wrong classes. One rolled her eyes. Another shook his head.

"Why were the Confederates in Gettysburg? Quickly! Quickly!" A hand shot up. Chris pointed.

"A road junction."

"That's one answer. What happened here? McPherson's Woods." Chris drew another x and pointed to Mr. Chopras.

"Reynolds was killed."

He asked another question. Another x appeared. He wrote names, asked questions. Hands rose, slow at first, then faster. Did he have their attention? "Why was Howard's move to the cemetery important?"

"It stopped the ..." the student began.

"Was he a hero? By the way, what do you think a hero is?"

Another hand rose.

"What do you think about 'Baldy' Ewell's decision?"

Chris rode a storm of questions. Energy filled his voice. "How would you have reacted? Why do you think?" Hands that had been tentative all year sprang up. They rose and rose and rose again. His pace increased until he was peppering students. Eyes lit up. Smiles appeared.

"What was he trying? What would you? How do you

think he felt?" Chris loosened his tie. His blazer came off. He pulled names, places, terms, and concepts from the depths of the story. The list on the board grew. Buford, Seminary Ridge, Howard, railroad cut, drunkenness, lines of communications, McPherson's barn, Longstreet, Peach Orchard, Cemetery Ridge, "practicable," Pickett, and others.

"Do you agree, Miss Hasan? Why?"

The board became a puzzle of lines and phrases as Chris filled in areas at the top and bottom and sides. Circles and arrows appeared everywhere.

"What happened here? And here?"

Students shook their heads. Eyes questioned. Hands rose. Chris erased the board and redrew the map.

"Let's talk about the spy." And he began asking new questions.

New names and circles appeared. The speed intensified. More discussion followed. New questions posed. Chris walked. Heads turned. During the half hour, Chris circled the room and the three-day battle, zeroing in on what the students thought the book was telling them.

The discussion ended as abruptly as it had commenced when Miss Amore said, "Time's up!" Chris walked to the window and looked past Municipal Auditorium toward Rensselaer Island. He took breaths like a runner at the end of a sprint.

"I guess we did it. No home work for a week and I think you understand the material. Any questions before we wrap up?" A single hand shot up. "Yes, Mr. Andover."

"Mr. Martin, I don't get it. Vermonters make so much of Gettysburg, yet the book doesn't even mention them. I guess they fought there, everybody did. But their role must have been minimal. They weren't at the Round Tops or Picket's Charge. It looks like the units from Maine, Texas, Alabama, Pennsylvania, and Virginia did the fighting. What's that all about?"

"Good question, Mr. Andover. Let's pursue it. Where did you get your information?" Michael held up the book.

"Any other sources?" Michael shook his head. Chris inhaled. Michael appeared to inflate. "Well, Mr. Andover, and any of you who may have based your opinions solely on *Killer Angels*, I applaud your efforts, but a lot more people were involved than just Chamberlain's Maine troops or Pickett's Virginians. The book doesn't mention places like Spangler's Spring, East Calvary Field or the area between the Angle and the Peach Orchard. This is one of the most studied events in our history. There was infinitely more action than Mr. Shaara's book portrayed. The author told an informative tale; the battle scenes provide some great detail. That's the reason we use it. But all that—and all the other books and movies—only provide glimpses into what happened. Your text book has five paragraphs on Gettysburg. *Killer Angels* has 345 pages. But it's almost impossible to tell the story of 160,000 men from Vermont, Virginia, and Texas who fought for three days across the farm country of Pennsylvania in a battle that determined the history of this country. There's so much more. Mr. Andover, you once said there was more to history than barrels of pork and supply lines."

Michael nodded and clasped his hands behind his head.

"Well, you were right. Just look around Queen City or take a drive through small towns in Vermont." Chris walked to the window. He pointed up Main Street. "There's a house up on the next corner. It's a fraternity house now, FIJI, but it once belonged to Gen. William Wells. He won the Medal of Honor at Gettysburg for rallying his men near Little Round Top. That's not in the book, but some Vermonters still tell how his son-in-law, Col. H. Nelson Jackson, was so moved by Well's courage, he raised money to build a statue of Wells at Gettysburg. My Uncle Jonathon delivered the paper to Col. Jackson. So many people contributed that Jackson bought two statues. One's at Gettysburg and the other sits in Bluff Park near Benny's French Fry Bus. Did you know that, Mr. Andover?"

"No sir."

"Mr. Glover?" T.D. Glover shook his head and lowered his eyes.

"A block further up Main Street hill on Summit is where General O.O. Howard lived after the War. Howard rallied his men on Cemetery Hill and prevented a Union defeat on the first day. That rally may have saved the Union. When Howard died, so many people came to his funeral the cortege stretched a mile between the church and Lakeview Cemetery. Did anyone know that?"

No hands rose. A few heads shook. Chris paced back and forth, his hands on his hips.

"General George Stannard lived in the Old North End. His Vermont units are credited with decimating General Pickett's charge. He ordered a flank attack that altered history." Chris picked up his copy of *The Killer Angels*. "But all the book says about Stannard's Vermonters is this." Chris flipped through his copy. "'General Armistead saw a long line of Union boys in blue, firing from the right.'"

Chris looked out the window. He lowered his voice. "Stannard came home after the war without an arm and became collector of customs. His wife fell and became a cripple. Stannard made some mistakes and lost his job. The man whose decision stopped Pickett's charge couldn't even take care of his crippled wife! Sounds like today's soldiers, doesn't it? Out of work, unable to care for their families. Some of Stannard's old friends heard about it and found him a job as doorman at the House of Representatives in Washington. That wasn't in *Killer Angels* either." Chris walked back to the front of the room. "The majority of those who fought at Gettysburg were ordinary men, not the kind of people text books or novels are written about. Many were just boys. Some were your ages. The First Vermont Cavalry trained over near Bluff's Park. Some were immigrants. Irish and French boys who came down from Canada for a better life. Their ideals were true and their blood was all the same color. They had snowball fights at night after drill, and they ate a big Turkey dinner on Thanksgiving. A thousand of them practiced riding in formation right outside the Academy on Main Street hill. When the time came, they rode their horses down to the station by the lake and boarded trains for Virginia. Many of them never came home. Their names filled our newspapers and cemeteries. If you look hard enough, plenty of reminders of that war remain. There's a monument in City Hall Park, statues in Milton and Brandon listing the casualties. If you stop and read the names, you wonder how communities so small could survive after losing so many.

Walk through Green Mountain or Mount Saint Brendan's cemeteries sometime and read the stones. You'll find lots of names and places not listed in any of your textbooks. That war left an indelible mark on our collective memory, a memory with deep scars and slow healing wounds." Chris's voice lowered again. "The scars still exist. Some wounds never heal. That's why textbooks talk about barrels of pork and lines of communication. It's a lot easier."

The metallic horn snapped everyone back into the school day. But, as the seniors gathered their belongings and started for the hallway, there was a church-like silence, making Chris think of monks walking to vespers. He put his blazer on and began tightening his tie, wondering what his seniors were thinking, when Mr. Chopras turned and gave him a thumbs up. For the first time that year, Chris felt at home in class and thought he could see the finish line in his long run. He felt himself smile as he picked up his tote bag.

After dismissal, Chris took a short nap and returned to the library. All the fiche readers were in use, so he graded quizzes for his European Traditions class in one of the empty cubicles. After waiting another hour for a reader to free up, he called it quits and left for a burger and a beer.

His mailbox at Wells Court was full. He grabbed his mail and climbed the stairs. Dylan watched him carry the mail to the kitchen table: clothing catalogues, an electric bill, a large envelope from Claudia Nichols, and an envelope from the GMU reunion committee. Chris slipped it into his pocket, turned out the lights, and walked down

College St. toward The Establishment.

The street was filled with runners practicing running hills in preparation for the coming marathon. The warm evening weather was perfect for training.

Jack, mixing drinks at the far end of the bar, drew a draft when he saw Chris arrive and carried it over in a mock ceremonial manner. "Haven't seen you much. You still be hiding out in the library looking for important relatives? I mean, they're all important. We history zealots joke about shit like that. Found any ghosts from your mysterious past?"

Chris took a sip and tipped his glass. "Did I tell you my grandfather and his brothers were community leaders in Weaverton? Bigwigs."

"In Weaverton? Sounds like an oxymoron."

"Yeah, Weaverton's had its ups and downs but…"

"Pillars of society. Salt of the earth. Roses among thorns."

Chris raised his hand. "You're hopeless, Jack."

"I hope so." He said, wiping some spills off the bar.

"Big weekend coming up!"

"What?"

"Memorial Day. The marathon."

"Oh, yeah. That's when the town fills up with yahoos who sip daiquiris on Center Street and criticize how much the marathoners sweat."

Chris reached into his pocket for the reunion packet and tossed it on the bar. "I received this today. It's the reunion schedule for Memorial Day weekend."

Jack glanced at the information then slid it back across the bar. "You keep forgetting. I didn't really go to GMU. I was just a social member of the fraternity. You might say, very social!"

"You were there as much as I."

"But I didn't pay. I just sat in on what I liked. You aren't going, are you?" Jack said pointing at the schedule.

"I've been thinking about it. "

"Don't! I went to one of my high school reunions. Big

mistake."

"You never told me that."

"You were busy with your sister's kids, Little League or something. We were the Big Blues of Port Huron High! The Big Blues. Division champs. I'd played linebacker, class officer, acted in the class play, dated a cheerleader—did all the stuff you're supposed to. Well, I was about 40 and suffering from remorse and thought I'd go back and parade around with the rest of the big cheese, but it kind of let me down.

"You're kidding."

"I met all the old yahoos, even danced with my old girlfriend to our favorite Brenda Lee songs. Most everyone's faces were reasonable facsimiles of what I remembered but everything was different. It wasn't just that we were older and overweight." Chris smiled. "Everyone wore nice clothes and some had accomplished stuff—like inheriting the family business or stealing lots of money on Wall Street. Some had even become successful." Chris laughed. "But they weren't the way they were, Chris. They weren't… pure anymore."

"Pure?"

"Yeah, everybody was trying to act like they had acted, but that can only really happen once. During that perfect time when everything's new. Once it's gone, trying to relive it always comes out wrong. Everything's distorted."

"It had been a long time, Jack. Maybe people found it difficult to converse."

"That wasn't it. The spontaneity was gone. The excitement was gone. People said shit like, 'Remember the championship game? We really creamed those Huskies, didn't we?' Trying to make it some earth shattering event. Like it was unique to the world. But it wasn't. Somebody wins and somebody loses. It's all just chance. We weren't special. We just thought we were because it was our first time. Anyway, I started feeling a little hollow. I don't know how to explain it. Nobody wanted to go beyond the past. Nobody wanted to say, I hope you're having a nice life, or I loved you, or I hated you, or I'm sorry I never got to know you. I'd moved so far away from Port Huron that I just couldn't reconnect. Hell, I'd lived in Europe by the time I was 19, and most of those bozos hadn't moved outside their zip code. The high point, you might say, came after my old football buddy asked me what I'd been up to. I actually thought about answering him for a second but most of my life has been pretty painful, so telling some clown in a Gucci jacket that after school I ran away from an abusive, alcoholic father, became a drunk myself, had a couple failed marriages, and had liens on everything I'd ever owned didn't really strike me as meaningful small talk, so I excused myself to go to the rest room and walked out of the hotel."

Chris waited.

"I felt a little better. I bought a six pack and drove over to the old football field. After I downed the beers, I pissed all over the bench just like I did the night we beat the Huskies in the championship game. My advice? Skip the reunion and save yourself some aggravation 'cause nobody's pure anymore. Better to return to the site of your victories than the site of your defeats." Jack looked up and down the bar for customers.

"Well, some of the guys from the house may show up at the reunion, and I was hoping to run into Susan Boisvert."

"What?"

"Yeah. I been thinking about her since I first learned about the reunion. It would be nice to see her…"

"Wait a minute. Something wrong here. Have you been reading Peter Pan up at the library? You're talking about never, never, Neverland now."

"It was just a misunderstanding, Jack. A lot was going on. I should've just sat down with her years ago and talked it all out, but that wasn't the way I'd been raised. If I had…"

Jack's face reddened and he gritted his teeth. "Doofus! You're the history man! Didn't you learn anything? If you don't, you'll do the same stupid shit over and over until you go crazy. " Jack walked down the bar and spoke to a young couple in a loud voice. He mixed two Bloody Marys then banged them down before the couple.

Chris reread the postcard. Yes, Susan Boisvert had walked away, bruised him, but that was long ago and he and Jack didn't always look at things the same way.

Jack pulled drafts for two new customers before walking back. "So, history man, are you serious about going?"

"Yeah, I think so."

"I still don't get it. You're always looking backwards."

"What do you mean?"

"The whole family research thing. It's as if you're trying to reclaim something you never had. And now Susan. Hell, even a dummy on a gallows knows something's wrong if his hands are tied behind him and he's wearing a blindfold. Reality check, Chris. Uncle and auntie are gone. Mommy and daddy are gone. The girl walked out on you over 40 years ago. And you're thinking, if only! You can't restart the past. Understand it, then kiss it goodbye."

"I didn't do anything. I just shut my mouth like Aunt Harriet taught me. If …"

"All these ifs," Jack said. "I'm sick of asking you about every new sack cloth you wear 'cause they're all the same. Every week you've got another booboo. The church is wrong, the principal's wrong, some student is out to get you. You're always making me feel guilty about something. You used to smile once in a while. You were on your toes. You used to have some fun, but now things fester inside you. You're always second guessing. Poor me, poor me. And to make matters worse, you want to go backwards."

Chris felt Jack's anger infect him. "How am I so bad off? You're brilliant but can't hold a decent job. You play bartender, fisherman—who knows what—and all you have to show is a dumpy apartment and a bunch of unfinished paintings. You babble about fishing or running away to paint. How real is that?"

"I'll tell you this, Chris. I may not have much, but I've still got a dream. That's better than being trapped in yesterday, history man!"

Chris chugged the rest of his beer, pounded the empty down, and threw a $10 on the bar.

"Doofus!" he heard as he was leaving.

Chris walked a roundabout route back to Wells Court, letting the spring evening gradually cool his boiling temper, but it flared back up after he returned to his apartment and listened to his answering set.

"Hey, Doofus. Put my money in an envelope and mail it to me. And I'm not drunk."

26

Did Dylan just blink, Chris wondered as he walked past the poster, or was it just a long day's imaginings? After nodding back at the young musician, he found in the fridge a half bowl of Catch's mac and cheese, which he popped it into the microwave. And while the timer ticked down, he looked through the mail that had accumulated on the table. The bills didn't temp him. He noticed the envelope from Claudia Nichols just as the timer went off. After setting the mac and cheese aside to cool, he returned to the brown envelope. A handwritten note was inside along with another smaller brown envelope.

"Chris, these just arrived. Also, have you looked at General Well's papers in special collections? Hope this helps! Claudia"

The smaller envelope's return address said National Archives Trust Fund Board, Washington, D.C. A number of photocopied pages were inside. Several were Company Muster Rolls. The handwritten data told Chris that Gordon, Christopher was mustered in to the First Vermont on November 19, 1861 for a three-year term as a saddler. His horse was valued at $112 and his equipment at $31.63. The cursive handwriting reminded Chris of Uncle Jonathon's Palmer script: flowing, curvy, bold. Two other sheets provided information Chris had hoped to find. He studied them as he ate the hot mac and cheese, then reached for the phone to thank Claudia but decided against it when he noticed the time. Instead, he dialed Catch. Her phone rang five times before she answered, sounding sleepy.

"Hi, Chris. I guess I was asleep."

"I shouldn't have called."

"No, never think that. What's going on? Did the Diocese give you directions to the graves?"

"Yes. The archivist said the LeClair lots were in the center near where the gazebo used to be."

"Gazebo? I don't remember that."

"It's been gone for years. When Logan Cassidy and I mowed lawns, he'd hide out from Mick Finnigan there. It was run down, covered with vines, but the ceiling looked brand new. Tongue-and-groove boards. Funny, makes me think of Cookie LaFromboise."

"Cookie who?"

"LaFromboise. This little French kid who lived near Uncle Jonathon's. We walked up to the gazebo one night. The guys always said she was 'snuggle friendly but huggle empty.'"

"What's that mean?"

"I'm not sure, but Cookie was a tease. She was always leading somebody on. She'd rub up against you or put her arm around your waist, then look up and close her eyes but she'd pull away and act surprised if you tried to kiss her. I won't tell any tales 'cause she's probably somebody's grandmother now. But before we left that gazebo, I carved my initials in the ceiling."

"Chris!"

"Sorry, that's not why I called. I found the LeClair stones all together near where the gazebo was. And all the things in Uncle Jonathon's letter are there."

"Amazing!"

"That's not all. The wording and dates on the stones looked familiar, so I compared them to the letter. He copied it right off the stones. When you asked him for information, I bet he drove over to the cemetery and just copied everything he saw down."

"What about Christopher Gordon?"

"I couldn't find him. The archivist said he was buried further to the south, but there'd been a water problem at the archives years ago. The maps were damaged. He gave me the section and plot number but couldn't tell where it was. Said I could look at the maps if I wanted to. I walked around for a while but couldn't find it."

"You've put so much time in this."

"There's something else, Catch. I went over to Saint

Brendan's Church."

"Uncle Jonathon and Aunt Harriet brought us to church there."

"I thought something about it was familiar."

"It's so pretty. I love the white marble."

"But it was kind of creepy. The only light came through the stained glass windows. Made everything look distorted. The dark paneling made it feel haunted. "

"I remember the big windows behind the altar. When the sun shined, you could see dust particles floating in the air. I thought it was pixie dust.

"And…"

"What?"

"I remembered the coffins! And all the firemen!"

"Chris! Are you OK?"

"Yeah. When the priest turned on the lights, I saw how beautiful it really is. The wainscoting needs to be touched up and the floors are mess, but it's still beautiful."

"Weaverton has always struggled. How did you feel?"

"I don't know. Like a dream, I guess. I remembered during the funeral looking up at the big trusses stenciled with gold and red and green designs. I remembered the singing. It was in Latin, like the chanting in monasteries."

"You sure you're OK?"

"Yeah. I'm sure. Before Mass, I walked around and found these tiny plaques under the windows engraved with names of people who'd donated the money to build the church. There are plaques listing Grandpa LeClair and his brothers. Do you remember those?"

"No, but it doesn't surprise me."

"I felt more comfortable there than I have in a long time. Even the homily! And all the priest said was to set your mind on the kingdom and everything else will take care of itself. Don't worry about what to eat or drink or wear. Everything will take care of itself. After, this little choir sang about the moon and stars. It was so peaceful."

"I'm so glad for you."

"I even thought about carving my initials in the bench."

"Chris!"

"Sis, I need some sleep."

"Me, too. Good night, Chris."

Chris then reread Uncle Jonathon's letter and the documents from Claudia. He wondered if he had overlooked something that might tell him more about Christopher Gordon. He skimmed through the names and dates until noticing Black Rock, Quebec again. Still a mystery. His great-grandmother Catherine Cecelia Gordon LeClair had been born and then had died there. The letter from the National Archives said Christopher Gordon came from Black Rock, Quebec, too.

Chris closed his eyes and wondered what stories Black Rock could tell if there were only time.

***

The following morning, Chris heard Honora's booming voice as he approached the teacher's lounge.

"...sandwiched between them. Little Honey can't find enough substitute work, and I certainly can't just kick Uncle Harry out. He's nearly 90. I'll probably have to work forever. Little Honey and I talked about opening a little catering business."

When Honora noticed Chris walking toward the hot-water pot, her voice dropped off and her face became porcelain. She picked up her books and went out into the lobby. K.J. was pouring Libby a cup of coffee as Chris walked over. "What's up?" he said.

"Let's see. The latest rumor is that graduation is going to be outside. It seems the Queen Brothers used to do it, so you know Brent. And Anita told me the malicious marker struck again. It's scary to think, but there's actually a student at the Academy who can write without a keyboard. Unfortunately, he's slow. Only one letter at a time."

"What was it?"

"O! O as in orange." K.J. said before singing the Mr. Rogers's theme song "It's a wonderful day..."

"K.J.! Be serious. Where was it?" Libby said.

"In the central artery. Serious?"

"Brent must be pissed," Chris said.

"He is. Anita said he called the sheriff again. They've been working on some sort of contingency plan, but how serious can it be? The letters spell ZOE. Sounds like someone's kitten."

Libby shook her finger at the gawky teacher.

"My bad. Mea culpa," K.J. said, pretending to pound his chest. "Time to go."

"Wait a second, K.J.!"

"What?"

"I'm having a devil of a time finding where my relatives came from. Black Rock, Quebec doesn't show up anywhere. I've looked through every map and geographical reference book at GMU. Any ideas?"

"Google it! You'll find something."

"I'm a textbook guy."

"I'll write some search ideas and leave them in your mailbox. The next time you use Anita's laptop, bring it over to your kitchen window. There are so many students in your neighborhood there's bound to be a Wi-Fi you can tap into. I'll write some ideas on guessing passwords, too."

"Thanks. And I'm going to need some help with Power Point."

"Power Point?"

"I've got an idea."

"Sure. We'll talk later."

As K.J. and Libby started for the door, Libby looked back over her shoulder and smiled. Chris had a feeling he was headed in the right direction and Libby's smile seemed to back him up.

***

During eighth period, Chris sat in the teachers' lounge and reviewed his to-do list. He added "Google Black Rock" under "call Mini; Gen. Wells; Papers; Recert Presentation:

and review exams." An hour later, he crossed off "review exams" from the list.

After everyone had left the lounge for the day, Chris used the conference room to call Mini. He thanked her for all her help and asked, "Can I ask you something else?"

"Sure. Go ahead."

"I have to give a presentation to the board about my department's projects. What advice would you give me?"

"First, I'd be really prepared. Dr. George loves charts and graphs. Next, I'd surprise them."

"I've been thinking about that myself and I've got a couple of ideas."

"Take charge right away, Chris. Don't let them push you around. I hear your board chairman's a bear."

They talked for over an hour before Chris walked out to his car.

The crocuses and tulips stood at attention outside General Well's former home, where some FIJI brothers were now sunbathing on its porch. The gardens of the other gilded-age mansions along Wilson Ave. were nearly as vibrant, most wrapped in warm blankets of red mulch. Students in shorts and t-shirts strolled the sidewalks. Others scooted down College on their skateboards as Chris waited for the College Street light to change.

He drove north to Archer Street, turned, and pulled off on to the grass outside Mount Saint Brendan's Cemetery. He reread the archivist's information before walking along the south fence. He passed familiar stones. McMahon, Casey, Shea, builders and bootleggers, the poor and the rich, from Cork and Cavan, Quebec and St. Jean. They blended together like old neighbors. Arms and legs mixed in old New England dirt formed fertile ground. Some graves stood tall and straight; others were forlorn, leaning, and broken. There were forgotten names and numbers, children without families, soldiers from the Wilderness, El Alamein, the Somme, the Thresher, and Cedar Creek. Born in 1846, 1823, 18-whatever. They came on the good ship Washington. He'd seen most before but one old soldier remained missing.

Beads of sweat dripped from his forehead. He loosened his tie and rolled his sleeves like some politician running for office.

The young leaves formed shadows that hadn't existed a week before. The grass crushed soft beneath his steps. Geraniums. Geraniums. Geraniums were everywhere. Bright red flowers with velvet green leaves decorated the gravestones like torches in the night. The plants added so much color that Chris nearly overlooked the tiny flags marking scattered stones. Veterans had placed the flags in honor of Memorial Day. That's why there were geraniums!

He paced looking, reading, searching, hoping. He slowed in the warmth, then stopped to sit on a granite bench with MILLER chiseled deep into its granite. A tiny ceramic angel rested on one end. He wished he'd remembered a water bottle, then wondered whether some child was buried there or if the cherub was a private thought between death-separated lovers. He breathed in the silence and the green.

A car horn sounded on Archer Street when a mangy Old North End dog dashed from a driveway across the street. When the dog disappeared back into the yard, Chris's gaze fell upon still another veteran's flag near the fence. It stood at attention before a cube-like stone. That stone, waist high, stood between two trees. He couldn't remember seeing it before. Perhaps the light had been wrong. Perhaps the shadows. He stood. He walked closer.

A crucifix was chiseled into the top of the squat monument. He couldn't decipher its words, though it appeared to have an engraved semicircle of letters. He stepped back and tilted his head. Damn leaves. Damn shadows. Something was written, but lichens smudged the letters. He got down on his knees and, using his handkerchief, began wiping 100 years of detritus away. Letters appeared. Christopher P. Gordon they said. Chris stood up and smiled.

"There you are, you old bastard. That's where you've been hiding."

His smile grew into a laugh. He was delighted at the discovery — as a child who'd found a coin or recognized an old friend. Chris ducked his head and bit back the laughter. No talking in church, he thought. Not seeing anyone, he began laughing again.

He circled the stone, chest puffed like a child with a secret. He had to share his excitement. A celebration was in order, so he hurried to his car.

He drove across Center Street on the way down College. The outside tables were filled with sun worshippers sipping their little umbrella drinks. Summer had informally arrived. He drove a block further before finding a parking spot outside The Establishment. Only a few patrons were inside when he sat down at the bar.

"What will you have?" A bartender said.

"A draft. Is Jack working today?"

"No. Sorry."

"Oh. When'll he be in?"

"Can't say."

"He's a friend of mine and …"

"You Chris?"

"Yeah. Why?"

"He said you might be by. He left something for you." The young man went into the back room and returned with a long flat package wrapped in a brown paper bag. He also carried Jack's old leather jacket and an envelope. CHRIS was printed across it. "Here you go."

Chris tore the envelope open and read the lines scribbled on a half sheet of paper.

I hate saying goodbye so I won't.

Alaska won't wait forever. I plan to stop in Port Huron and kiss a pretty girl.

It's time to move on.

Jack

Chris pushed away his untouched draft. He tossed a $5 on the counter, picked up the package and jacket, and walked out. College Street was energized. He heard laughter and parts of stories as people, filled with purpose and summer, walked by. A woman with white pillowed hair and sun glasses sold hot dogs from her cart at the corner. A street artist drew caricatures while teasing his subject, coaxing him to smile. Someone strummed a guitar across the street, standing by an overturned Stetson.

Chris wasn't expected anywhere, but he felt some urgency. The sun was falling, so he turned westward. Down College Street, beyond the water, the Adirondacks waited. An olive-yellow hue embraced the mountains in warmth more imagined than real, a painter's vision. The Adirondacks appeared so close Chris thought he could reach right out and touch them. He lifted his hand as if to try.

> O'Driscoll scattered the cards
> And out of his dream awoke:
> Old men and young men and young girls
> Were gone like a drifting smoke;
>
> But he heard high up in the air
> A piper piping away,
> And never was piping so sad,
> And never was piping so gay.

27

Early Saturday morning, Chris reviewed his recertification presentation. When he discovered a spelling error on one of his PowerPoint slides he panicked and then called Anita for assistance. She guided him through the corrections and resolved them in a short time. Then he drove to the Academy and made paper copies of the presentation just in case something went wrong on Tuesday. It was approaching noon when he checked PowerPoint off his list. With several hours remaining before the reunion, he decided to return to the library, hoping to check still another item of his list. A half hour later, he walked into special collections.

"I'd like to look at General Well's papers."

"We're closing early for Memorial Day but you have about 45 minutes," the receptionist said.

The woman returned with a cardboard box that looked as if it had once held reams of copier paper. WELLS was typed on its white label. Inside were file folders hanging on a metal frame. The first said inventory. The subsequent folders titles were correspondence, personal 1861–65; correspondence, personal 1866–85; correspondence, military 1861–65; correspondence, requisitions 1862–1863; and others.

Unsure where to start, Chris opened the requisitions folder. It contained long yellowing forms with entries written in pencil. The first sheet listed military statistics: numbers of men present, numbers on sick call, and numbers of men assigned to guard duty. Other sheets indicated quantities of horses, sabers, pistols, blankets, and other accoutrements available to the regiment on any given day. He put that one away.

Chris skipped General Wells's personal correspondence file and looked through the correspondence, military folder hoping to find duty rosters, names of wounded, commendations, lists of any kind that might add to his knowledge of his relative. As he glanced through it, he noticed a folder labeled G.A.C. between correspondence and personal folders. It wasn't listed on the inventory. He opened it to find a single sheet of lined paper written in pencil. The white had faded to a smoky hue, and the date indicated it was written after the war. It was signed by General George Armstrong Custer.

"Dear General Wells," began the message, congratulating Wells on the fine job he had done commanding the First Vermont Cavalry. It mentioned Wells's bravery and stated that long after the war was over, Wells's deeds and those of the First Vermont Cavalry would live on.

"We're closing in five minutes."

"Have you ever seen this?" Chris said, holding up the letter. "It's from Custer! General George Armstrong Custer!"

The receptionist nodded. "There are a few ghosts in this place."

"I've been looking for information on a relative, and I found a Custer letter. A handwritten Custer letter! This is amazing."

"Sorry, but I have to close. Please put the files back in the box."

"Sure. Sure." Chris returned the letter to its folder.

Then he noticed another hanging folder lying on the bottom of the box. It must have detached from the frame and fallen. He parted the folders enough to retrieve it. The tab was unmarked. Inside were three handwritten pages. The first listed engagements the First Vermont Cavalry participated in. The names Brandy Station, Buckland Mills, Yellow Tavern, Gettysburg, and Cedar Creek were listed among others he didn't recognize.

"Vermont Cavalry 25-26-27-28 August 1874 Reunion Montpelier" was written across the tops of the next two sheets. Listed were the names of men who attended the reunion. Near the middle of the second sheet, another piece of data was revealed. C. Gordon, Company A, Weaverton was printed across the line.

"Can I copy this?"

The attendant nodded before glancing at her watch.

Chris copied the pages, refiled the originals, and handed the box back.

"Did you find what you were looking for?"

"A little bit more," he said as the woman locked the door behind him.

***

A steady stream of people in casual summer attire were entering the Hotel Champlain's rotary glass doors. Chris had expected a crowd. Marathon weekend was Queen City's biggest event each year. Rooms for 20 miles were booked months in advanced. Chris stepped aside as a pushy bald man in a Hawaiian shirt barged through. The white-marble lobby was crammed with guests and smelled of gladiolas. Chris found the events board, which listed the evening's schedule. He ran his finger down the items.

Green Mountain University Reunion	Over Lake 3	6 pm
Queen City Marathon Pasta Dinner	Over Lake 1	5 pm
Queen City AGLO	Over Lake 2	6 pm
Running Shoe/Attire Display	Courtside 4	9 am–7 pm
Wild Flower Festival Headquarters	Courtside 3	10 am–5 pm

He followed the arrows down the hall to the function rooms. There was a shorts and t-shirt crowd outside Over Lake 1. The smell of meatballs and fresh garlic bread permeated the air. The carbo loading crowd inside was noisy and energetic. Chris wondered whether Libby was inside somewhere or back at her apartment following her own routine. He guessed the latter.

A more subdued group lingered outside Over Lake 2. They were dressed in short-sleeve shirts and ties and speaking in low voices. Most appeared more interested in the sunset than the hors d'oeuvres table. As Chris walked passed the registration table someone called, "Hi Chris."

"Hey, K.J."

"Did you finish making those corrections?"

"Yeah. Thanks for the help. Just have to practice operating the slideshow."

"Great! Remember Lucien?"

The short round-faced man in the white shirt and yellow tie shook Chris's hand

"Hi, Lucien. Nice to see you again." Chris said and turned back to K.J. "Big night?"

"Lu says we don't get out enough. He thinks I spend too much time online."

"And reading comics!" Lucien said. "He's a grown man for Christ's sake."

"I hate to run guys, but I'm already late for my reunion." Chris pointing toward Over Lake 3. "See you Tuesday, K.J. Have a good time."

"Chris, before you go…" Lucien said.

"Yeah?"

"We want to thank you."

"Thank me?"

"Oh, you know. Brent's never approved of us." Lucien pointed between K.J. and himself. "He made such a big scene when K.J. came out last year that it's made his life at the Academy difficult. But you've always been supportive. I know you've taken some heat, but we appreciate it."

"We do." K.J. said.

There was only one person ahead of him when Chris reached the registration table outside Over Lake 3. As he waited to sign the guest book and fill out his name tag, Chris saw in the room about a dozen people gathered near a large easel covered with black-and-white photos. After signing in, he went over to the easel. One picture was taken at a basketball game in Municipal Auditorium. Another showed the winning sculpture at an old Snowflake Follies, GMU's winter carnival. A group of PHI NU GAMMA brothers held a trophy up in front of a large snow castle.

Groups of people were scattered around the room. Others stood by the windows and out on the balcony that overlooked the lake. The sun reflected orange-red off the water. Because GMU used a multi-class format for its reunions, Chris didn't recognize anyone he knew, so he ordered a beer from the bar and spoke with a former classmate who'd been in line behind him. He knew the local fellow well enough to be on the offensive, invoking the Red Sox in order to avoid an aches-and-prescriptions conversation. Eventually, the man ran out of excuses for another poor season start and walked away.

Chris recognized one couple near the center of the room and noticed Susan standing just beyond them. She was holding a Bloody Mary and talking with a woman in a black dress. Chris walked over to the couple.

"Hi, guys."

"Chris. How good to see you," the woman said, leaning forward to kiss his cheek.

After sharing a few college memories, his former classmates rambled on about their family business. As they described the finer points of a new point of sale program, Chris glanced toward Susan. Her once light brown hair had turned white. Her movements were still familiar and her hazel eyes just as bright as he remembered, but her face had changed. He recognized the tiny lines from years of worry and frustration that appeared in his own mirror each morning. The difference was Chris had no idea what had caused hers. Chris didn't do well with small talk. He never had. At best, he found it a gap filler or time killer. At worst, he thought it was an excuse to spread around the secrets everyone promises to keep. "You still teaching?" The man asked.

"Yes. I'm still at the Academy." Chris looked around but Susan was gone.

"You should retire," the wife said. "We did and all we

do is play."

The couple looked at each other and began laughing just as a stocky, gray-haired man with thick black-rimmed glasses walked over and extended his hand.

"Hi, Chris."

"Hi…" Chris said, looking for the man's missing name tag.

"Jim. Jim Underwood. From TAC."

"Oh, sorry, Jim. I guess I didn't recognize you. You look different. It's been so long…" Underwood waited, but the other man commented instead.

"You didn't wear glasses in school, Jim, and you were thinner!"

"You think so!" Jim looked down at himself and unbuttoned his jacket.

"Everyone's changed, Jim, everyone," the classmate said.

Chris felt awkward standing beside Underwood and couldn't think of anything to say. Underwood seemed voiceless, too. His face tightened, and he looked around. Finally, he nodded his head at no one and looked away. "Excuse me for a moment. Nice seeing you," he said, moving toward the bar.

"We're going to be around for a few days, Chris. We should do lunch," the woman said when Chris heard a familiar voice from his right.

"Hi, Chris." He turned to find Susan standing beside him. She gave him a hug, holding on for an uncomfortable amount of time. "I'm so happy to see you," she said. He stepped back. Another couple walked past. "Oh, hi, Elaine. Save us a seat. Be there in a minute." Susan reached into her purse. "Look at what I brought!" she said, sorting through a stack of pictures. Her movements, though familiar, were from some dream time.

"Do you have grandchildren?" she said, snapping Chris back into the present.

"No. Grand nieces."

"These are mine. This is Bristol. And Andrew. Do you

and your wife …" He shook his head. "They're six and four. She just started school. You're not married?"

"I never found," new wrinkles formed around Susan's eyes, "the right girl."

"But I thought you and Mini were…"

"Mini? Where did you get that idea?"

Susan's smile faltered. "Jim said you and she—"

"No."

"No?"

"I haven't seen her since graduation."

"Oh." Susan's eyes darted about the room until they found Underwood, talking with the woman in the black dress. The tension lines around them dissolved, leaving her expressionless until the beginnings of a smile emerged. It was as if some recovery protocol sequence had been initiated. She cleared her throat and held the pictures back up. "Well, these are mine. I take care of this little girl every Thursday. Her name's Bristol." She handed the picture to Chris. "We took this at her baptism." Chris looked at the photo. Susan handed him another. "This is Bristol at her first Communion party. See Andrew there. We call him Drew."

The protocol was working. "It's so wonderful! What an opportunity! I can't believe…such angels…Florida… bridge…pickle ball…index funds…" Her words were precise and exact; the bland, gap-filling details or her life exposed themselves in a colorless brocade. Chris tried to listen, but as Susan's recitation turned to litany, he realized how far their lives were from where they'd once been. And how deep the chasms between them had grown. He wondered why he'd been drawn back. Did he hope to rekindle some old chemistry with Susan and clear up decades of distance? Did he think he could reverse the results of their youthful decisions? Was he being nostalgic? Did he think he still loved her? Or was he just chasing phantoms?

As she spoke, Chris thought back over their time together. He'd loved Susan during a time in his life when everything was fresh and pure-a time of escape and discovery. He'd never wanted that time to end, but when it did, he was devastated. To deal with his emotions, he'd locked them unresolved away. But they resurfaced after Walt's passing. His loss, the turbulence at the Academy, and his search through family history created a need for simple answers. The memory of Susan filled that need. But, seeing her again, he realized he didn't even know her. He knew an apparition from a romanticized, unchangeable past. The reality left a strange taste on his tongue but told him what he already felt. There was only one direction to go: forward.

"…and at Christmas, we all get together to…"

"Susan, I'm sorry to interrupt, but I really have to leave."

"You're leaving?"

"I'm working on a big presentation that's due on Tuesday. My job depends on it."

"Join us for dinner first. You have to eat and we haven't had a chance to…."

"I'm sorry."

"It's been so long, Chris. There's so much to say."

Chris knew there really wasn't, so he shook his head. "Thank you but it's getting late. But I do want to tell you something." He took both her hands in his and looked into her eyes. "I loved you once, Susan. That was a very special time for me. I've thought about it a lot, and I'm glad it happened." He smiled. "I hope you have a nice life."

"Chris! I don't know what to say. That was so long ago. I mean, everything's changed.

"I know it has. Good bye, Susan."

A few minutes later Chris parked beside the GMU green and climbed Sci Hall's fire escape. He sat outside the quant lab window. The college green below wore an emerald tint beneath the street lamps' glow. The flag hung still and the rich smell of mulch permeated the night. The old hospital across the way appeared empty. Chris looked to the west where the lake and shadowy Adirondacks lurked, loving what was beyond the darkness.

28

The Daily Freeman lay on the grass just off the front step of 25 Wells Court. Chris picked up the newspaper and scanned its front page. It was crammed with predictable stories and pictures of first-time marathoners, marathoners planning to carry flags, marathoners planning to dress like Uncle Sam, and marathoners running in someone's memory. He'd seen so many versions of those stories he knew he wouldn't read beyond the headlines.

The mail was different, however. Mixed in among the junk mail were two postcards and an envelope from Claudia. Chris read the postcards on his way back up the stairs. The first, dated the previous Wednesday, pictured a car-sized trout tied atop a trailer and pulled by an aging station wagon. The block letters above a smiling angler said, "Welcome to Port Huron." He flipped it over.

Doofus,

My Father's still dead, God bless him! Mother's still in the home, God bless her! Anchorage is still 3912 miles. God damn!

Jack

The second card, dated the following day, pictured a vast expanse of empty stockyards.

Doofus,

Stopped in Sioux Falls to pee by the old stockyards and climbed up on an elevated walkway over the piggy pens. John Morell Meat Packers is printed across a building next door. Thank goodness the poor little porkers couldn't read.

I can almost see the Grand Tetons.

Jack

Claudia's envelope contained some typed notes about the GAR, a Civil War Veterans organization, and copies of pages from the Vermont Historical Society. After glancing at them, Chris showered, dressed, and walked down College Street.

The Queen City Marathon was a perfect race on a perfect day. The streets were filled with thousands of fans cheering the runners on beneath a crystal-blue sky. The lake and Adirondacks formed the backdrop for the photo finish. Chris yelled and clapped as runner after runner sprinted along the lake front toward the tape. He ate hot dogs and drank too much soda. He sat and watched children throwing breadcrumbs at the mallards swimming near the boardwalk. Later, he wandered the crowds looking for Libby but couldn't find her. Eventually, he resigned himself to the long walk back up College St.

Back at Wells Court, he sat in front of the television and watched films of the race but felt restless. He felt as if he had more to do on his recertification presentation, so he picked up his papers and read through the demography section again. Everything looked good. As he put his work away, he remembered K.J.'s search ideas for finding out more about Black Rock, so he carried Anita's laptop over to the kitchen window.

K.J.'s directions were simple enough. In just a few minutes, Chris had accessed the wireless connection for an account named LOVERBOY, found Anita's browser, and began typing in searches. He tried the obvious. Black Rock, Quebec. No luck. Black Rock, Canada. Nothing. Quebec, Black Rock.

He entered at least a dozen alternatives without success. One result showed promise, pointing to an area on the St. Lawrence east of Tadoussac, but that couldn't be it. It was too remote and had a tiny population.

He remembered a librarian in the GMU map room saying names had been changed back to the French when the separatists gained influence in Quebec, so he used the little French he knew. Noir Roc, Roc Noir, Noir Roche, and other variations didn't produce anything useful. St. Roch turned up an area of Quebec City, but dozens of other combinations proved fruitless.

Chris took a break but was back at the computer after a peanut butter and jelly sandwich. He tried numerous searches before considering that if St. Roch was an area of Quebec City, then Black Rock could be an area, or a nickname, or a neighborhood of some other city. He typed Black Rock area of Montreal into the search engine.

Bingo! The site disclosed another small piece to his puzzle. The Gordons had come to Weaverton through Montreal. Other searches opened other doors and filled in more blank spaces. He opened Word and inserted the new details into LeClairHistory.doc. It was nearly 11 when he turned off the pc. The phone rang.

"Hi, Catch. How are you?"

"Mr. Martin?"

"Is that you, Catch?"

"No. It's Suzie Thomas."

"Who?"

"I'm sorry. Suzie McEdward, class of '82 at the Academy."

Chris didn't remember anyone by that name. Was this some sales call from the west coast?

"I'm sorry, Suzie. It's pretty late. Can you call…"

"Mr. Martin, I apologize for calling so late, but I had to tell you something. It'll only take a minute. OK?"

"OK."

"It probably doesn't mean anything but I enjoyed your U.S. history class when I was at the Academy. Not at first. It was all so cold and factual. But it began to grow on me. Things came alive." Chris began drumming his fingers and looked around for the remote. "At first, I thought history was nothing but stories about dead people and old rocks. That was until you did that unit on memories of historical events. What do you remember about Kennedy's assassination vs. what are the real facts? That type of thing. Do you remember doing that?"

"I did that unit for years."

"My project was to interview a veteran and compare what the veteran said with the textbooks. I interviewed my dad. He'd been with the First Marines at Cape Gloucester during World War II. He wouldn't talk at first, but then he broke down and said things he'd never told anyone. Nobody knew. My brothers still don't. That changed everything for me."

"That's nice, Suzie. I'm glad I helped." Chris clicked the TV.

"You really did. It made me understand things that had been nothing but words in books before. History changes us. I minored in history at GMU. I never did anything with it, but I thought it was important for me to do."

The TV flashed runners crossing the finish in the background. "It was really nice of you to call. I hope we can speak about this some other time."

"Wait! Please."

"But it's late."

"I really called about my son. When he was growing up, I told him stories about what I'd I learned. I took him to places I'd read about, like Fort Ticonderoga and Philadelphia. We saw the Liberty Bell. We went to Antietam. Can you believe that? Antietam." Chris muted the volume on the TV. "I read whenever I could. I always liked nonfiction, but this isn't about me. I called to say I just got home from Madison. My son graduated from the University of Wisconsin on Saturday. And guess what? He majored in history. Can you believe it, Mr. Martin? My son majored in history. That's all, Mr. Martin. I just had to tell you my son majored in history. Thanks for answering."

"Thanks, Susie." Chris sat back on the couch and stared at his TV. The newscaster mouthed silent stories as pictures of unnamed runners crossed the finished line. Spectators jumped up and down. Runners collapsed into the arms of volunteers. But Chris had trouble seeing them because he was peering back through dark decades of faces with forgotten names.

29

Chris had showered and dressed an hour and a half before he normally began tapping the snooze button. After a bowl of cereal, he reread his presentation, then placed his materials into his tote bag. Folders, discs, handouts: yes, everything was there. All the while, Dylan watched. Dylan was always watching, commenting without words, criticizing without speaking from another lifetime.

Chris paused before the old poster. Dylan was still curly haired, young, and rebellious. He stood before the microphone, waiting to tell Chris again how it felt to be alone—unchanged a half century later. But Chris had changed. The transition may have begun when Walt died or during the time he'd searched through graveyards and records rooms. Perhaps seeing Susan at his reunion, or talking with Suzie McEdward, or sitting in St. Brendan's Church had unlatched some doors that had closed years before. Perhaps it was spurred on by Libby's spirit, or the anonymous letter, or Jack's dream. It didn't matter. What mattered was that Chris remembered his feelings the first time his life had changed, when he walked into Uncle Jonathon's living room and saw the photos of people he didn't recognize and trophies for teams that no longer competed. He felt that way again. Dylan belonged back in some old living room now, not his. Chris dropped his tote bag and lifted the poster from the wall, then carried it into the kitchen and placed it beside the trash.

"Sorry, Bob. It's the times," he said with a wisp of a smile.

Just then, the alarm clock went off in his bedroom.

The Academy's final assembly inched forward. Chris drummed his fingers on his knee through the speeches, but as the chaplain approached the podium Chris rubbed his hands together in anticipation. As soon as the tiny chaplain challenged the seniors to "…go forth to the four corners of the earth," Chris bolted down the central artery toward Old Hall. He adjusted the blinds in C44 to the prescribed height, gathered his overdue library books, and locked his coffee mug away before turning off the lights. T.D. Glover and Michael Andover were emptying their lockers as Chris hurried by. "Have a nice summer, boys." Chris paused to shake their hands.

Neither said a word. Nor did Madison Amore when he passed her in the central stairway and wished her good luck in college.

Libby was leaving the teacher's lounge as Chris passed by. "Today's the day?"

"Yeah, today's the day."

"Good luck, Chris." She reached across the void, kissing him on the cheek. "I probably wasn't supposed to do that to the new department chairman. It must be against some Academy protocol."

He felt a boyish flush across his face, smiled, and stepped back. "I haven't got it yet but thanks for the support. It means a lot."

Libby walked off toward the central artery. Brent had left copies of two memos in Chris's mailbox. The first notified teachers of a substantial donation made to the Academy, which would let the Academy purchase tablets for every student. The other summarized next year's PBR guidelines and announced a two-week workshop in August to plan for the changes. Chris returned the memos to his mailbox. Honora was leaving the principal's office when Chris reached the door. She lowered her eyes and walked toward the teacher's lounge. Chris opened the door to the principal's office to find Brittany Newport sitting behind Anita's desk.

"Hi, sugar!"

"Hi Brittany. Where's Anita?"

"I'm the new secretary."

"New secretary?"

"Well, for today. Anita's brother died."

"Oh my God! What happened? How is she?"

"I don't know, sugar. That's all Brent said." As Chris pondered the volumes of things Brittany didn't know, she picked up the phone and began searching the console. "Did you ever see so many colored buttons? I wonder what they're all for." She tapped the automatic intercom. "Brent, sugar, Chris is here. Sure. They're waiting for you, sugar. Go right in."

"I'm using Anita's laptop for my meeting. I'll bring it back when I'm done."

"Sure, sugar. Whatever."

Chris tapped on the principal's door and entered, finding Brent on the phone. Regan Andover and Dr. George were sitting in the Cardiff-house wingbacks. A large plate of chocolate-chip cookies sat on Brent's desk. Dr. George was stroking his beard, his lips puckered. Regan was watching Brent. Michael Andover strongly resembled his father though Regan was taller and wore his salt-and-pepper hair closely cropped.

"Sit down, Chris. Be a second." Brent pointed to a side chair. "Yes, sheriff, the janitor found an L painted just inside New Hall by the entrance to the parking lot. This one is different from the others. Along with the letter and flames, there's also an arrow pointing down the central artery toward the lobby. I called a code blue. Yes, your deputy came over and took pictures."

Wrinkles appeared around Regan's eyes. "Code blue?" he whispered.

Dr. George shrugged.

"Three will be fine. The students are gone. I'll be waiting. Goodbye." Brent hung up and turned to Regan. "It's one of the alert levels in the new emergency-procedure manual the sheriff and I developed. Code blue means we called for an officer to walk the hallways, evaluate the situation."

"I want a copy of those guidelines. The board needs to know," Regan said.

"I'll get you one once the sheriff and I finalize things. Today was the first time we've followed the protocol."

"Be sure they're DBUG'd. Keep us in the loop. "

"It's under control, Dr. George, except that our pubescent Pollack defaced our temple again."

"What are the other letters?" Dr. George asked.

"Besides the L today, there was already Z, O, and, E."

Dr. George shook his head. "Must be a code." He shook Chris's hand. "Good to see you. You remember Regan Andover?"

Andover leaned forward and shook Chris's hand.

"Chris, Dr. George and Regan want to know where things stand in the history department. Changeovers can be tumultuous. Please bring us up to speed." Brent winked at the others, making Chris wonder what was said before he'd arrived.

"And there's the matter of your reappointment to the history chair but we'll discuss that afterwards," Dr. George added.

"Show us what you've got," Brent said, rubbing his hands together.

"Is the rest of the board coming?" Chris said.

"Rest of the board?" Andover said, turning to Brent.

"I may have misrepresented this meeting, Regan but I'll explain it all later at the club."

Chris took some folders from his tote bag. "I guess I don't need to do a full PowerPoint slideshow, seeing it's just the four of us, but here are disc copies if you wish to review it later."

"PowerPoint?" Dr. George said, looking to Brent. "You said he didn't... "

Brent shrugged but kept his expression neutral.

"I'll keep this informal," Chris said.

"Yes! Yes! This is just the right group for informality," Dr. George said.

Brent stared at the disc as if he'd been handed a road map through an eastern Slovakian sub province.

"I created folders about the teachers who chose the one-time option. Honora is the only one who opted for traditional certification."

"Is she still doing those silly-ass dinners?" Regan whispered to Dr. George. He nodded.

"The first sheet in each folder is an outline of the individual's recertification project. Everyone meets the criteria. I discussed each of them with Mini Contois at the Department of Education."

Brent leaned forward. "Mini Contois! Who is she?"

"Oh, sorry, Brent. Myra Spelling at Professional Standards. We attended GMU together. I've always called her Mini. She dated Walt for a while and, boy, could she dance. Since Walt passed we've talked several times."

"Oh!" Brent's eyes closed.

"The following pages are the individual's working documents. Objectives are listed first." Chris thumbed through a folder. "There's a resource page and bibliography. The last sheet details the metrics. The proof is in the pudding, so to speak. Now, let's talk about each individuals' projects." Chris started with K.J., saying K.J.'s idea would benefit nearly every student in the state. "Please open his folder."

Brent lifted his copy using his thumb and forefinger.

"K.J. has 30 creative years with the Academy. He and his students teamed up with IT to construct a database." Chris winked at Dr. George. "It lists library and historical society resources from across the state. As a result, he's located and defined lesser known resources. I told Mini about the idea. She wants us to expand it using funding from the state interlibrary task force. No budgetary effect on the Academy, Dr. George. In fact, Mini said she'd fund a couple of new servers for the Academy, if our IT agrees to maintain the database. What do you think?"

"That's an easy sell. Helps us keep the old budget in check. Doesn't it, Brent?"

Brent struggled to force a smile.

"Here's how to use K.J.'s idea. Say for example, a student is looking for resources on the Battle of Bennington. He can go to the database…"

Regan waved his hand. "Sounds great, Chris, and I'm

sure Dr. George and Brent have more detailed questions, but I only have a few minutes. I thought this was about something else." Regan looked at Brent. "I'd like to change the subject."

"What to, Regan?" Dr. George said.

"Chris's role." He turned back to Chris. "What about your recertification? The board hears things." He glanced at Brent. "Rumors are that you haven't distinguished yourself recently, not up to Academy standards."

"Here's my folder. Take a look. The documentation is the same as the others with one exception. There's a copy of a letter signed by both Brent and Dr. George that they sent to the Department of Education recognizing all my credentials."

Regan Andover looked over the letter and nodded. "Very impressive!"

"I've had a tough year. I lost a friend. But I've designed a demography unit for freshmen." Chris pointed to another sheet. "It begins by collecting raw data from gravestones in cemeteries. Then students are taught to form suppositions based on that information. We move on to town records, church records, and census data. Simply put, it's about collecting data, making predictions, collecting better data, making better predictions."

Regan glanced over the paper and began reading aloud. "History Foundations Course. Objective: Introduction of data-collection methods, data analysis, and interpretation techniques. Methods include..." Regan's lips continued moving but his voice faded. He looked up. "Pretty comprehensive, Martin."

Brent's eyes lit up. "It doesn't list any texts. We have some great texts at the Academy!"

"I know, Brent. I selected them myself when I chaired the textbook committee a dozen years ago. But they don't go far enough these days. Besides, texts without technology are incomplete. We need greater diversity and a hands-on approach does that."

"He's right!" Dr. George said "This is just what we're

after. A flagship! Look! Rather than just read those old texts and take notes on how to collect data, students do the footwork. They're searching, identifying data, building databases. Sink or swim. Hands on. Look at the metrics sheet. Myra is going to love this."

"She already does, Dr. George."

"She does, doesn't she?"

"Not bad, Martin." Reagan said. "This type of approach will have a big payoff later. My own department complains that freshmen don't know how to do research, so we teach a similar course. Your courses could affect GMU's bottom line by cutting remedial work."

"Thank you, sir."

"I've seen enough. The board is satisfied and I've got to run to another meeting, but before I go, one other question, Chris. Brent mentioned that someone in your family fought for Custer at Gettysburg—that he was a hero. What's the story?"

Chris looked at Brent. "He wasn't with Custer at Gettysburg. As you know, Custer led the Michigan troops there, not the First Vermont."

"That right. East Cavalry Field."

"I don't know much about him. His name was Christopher Gordon. His enlistment papers say he was 5′ 8″ with gray eyes. The company surgeon verified he was 'sober' when he enlisted."

"I love that 19th-century detail," Regan said.

"After the war, he ran a harness shop and became postmaster of Weaverton. His descendants must have thought a lot of him, because they named children after him for two generations. I'm one. Christopher Gordon Martin. I discovered one other interesting thing."

"What's that?"

"Where my ancestors lived—Black Rock, outside Montreal. Its real name was Goose Village. It was a tiny spot packed with immigrants."

Chris told them how Windmill Point on the edge of Goose Village became a typhus or 'ship fever' quarantine area in the late 1840s when the sick, escaping the Potato Famine, needed care. Large hospital sheds were built to house them, and nearly 7000 victims died there. Years later, workers building the Victoria Bridge rediscovered the mass graves and were so moved they placed a large Black Rock on Bridge Street in memory of the dead. Crowded neighborhoods sprang up. Some of his ancestors lived there. When the city needed parking for the '67 Olympics, Goose Village, Windmill Point—all of it was bulldozed over. The Black Rock is all that remains.

"The irony is that the same thing happened to my ancestors who moved to Weaverton from Montreal. In the '40s, my grandfather's house on East Central St. was destroyed in the big fire. Then, in the '70s, the rest of the neighborhood was bulldozed. Christopher Gordon's house became a parking lot behind a bank. Searching for my family history has been like trying to catch shadows."

"Are you going to continue your family research?" Regan said.

"I'll work on it when I get a chance, but now just reading the old newspapers is more interesting."

"Sounds pretty superficial," Brent said. "Don't you want to know the details?"

"I'm not sure. That's the end of the process. I think the race is in the running, not the finish line. I don't know where I'm going but I'm still running."

"Thanks, Chris. Good luck running the department," Andover said as he stood. "By the way, you've done a good job with Michael. He's needed his ears pinned back. A year at Mansfield Prep will finish what you've started. He's a lot like me, the little snot."

Dr. George took an envelope from his briefcase.

"Here, Chris. Get this back to me when you can."

"But contracts are due today!"

"Give him a break, Brent! Have a cookie. Come on, Regan, I'll give you a lift."

While Dr. George and Regan were shaking hands, Chris gathered up his materials and walked out toward

Brittany's desk. The tension that had been building inside him over the last few months subsided. He felt as if he'd just reached the top of a steep climb and been rewarded with sight of the vista beyond.

"Big smile, sugar. Did you win the lottery, sugar?"

"No, thank goodness."

He had little time to enjoy the feelings of liberation though, for as he handed the laptop to Brittany, Barney, the janitor, entered the office.

"Our painter is at it again, Brittany," he said.

"What?"

Brent heard the commotion and emerged from his office. "What's going on?"

"The painter struck again," Barney said. "I just found another flaming arrow. It's pointing up the central stairway. Do you want me to repaint it, Brent?"

"Brittany, call the sheriff. Tell the dispatcher code red!"

"What the hell's a code red?" Chris asked.

"The sheriff's tactical team!"

"Brent, this is just some kid with a can of spray paint!" Chris said.

"We can't take any chances! If it's a senior, the little turd will never graduate! He's defiling the temple. I'll be in the command center, Brittany."

"Where, sugar?"

"My office! My office! Lockdown, Brittany. Code red!"

Brittany appeared dazed. "Sugar, this is my first day. Code Red? I don't get it! And this phone has so many buttons."

Brent turned red. "Think, Brittany! The flaming mushrooms on the back of Municipal Auditorium! Emergency response to code red?" He said, slamming his office door behind him.

"Oh!" She said and looked down at the console. She turned the speakerphone on and pushed the first red button on the automatic dialer. As the phone rang, she reached into her purse for a stick of Minty Mint Gum.

"Fire department! What's your emergency?"

"This is Brittany. Code red!"

"What?"

"Oh, sugar, Brent said there are flaming mushrooms on the back wall of Municipal Auditorium. This is an emergency!"

Chris could have just walked away. The school year was over. He was recertified. His contract read department chairman. Still, something held him. A thousand memories from the past year competed for prominence in his head. He remembered someone calling the mystery painter Pollack and had thoughts of Christopher Gordon. There was an L and flaming mushrooms, a command post, Barney the janitor, code red, Dr. George, Z, Regan Andover. The facts came faster and faster still. Michael Andover, O, Walt's funeral, Susie Thomas, chocolate chip cookies, contracts, databases, E, Little Honey, boring lectures, Weaverton, tactical team, Gettysburg, Killer Angels, loser, cup, senior prank, graduation!

The puzzle pieces assembled and disassembled, again and again, until Chris realized one piece was still missing. The R! LOZER. And T.D. never could spell. He was trying to write LOSER. The letters had begun at the New Hall entrance, followed the central artery, and climbed the central stairway. T.D. was probably up in Chris's homeroom, painting an R on something.

Chris could have explained to Brent then argued about what to do. He could have tried to explain to Brittany, but instead, he dashed out of the office. The lobby was empty as he sprinted through. He pushed aside the door to the central stairway to find a new arrow painted above the handrail and pointing upward. He heard sirens when he reached B Level. The fire department was headed to Municipal Auditorium. He took two steps at a time between the B and C Levels. The door to the C Level corridor was still swinging as he banged through to find another new arrow painted on the opposite wall. It pointed down the corridor toward the only open door, C44. The sirens went silent.

Chris dashed the length of the hall and burst into C44, where he found T.D. leaning over his desk. A screwdriver lay on top. Across the street at the auditorium, the fire chief yelled commands into a bull horn as Queen City's super ladder truck's motor began to wail.

"What the hell are you doing, T.D.?"

T.D. stood up. He held Chris's GMU coffee mug and a can of red spray paint. A large red R had been sprayed on the white board behind the desk.

"Mr. Martin!"

"T.D., this isn't funny!"

"It's just a joke. It's really nothing. We had a couple of beers. I didn't think anybody would…" T.D. said and started backing toward the window as Chris moved forward.

Chris looked past T.D. and noticed a fireman on the roof of the Municipal Auditorium scratching his head.

T.D. reached the window ledge and looked down. "I'm not in any trouble, am I? I mean it was just a joke. I was just playing. I wasn't being malicious or anything."

"T.D., put the can down!"

"No!" he said with the composure of a frightened child.

The fireman started back down the ladder, and the unfolding sequence became as obvious to Chris as T.D.'s guilt. In moments, the fire department would call the school back, and the sheriff would be on his way.

Chris looked into T.D.'s face and saw his own from a long time ago. He remembered doing silly things, not worrying about consequences, not thinking beyond the next few minutes. He looked at the cup T.D. held and then reached inside himself, understanding for the first time in a very long time what his job really was.

"T.D., do you want to graduate?"

"Yeah."

"Then listen to me. I know how we can get out of all this."

C44 was empty when Sheriff Flanagan and the technical team arrived a few minutes later.

30

The No Dogs Allowed sign outside Mount St. Brendan's third drive had a new dent in it, as if some child had thrown a stone. Chris felt himself smiling. At least there were other visitors. He turned off his engine and glanced at the dashboard clock. There was still time enough, so he finished the decaf in his GMU mug before getting out. Across the street, he could see familiar names—Fitzsimons, McMahon, Cassidy, Finnigan, Shea, and Cashman—awaiting him.

He stopped at the Cassidy lot before walking around behind the granite marker, where the names of previous generations were stacked on top of Logan. His father, Michael, came first—then his grandfather, Ryan, and grandmother, Katherine Queen Cassidy. Generations of life too short, generations of stories, the kinds of stories Uncle Jonathon told over and over.

Muffled church bells riding the breeze reminded him of his task, so he cut west across lots while glancing at familiar words along the way. Born in the City of Dublin. Born in 1847. A native of County Down. Apoplexy. Age 34 years. Died in Shelburne. 1840–1863. 1844–1862. 1874–1878. Each told a tale. He knew his path now.

He stopped beside the Gordon Stone. The small flag he'd first noticed in the spring showed the wear of five months exposure to the elements. He took a deep breath, inhaling the autumn air. It calmed him.

A school bus, rounding the corner from Wilson, revved its engine. As it lumbered up Archer Street, Chris thumbed through his notes. The bus reached the second drive, turned into the cemetery, and bounced over a few potholes before pulling to a halt.

Several of the freshmen inside noticed Chris standing beside the Gordon stone. One began waving to him. Chris smiled and waved back. The door opened and a tiny girl, wearing a pink fleece, disembarked and walked toward him. Other students milled about the doorway, waiting for friends so that parts of WEAVERTON written on the bus were obscured. They filled in when he called, "Come on up!" The students walked toward him, some kicking the fallen leaves.

Everyone's attention shifted to the gate when the putt putt of an old VW microbus sounded as it stopped behind the school bus. Inside it, Principal Rich Hillsborough and Claudia Nichols were talking. Chris ran his fingers over the carved crucifix on the stone as the students finished gathering around him.

"Hey, Mr. M. What's happening?" a girl, wearing a multicolored hijab, said.

"Fatima, today we're going to try something different. We're going to hold class right here in the cemetery."

"Ugh."

Some of the students began laughing. Chris did too. As he did, he thought he felt drumbeats in his chest.

***

Later that afternoon, Chris unlocked his apartment and switched on the lights. He stopped by the new painting in the hallway. Split Rock Island glistened beneath an afternoon sky. He placed his tote bag on the table. Dozens of postcards were tacked above it on the bulletin board, each one a different mountain. After grabbing an apple from the fridge, he sat on the couch and took out his smartphone. He stared at the dialing screen for a moment before punching in the numbers.

As the phone rang, he pictured her sitting on her couch, curling her legs under herself like a cat. She'd raise her chin and push her hair back behind her right ear, exposing the freckles on the side of her neck. And across the street from her apartment, he imagined a light breeze whisking the leaves between the stones at Elmwood Cemetery.

"Hello."

"Hi, there."

"Oh, hi. I didn't know if I'd hear from you again."

"I can understand that. And I'm sorry. I really am. But a...a...about that steak."

"Yeah. About that steak."

The sound in Libby's voice reawakened some phantom inside of Chris. He felt his hand rising toward his heart, but this time, it made him smile.

If you wish to make comments to the author, go to the comments section at:
www.GordonRLawrence.com